Praise for *New York Times* bestselling author B.J. Daniels

"The first book of Daniels' new Montana Hamiltons series will draw readers in with its genuine characters, multiple storylines and intense conflict set against the beautiful Montana landscape."
—*RT Book Reviews* on *Wild Horses*

"Truly amazing crime story for every amateur sleuth."
—*Fresh Fiction* on *Mercy*

"Daniels is truly an expert at Western romantic suspense."
—*RT Book Reviews* on *Atonement*

"Romantic suspense that will keep readers guessing. If you like *Longmire*, this is the book for you."
—*RT Book Reviews* on *Forsaken*

"Will keep readers on the edge of their chairs from beginning to end."
—*Booklist* on *Forsaken*

"Action-packed and chock-full of suspense."
—*Under the Covers* on *Redemption*

"Fans of Western romantic suspense will relish Daniels' tale of clandestine love played out in a small town on the Great Plains."
—*Booklist* on *Unforgiven*

B.J. DANIELS

REDEMPTION

HQN™

Recycling programs
for this product may
not exist in your area.

ISBN-13: 978-0-373-60213-1

Redemption

Copyright © 2013 by Barbara Heinlein

www.Harlequin.com

Printed in U.S.A.

Dear Reader,

I couldn't help thinking of my dad,
Harry Burton Johnson, as I wrote this book.
I grew up on stories of lost treasure. What could
be more exciting than finding a river of gold
hidden in the rocks on some remote mountain?

Dad loved to travel and believed it was the best
education there was for children. Because of that,
I've tromped around with him all over the West
looking for artifacts and other lost treasures.

If there is anything I've learned it's that the
journey really is more important than what lies
hidden at the end. I cherish those times with my
father—and I love that we live in a world where
there is still lost treasure.

B.J. Daniels

This book is for my father, Harry Burton Johnson, the best storyteller I ever knew.
He loved nothing better than treasure-hunting stories after spending most of his life searching for lost treasure of one kind or another.

Born in a time when women had few choices, he encouraged me to live life to its fullest and loved that I became a writer. He taught me to dream that anything was possible. Thanks, Dad. I sure miss you.

CHAPTER ONE

JACK DIDN'T WANT ANY TROUBLE. He couldn't afford any. That was why he decided to keep walking right past the Range Rider bar and the blaring Western music, through the darkness that shrouded the long-ago abandoned buildings of his hometown.

A sliver of moon hung over the top of the mountains among a plethora of stars in a midnight sky bigger than any he swore he'd ever seen. He could smell spring in the pines and on the snow-fed water as the creek rushed past town.

When he was a boy he used to imagine what Beartooth, Montana, had been like in the late 1800s. A gold-rush boomtown at the feet of the Crazy Mountains. Back then there'd been hotels and boardinghouses, a half dozen saloons, livery stables, assaying offices and several general stores.

Once the gold played out, the town died down to what it was today: one bar, a general store, a café, a church and a post office. Many of the original buildings still stood, though, ghostly remains of what once had been.

As isolated as the town was, Beartooth had survived when many Montana gold-rush towns had completely disappeared. Towns died off the same way families did, he thought, mindful of his own. His roots ran deep here in the shadow of the Crazies, as the locals called the wild, magnificent mountain range.

Over the years two stories took hold about how the Crazy Mountains got their name. Native Americans believed anyone who went into the frightening, fierce winds that blew out of the inhospitable rugged peaks was crazy. Another story was about a frontier woman who had wandered into the mountains. By the time she was found, the story went, she'd gone crazy.

Jack believed being this close to all that wildness could make anyone crazy. His great-grandfather used to tell stories about gunfights and bar brawls on this very street. Of course, his great-grandfather had been right in the middle of it.

Blame the mountains or genetics—this was his family legacy. Trouble was in his genes as if branded to his DNA. But hadn't he proven tonight that he could change? He'd been tempted to stop in for just one beer at the Range Rider. Why not, since it was his first night back in town?

But a two-year stint at Deer Lodge, Montana State Prison, for rustling a prized bull, had made him see that it was time to break some of those old family traditions. Didn't matter that he hadn't taken the bull. He'd been living as wild and crazy as the wilderness around Beartooth and it had caught up with him. He'd just made it easy for whoever had framed him.

He'd had two years to think about who'd set him up for the fall and what he was going to do about it. Or whether he was going to forget the past and move on with his life. Not that prison had been that bad. He'd spent those couple of years on the prison's cattle ranch, riding fence, chasing cattle, doing what he had since he'd been old enough to ride.

But now he was back in the only place that had ever been home.

A pickup roared past with a glow-in-the-dark bumper sticker that read: Keep Honking, I'm Reloading. Jack breathed in the night and the scent of dust along the narrow paved road, which turned to gravel just past the abandoned filling station and garage at the edge of town.

As the truck's engine roar died off, he heard raised voices ahead, coming from the alleyway between the Branding Iron Café and the skeletal stone remains of what had been the Beartooth Hotel.

As his eyes adjusted, he saw a man standing in the ambient light of the café sign. At first he didn't see the second figure. Jack caught only a few phrases, just enough to realize the man was threatening someone he had pressed against the stone wall of the café. It was too dark to see who, though.

"I've been looking for you," the man said. "I just didn't expect to find you here." The voice didn't sound familiar. Even after being gone for two years, Jack figured he probably still knew most everyone in this part of the county. Few new people moved here. Even fewer left.

Good sense told him to keep walking. Whatever was going on, it had nothing to do with him. The last thing he wanted to do was get involved in some drunken fight in an alley his first night home.

Earlier tonight he'd moved his few belongings into a small log cabin on the edge of town in the dense pines. The place was habitable and only a short walk from the café and the Beartooth General Store. It would work fine for the time being. He wasn't sure he was ready to go out to the family homestead just yet.

Walking on past the alley, Jack congratulated himself on staying clear of trouble tonight. He would have kept going—at least that's what he told himself—if he hadn't heard her voice.

"Let go of me." Definitely a woman's voice. "I already told you. You have the wrong woman. But if you don't leave me alone—"

Jack had already turned to go back when he heard a smack and her cry of pain. With a curse, he took off down the dark alley.

The man turned when he heard Jack's boot soles pounding the hard-packed earth, coming fast in his direction. "Butt out. This isn't any of your bus—" That's all the man got out before Jack hit him.

The man was a lot bigger than he'd appeared from a distance. He had the arms of someone who'd spent a lot of time lifting weights. Jack caught sight of jail-house tattoos on the man's massive arms below the sleeves of his dark T-shirt, and swore. He was already thinking that getting beat up wasn't exactly what he had in mind for his first night home. That was if he didn't get himself killed.

The man staggered back into a slice of darkness,

rubbing his jaw. He'd lost his Western hat when Jack had hit him. The hat lay on the ground between them.

"You just messed with the wrong man, cowboy," the stranger said.

Jack couldn't have agreed more as he braced himself for the man's attack. He'd been in his share of fistfights in his younger days and figured at thirty-one he could still hold his own—at least for a little while. He just hoped the man wasn't armed. That thought came somewhat late.

But to his surprise, the man looked past him in the direction of the woman, then turned, retreating into the pitch-blackness at the back of the alley. Odd, Jack thought, since the man hadn't even bothered to pick up his hat. Was he going to get his gun? Jack didn't want to find out. But a moment later, a vehicle door opened and slammed, an engine revved and the driver took off.

Jack leaned down and picked up the Western straw hat from the dirt before turning to the woman. "Are you all right?"

As she stepped away from the wall and into the diffused light from the café's sign, he was taken by surprise. She appeared to be close to his own age, and definitely not someone he knew since she was dressed in jogging gear. No one in Beartooth ran—unless there was a bear after her. No one wore Lycra, either—at least not in public.

But that was the least of it. Dark hair framed the face of an angel, while ice-cold fury shone in her dark eyes. It took him a moment to realize that her anger was directed at him.

"What do you think you're doing?" she demanded.

"I beg your pardon?"

"I can take care of myself," she said, snatching the hat from his fingers. "I didn't need you coming to my defense." She started to storm down the alley in the direction the man had gone.

Jack mentally kicked himself for getting involved in what now appeared to be a lover's quarrel. He should have known better. Just as he should have known to let well enough alone and let the woman leave without another word.

"From what I heard, it sure didn't sound like you didn't need my help," he said to her retreating back.

She stopped and turned to look back at him. Her eyes narrowed into slits as she stepped toward him, back into the faint glow of the café sign. "What you *heard?* What exactly is it you think you heard?"

He raised both hands and took a step back. "Nothing. I should have just left you alone to take care of yourself."

"Yes, you should have."

He nodded. "I won't make that mistake again."

With that, he turned and walked away, shaking his head at his attempt at chivalry. Still, he couldn't help but think about the slash of red on her one perfect cheek where the man had obviously hit her. Well, whoever she was, like the man she'd been arguing with, she wasn't from around here.

He told himself he wouldn't be crossing either of their paths again—which was just fine with him.

"Welcome home," he mumbled to himself as he headed for his cabin.

CHAPTER TWO

SHERIFF FRANK CURRY SHOVED back his Stetson as he watched the assistant coroner inspect the body. The sun was high and hot, another beautiful spring day in southern Montana. A breeze stirred the new leaves of the cottonwoods along the crystal-clear Yellowstone River. In the distance, the snowcapped peaks of the Crazy Mountains gleamed like fields of diamonds.

A fisherman had stumbled across the body in the weeds this morning after hooking into a nice-sized cutthroat. He was trying to land the fish when he'd practically fallen over the dead man.

From a nearby limb that hung out over the water, a crow cawed, drawing Frank's attention away from the body for a moment. The bird's dark wings flapped before it settled its black, beady eyes on him, as if to say he'd seen it all and could tell volumes if only Frank were capable of understanding a bird.

The crow cawed once more and flew off as Assistant Coroner Charlie Brooks stepped out of the weeds, rubbing the back of his neck. He was a short, squat man with timber-thick legs and a bald cue-ball of a head.

"I'd say he was killed sometime in the wee hours of this morning. Cause of death? Strangulation." Charlie, like a lot of coroners, was a huge mystery fan. "The body hasn't been here more than a few hours. Dumped, I would imagine, from up there." He pointed to an embankment that led up to a gravel access road into Otter Creek. "Appears he rolled down, to come to rest at the edge of the river."

Frank nodded—that had been his opinion as well. That was why he had one of his deputies up on the road making plaster casts of the tire prints closest to the edge of the embankment.

"Going to need to take some fingerprints once you get him to the morgue," he told the coroner. "No identification on him that I could find."

"We'll put him on ice until you can get a positive ID and notify next of kin."

Frank figured it shouldn't take long. The man had spent some time in a penitentiary somewhere, given the array of prison tattoos on his arms and neck. His prints should be on file.

"What's that he was killed with?" the coroner asked. "Appears to be some kind of fancy braided rope."

"Hitched horsehair," Frank said. "They make a lot of this up at Montana State Prison. That's why around here, hitchin' is synonymous with doing time. You ever heard the legend of Tom Horn? It's said that he was hung with a rope he hitched while doing time in a territorial prison."

"Horsehair dyed bright colors, huh? I'll be damned." A retired doctor, Charlie was new to Montana after living all his life in the big city.

Standing back, Frank watched as the assistant coroner and one of the local EMTs put the victim into a body bag and carried him to the fishing-access parking lot. In the distance he could hear the thrum of traffic on Interstate 90. Closer, a trout rose out of the water, the splash sending sparkling droplets into the morning air.

Frank watched the wavelets from the fish spread across the smooth surface. Murder had its own ripple effect. Shaking off the thought, he followed the path the body had made tumbling from the road. He hoped to find a wallet or something that might have fallen out of the man's pockets.

Fortunately, in Montana, few people littered, so there were only a half dozen rusted beer cans, a couple of plastic water bottles and several pieces of dew-wet cardboard in the weeds. He was about to give up when he spotted what looked like a scrap of white paper caught high in the grass.

His hands still covered by the latex gloves he'd donned earlier, he plucked the scrap up, surprised to see that it was a photograph folded in half. Yellowed with age, the snapshot was also cracked down the middle because of the fold and worn at the edges as if it had been handled a lot. The people lined up in the shot appeared to be a family, the youngest still in Mama's arms.

Frank turned the photo over and saw that something had been written on the back. The faded marks were impossible to read. But what made his heart beat a little faster was the realization that the photo hadn't been in the grass long. It wasn't even that damp from the morning dew.

All his instincts told him it had belonged to the unidentified dead man.

JACK WOKE TO POUNDING on his cabin door. He pulled on his jeans and stumbled barefoot to the door. "What in the—" He cut off his words with a grin as he saw who was standing there.

"Sorry to wake you so early, but I'm hungry," Carson Grant said, smiling.

Jack reached for his friend's hand, clasped it and pulled Carson into an awkward quick hug.

"It is so good to see you," Carson said.

"You, too. Come on in."

Carson had offered to come up to the prison and pick him up when he got out.

"Actually, the warden had my pickup released from Evidence and sent up here along with my horse and horse trailer, right after I was sent to prison. So I'll be traveling in style," Jack had joked about his old truck. "I will need a place to corral my horse, though, until I get settled."

Carson had laughed. "That was awfully nice of the warden. Hell, Jack, you really do make friends everywhere you go. Just drop your horse at the W Bar G. I'll tell my sister."

"Give me a minute," he said now as he snapped on his Western shirt. "I'll get dressed and we can walk down to the café."

"I was surprised to hear you weren't staying out at your folks' place," Carson said as Jack pulled on his boots.

"Just needed a few days in town," he said, hating to admit even to his best friend that he wasn't prepared for the memories the homestead would evoke. He'd kept the property taxes up on the place, but still wasn't sure he wanted to stay in Beartooth. "Ready?"

They walked down the mountainside through the pines, the morning sun shining through the branches to make golden puddles in the dried pine needles. A cool breeze blew down from the still-snowcapped peaks, but the sun felt warm as they walked to the Branding Iron. Jack swore he'd never smelled any air that was better than this.

Overhead, Montana's big sky was a clear brilliant blue that stretched across the vast horizon. It was the kind of day that made a cowboy glad he was alive— and in Montana.

As Jack pushed open the café door, a bell tinkled overhead. The cook waved from back in the kitchen. Lou had been a permanent fixture at the Branding Iron for as long as Jack could remember.

"Sit wherever you like," Bethany Reynolds called as she came out from behind the counter carrying a half dozen plates filled with food. Bethany, now close to thirty, had been waitressing at the café off and on since high school.

Jack breathed in the scent of coffee and crispy fried bacon as he slid into a booth across from Carson. "Bethany's looking good," he said.

"I wouldn't let Clete hear you say that," Carson warned. Bethany had married Clete Reynolds, a former football star. Clete owned the Range Rider bar and kept a variety of weapons behind the counter.

Jack was just marveling at how nothing in Beartooth ever changed when another woman came out of the kitchen. Her hair and eyes weren't as dark as they'd appeared last night in the alley. Her slim body under her apron was tucked nicely into a pair of jeans and a Western shirt that set off her assets—something else he hadn't gotten a good look at last night.

As she swept up to his table with two cups and a pot of coffee, she gave no indication that she recognized him.

"Good morning," he said, studying her as he removed his Stetson and placed it on the seat next to him. She had a bruise on her cheek that she'd done a pretty good job of covering with makeup.

She put down the cups and filled them without looking at him or Carson, but Jack noticed that her hand trembled as she filled his. There was no doubt in his mind that she recognized him. Without a word though, she headed for a large table at the front of the café where a group of ranchers were seated.

Jack's gaze followed her before finally turning back to his friend. "Who is *that?*"

Carson, who'd apparently also been watching the woman, gave a secretive smile. "You heard Claude Durham died a few months ago, right? That's the new owner of the café, Kate LaFond. At least that's the name she's going by now. I swear I know her from somewhere and, wherever it was, Kate LaFond was *not* her name."

"Really?" Jack said, letting his gaze return to the woman.

"Just saying you might want to stay clear of that one."

Jack turned back to his coffee and took a sip. He

figured that was probably good advice given what he'd seen last night, and yet his gaze strayed to her as she disappeared into the kitchen.

"So how are you settling in?" Carson asked after Bethany had taken their orders.

"It's as if I never left." Jack could feel his friend studying him.

"You aren't still thinking about getting even with whoever set you up for the rustling fall, are you?"

Jack smiled and glanced toward the group of ranchers at the big table at the front of the café. He recognized all of them, including Hitch McCray. "Water under the bridge."

Carson laughed. "If I didn't know you so well, I might believe it. I just don't want to see you end up back in prison."

"That makes two of us." Jack smiled as he leaned back in the booth and stretched out his long legs. "So how are *you* doing?"

"Gamblers Anonymous meetings in Big Timber once a week. Working the ranch the rest of the time."

Jack nodded. He knew Carson had been through hell the past twelve years. First, the woman he'd loved had been murdered. Everyone in the county thought he'd killed Ginny West. To keep from losing his son to vigilante justice, Carson's father, W.T., had sent him away for eleven years. Carson had ended up in Vegas, of all places, and gotten into trouble gambling.

Just recently he'd been cleared of the murder. But Jack knew that Carson was still paying off gambling debts and dealing with his father's death. It didn't matter that he'd never gotten along with W.T. Blood was always thicker than water, even when you wished it wasn't, Jack thought, with his own regrets.

"So you're sticking around?" he asked. Carson had sworn that the last thing on earth he was going to be was a rancher, and yet Jack knew for a fact that his friend was now wrangling on the family's W Bar G ranch with his sister, Destry.

"For now," Carson said. "Have you made any plans?"

Jack shook his head. He'd purposely not let himself think about the future, or the past, for that matter. Especially about how he'd ended up in prison. Or who might have put him there. Or maybe more to the point, what he intended to do about it.

"Interested in a job?" Carson asked.

"What do you have in mind?"

"Wrangling on the W Bar G."

"Destry offered me a job when she heard I was getting out, but I thought she was just being nice."

Carson laughed. "When it comes to the ranch, my sister doesn't offer anyone a job just to be nice. If you're serious about sticking around and staying out of trouble, I know she'd be happy to hire you on. Or maybe you're planning to start ranching your folks' place."

"I'm not sure what I'm going to do, to tell you the truth."

"Well, we're going to be working the roundup the next few days and sure could use your help with branding if you're going to be around."

Jack considered Carson and Destry's generous offer,

then studied his worn but lucky cowboy boots for a moment. Was he staying? He knew it could mean trouble if he did and yet… He watched Kate LaFond walk past their table again.

"Thanks for the offer. I'll give it some thought."

"You do that." Carson seemed to hesitate as if afraid to broach the subject. "Have you seen Chantell yet?"

Ah, Chantell Hyett. Jack knew it was just a matter of time before he crossed paths with his former girlfriend. "The only letter she sent me in prison made it clear she wouldn't be waiting around for me."

"You don't sound all that broke up over it."

He laughed. Chantell's father was the judge who'd sent him up—and the only one who'd taken their relationship seriously. Maybe too seriously. Two years at Deer Lodge was a stiff sentence for rustling one bull that was returned unharmed within twenty-four hours after it had gone missing. Jack recalled the self-satisfied gleam in Judge Hyett's eyes the morning he'd sentenced him. Jack had felt lucky he'd gotten only two years.

As the large table of ranchers paid and began to leave, Jack saw Hitch McCray headed for their table and swore under his breath.

"Jack French," Hitch said, smiling around a toothpick stuck in the side of his mouth. The rancher was on the south end of his thirties. He ranched with his mother on land just down the road from the French place. Ruth McCray ran her son and her ranch with an iron fist. When Hitch could escape her, he sneaked away to chase women and drink, both to excess.

But none of those were the reasons Jack couldn't stand the sight of the man.

"Hitch McCray," he ground out through gritted teeth.

Jack had heard all the stories, even while in prison, including Hitch's driving-while-intoxicated arrests. Not that he could blame the man for drinking. If Ruth McCray had been his mother, he would have tried to stay drunk, too.

Word around town was that Ruth was on the warpath over Hitch's brushes with the law, as well as his drinking and his taste in women. Hitch chased after any woman he saw. But if he ever caught one, his mother wasn't about to let him keep her. Ruth had never approved of any woman her son had brought home—and, no doubt, never would.

"So you're back?" Hitch said, sounding surprised.

"This is where I was born and raised. Why wouldn't I come back here?" Jack asked.

Hitch shrugged, his gaze sliding across the table to Carson. "Well, if you decide you want to sell your family's place... I know it's not much, but I might be interested." He looked at Jack again. "You let me know. You two have a nice day," he said, and laughed as if he'd said something funny.

"Don't pay any attention to him," Carson said as Hitch left. "You don't know for sure that he had anything to do with you going to prison *or* what happened to your old man."

Jack nodded. No, he didn't know. Not yet, anyway.

Bethany brought out their breakfasts. They ate, talking little. Jack found himself watching the woman he'd met last night in the alley. Kate LaFond. At least that was the name she was going by now, apparently.

It wasn't until he and Carson had finished their breakfasts and left that Jack could no longer help himself. He had to ask more about the new owner of the Branding Iron.

"I've been trying to place her since W.T.'s funeral," Carson said. "I know I met her somewhere in the eleven years when I was away from Montana. But I'd swear her name wasn't Kate LaFond."

"You can't remember where?"

"No, and it's driving me crazy."

"Why don't you just ask her?" Jack suggested. When Carson said nothing, Jack eyed him more closely. "You think she was in some kind of trouble back then?"

"Or now. Why else change your name?"

Good question, Jack thought. "Maybe you have her confused with someone else." Hadn't he heard her say something like, "You have the wrong woman," to the man in the alley last night? "She could just have one of those faces."

Carson laughed. "Yeah, right." Kate LaFond had the face of an angel. "But I suppose it's possible," he added doubtfully.

"Is that the rig she drives?" he asked as they walked past a newer model red pickup.

"Yeah," Carson said and frowned. "Jack?"

"What?"

"I know that look. Don't get involved with this woman."

Jack nodded. Clearly the woman had secrets and some questionable acquaintances, considering the man she'd been arguing with last night. But right now he was more curious about what he'd seen in the bed of her pickup. A shovel covered in fresh dirt. Kate La-Fond had been doing some digging—but not in the flower beds at the front of the café, which she'd let go to weeds.

"Where does she *say* she's from?" he asked Carson.

"She doesn't. No one seems to know anything about her. She just showed up after Claude Durham died and took over the café. Not even nosy Nettie Benton at the general store has been able to find out anything about her."

"A woman of mystery," Jack said, smiling with relish.

Carson swore under his breath. "Why did I bother warning you?"

How could Jack not be curious about her? He'd been warned to keep his distance by not only his friend, but also the woman herself.

KATE LAFOND WATCHED the two cowboys leave. She didn't have to ask about the blond, blue-eyed handsome one who'd come in with Carson Grant. She'd already heard more than enough about Jack French.

"Just like his father," one of the older ranchers had said, with a shake of his head, this morning before Jack and Carson had come in. She'd been busy refilling coffee cups at the large table of regulars who met in the café each morning. They'd mentioned they'd heard Jack had gotten out of prison and was back.

"Delbert French was one wild son of a bee in his day. He could ride anything and damned sure wasn't afraid to try. But he couldn't stay out of trouble for the life of him. The acorn didn't fall far from the tree when it came to Jack."

"Sad what happened to ol' Del," another rancher agreed. "Wonder if his boy plans to keep the family place."

Hitch McCray had spoken up. "Smartest thing Jack could do is clear out. His father never amounted to anything on that piece of land. I doubt Jack will take to ranching any better than his old man did. He'd rather be a saddle bum." Apparently, it was no secret Hitch wanted to buy the old French place.

Kate remembered how the others had gone quiet with disapproval. Hitch was the youngest of the regulars. She got the feeling that they didn't particularly like him but put up with him because of his mother.

"Jack has as much right to be here as anyone," Taylor West had said into the silence. "He's paid for his mistake. If he really was the one who took that bull to start with."

"Why would you say that?" Hitch had challenged. "He was caught dead to rights."

"If Jack did rustle that bull, he was either drunk or just foolin' around," Taylor said. "Either way, Judge Hyett went awful hard on him. I suspect if Jack hadn't been dating Judge Hang 'Em Hy's daughter he would have gotten off with jail time served."

The table had gone quiet after that. Kate had finished filling the coffee cups and gone to pick up their orders. By the time she'd returned with their breakfasts, the conversation had moved on to the weather.

Overhearing the earlier discussion now made her more curious about the man who'd come to her rescue last night. She'd been angry that he'd thought she needed rescuing. She'd been taking care of herself for so long she resented any help. The last thing she wanted was to be beholden to any man—especially one like Jack French. And now the cowboy thought he'd saved her last night.

She'd seen how surprised he'd been when her attacker had taken off without a fight. What Jack *hadn't* seen was the small gun she'd pulled. The other man had seen it, though. One look at her and the gun, and he'd hightailed it.

Kate shuddered inwardly at the memory. She'd hoped she would have more time before one of them showed up. But she couldn't let it rattle her. She'd deal with it, the same way she'd dealt with everything else in her life. But it did make her all the more aware that she needed to speed things up.

Late last fall, she'd barely gotten settled in before winter had hit with a fury. She'd realized quickly that she would have to wait it out. But now that spring had finally come to the mountains, she wasn't about to let anything stop her. Or anyone.

Kate watched Jack French and his friend Carson Grant meandering up the street. She saw Jack peer into the bed of her pickup, then turn to look back as if he knew she'd be watching. She quickly turned away.

Across the street, she saw movement in the room over the general store and groaned.

Jack French wasn't the only one who was too curious about her and her personal business. Nosy Nettie Benton had been spying on her for months.

CHAPTER THREE

NETTIE BENTON TURNED OFF the vacuum and surveyed the room. She'd been talking for years about turning the storage area over the Beartooth General Store into an apartment.

It had taken her husband leaving for her to do more than talk. Bob had been gone four months now after packing up his pickup and leaving for Arizona, with no intention of ever returning. Not that she would take him back if he did.

She hadn't expected to hear from him, given the way he'd left, but a few weeks ago she'd received a postcard. It had a cactus in bloom on the front and the words Greetings from Arizona. She'd turned it over, easily recognizing the handwriting of her husband of thirty years.

> *Just wanted to let you know that I made it without any problems. Hope all is well with you. Sorry about everything— Bob*

She'd stared at the scrawled words for a moment and then dropped the postcard into the wastebasket without another thought. She felt guilty enough that she hadn't given him a thought all these months, let alone missed him. But she was through with Bob Benton and realized she had been for years.

Bob's parents had given them the store as a wedding present. Well, they'd given it to her, since Bob had no interest in being a shopkeeper, or anything else for that matter.

She was the one who worked in the store seven days a week, short days on Sunday because she had to go to church first. She prided herself on having a general store that carried everything from canned goods to diapers, muck boots to fishing tackle.

Nettie also prided herself on knowing everything that was going on in the small community. Most days, with business slow, she would perch in the front window of the store and watch what life there was pass by. She learned a lot doing that and liked to brag that she knew more about the people of Sweetgrass County than they knew even about themselves.

The bell over the front door of the store sounded below her. Nettie glanced out the window, saw Sheriff Frank Curry's patrol pickup parked out front, then hurriedly checked her short, dyed-red hair in the mirror on the wall before she went down the stairs.

Her pulse jumped as it always did at the sight of the sheriff, who was standing just inside the door. She straightened, fighting a ridiculous grin, and did her best not to fuss with her new haircut.

"Mornin', Lynette," Frank said, tipping his Stetson. He was the only person who ever called her by her given name.

A big, broad-shouldered man, he looked as if he'd stepped out of an old Western movie with his thick, drooping mustache. Now in his late fifties, like her, he was even more handsome than he'd been when the two of them were young and in love. There were tiny laugh lines around his eyes, his face tanned from working outside when he wasn't working for the law.

"Frank," she said, still trying to hide how happy she was to see him. After all, legally she was still a married woman and, while Frank had done his share of flirting with her since Bob had left, he hadn't even gone so far as to ask her out. The fact that she'd broken his heart thirty years ago seemed to have made him leery of going back down that particular trail.

"What can I get for you?" she asked as she watched him head for the cooler. He took out his usual orange soda and popped the top before taking a long drink. He smiled at her as he swallowed and reached for his usual candy bar.

"Just needed somethin' cold," he said.

She suspected he'd stopped in for more than orange soda and a candy bar. She hoped it was an excuse to see her. That she could be wrong, though, kept her from calling him on it.

"Warm for spring," she said, glancing toward the front window of the store, with its view of the sharp peak in the distance that had given the town its name. Closer, she caught sight of the café across the street and Kate LaFond. The young woman was like a burr under her saddle and had been since the day she'd shown up in town.

Nettie was about to ask the sheriff if he'd checked up on Kate, something she'd asked him to do before Christmas. She imagined that he'd forgotten, given everything that had been going on back then.

But when he spoke, all thought of Kate LaFond vanished.

"There's something I need to ask you," Frank said as he moved to the counter. He put down his soda can and with obvious reluctance took a small plastic evidence bag from a pocket. "I need you to keep this just between you and me, Lynette. I'm going to need your word on that."

She nodded, wide-eyed. He knew her too well. People considered her a terrible gossip, Frank included. But she would do anything for Frank. Even keep a secret.

He flattened what appeared to be an old photograph inside the bag and pulled a magnifying glass from his other pocket. "I know it's hard to see through the plastic, but I'd prefer the snapshot not be handled too much."

Her curiosity piqued, Nettie took the magnifying glass he offered her and leaned over the photo. As it came into view, dread filled her.

"You know those people?" Frank asked.

She knew he'd seen her reaction. She suspected he'd had much the same reaction himself when he'd gotten a good look at the photo. "Where did you get this?"

"Can't say."

The fact that it was in an evidence bag meant it was part of an investigation. Her pulse pounded as she took another glance at the faces in the photo, turned the bag over to look at the back of the snapshot, then handed him the magnifying glass.

"Well?" he asked.

"You know as well as I do it's the Ackermann family." She couldn't imagine what he was doing with that photo, let alone what it was doing in an evidence bag or why he was warning her she had to keep quiet about it.

"Who else have you shown this to?" she asked. All that awful stuff had happened more than thirty years ago. Only residents as old or older than her and Frank would remember. But it wasn't as if everyone else hadn't heard about what had happened up there in the hollow outside town.

"You're the only person I've shown it to." He shook his head. "I was hoping you'd tell me I was wrong."

"I just don't understand why you'd be asking about the Ackermanns. They're all dead." She saw his expression and her heart fell. "Aren't they?"

"I don't know what this photo means, if anything. I just had to be sure I wasn't wrong. I need you to keep quiet about this, Lynette. I'm serious."

"You don't have to worry about me saying a word." She shuddered at the memory of what Frank's father, who was sheriff back then, and his deputies had found up in that valley more than three decades ago.

"I knew I could trust you. That's why I brought it to you," he said.

His words made her heart beat a little faster as he put both the evidence bag and the magnifying glass back in his pocket. She watched him finish his soda, seeing the weight of this on his broad shoulders.

"What's that written on the back?" she asked.

He shook his head as he paid for the soda and candy bar. "It looks like hieroglyphics to me."

"Or a map of some kind."

He looked up at her, and for the first time, his gaze seemed to brighten. "A map? You know you really are an amazing woman."

She wasn't actually blushing, was she? Nettie quickly scooped up the money he'd put on the counter and busied herself putting it in the cash register.

"I'd better get going." As he glanced toward the street, he let out a curse. "I promised you I'd check on your new neighbor." The Branding Iron Café was directly across the narrow strip of pavement from the store. "I'm sorry, it completely slipped my mind."

"You've had a lot on your plate with the Ginny West murder case." The murder had gone unsolved for eleven years—until late last fall when some new evidence had surfaced.

"Still, that's no excuse. I told you I'd do it and I will." He frowned. "Did I see an Apartment for Rent sign in your front window?"

"You know I've been threatening for years to use that old apartment upstairs for something other than storage." She and Bob had lived up there when they'd first gotten married, but only until their house on the mountain behind the store had been finished. "I know I can't get much rent for it, but I thought I'd try. Would be nice to have someone living up there who can help keep an eye on the store," she added quickly. She didn't want him to think she needed the money. Nor did she want him to think she missed Bob.

"Good idea," Frank said, but she could tell he was distracted. "Lynette, if you ever need anything—"

"You don't have to worry about me. I'm fine, Frank."

He smiled, the warmth in his eyes making her feel like a schoolgirl again. "Yes, you are fine. By the way, I like your new haircut." Then he hesitated. "You won't say anything about—"

"*No.*" She swallowed back the bad taste in her mouth at the mention again of the Ackermann family. She almost wished he'd never shown her the photograph. When she'd looked past the faces, she'd seen the cave behind the house, a thick wooden door covering the opening, and remembered what had been found in the cold, damp darkness behind it.

She shuddered, hugging herself, and said a silent prayer for all of them as she watched the sheriff leave.

JACK REINED IN his horse to look out across the wide, green valley. He breathed in the day, never more thankful than right now that he'd come back here. Next to him, the creek roared as it tumbled through large granite boulders. Farther away, calves bawled for their mamas in a field of tall, new green grass and wildflowers.

He loved helping with spring roundup on the W Bar G, gathering the cattle in order to tally the calf crop and getting ready to tag and brand. It was a big operation on this huge ranch. He'd been riding for two long days now, combing the breaks and coulees for cattle and heading them toward the central point where other riders kept the herd together until they could be moved down to the corrals for branding.

Each night he'd fallen dead asleep, saddle sore and exhausted, hearing the sound of lowing cattle even when he closed his eyes. The work had kept him from thinking about anything other than cows. But the spring roundup was now over, and he had to make a decision whether to stay on at the W Bar G, ranch his own place, or sell out and move on.

"You're good with horses and cattle," Destry Grant said to him now as they rode back down toward the main ranch house. "I need someone I can trust, and my ranch manager likes you. Not that Russell will go any easier on you than he does on the rest of the wranglers."

He grinned at that as they dismounted. "I wouldn't have it any other way."

Destry gave him a hug. "I'm glad you're back. So is Carson." Carson had been his best friend since they were kids. Jack had lied for him eleven years ago, knowing that Carson had nothing to do with the death of his former girlfriend Ginny West. He would do it again, since Carson was the closest to a brother he'd ever had.

But being under suspicion of murdering his girlfriend had been rough on his friend. Carson had enough to overcome after being raised by W. T. Grant, an overbearing, controlling father. *Rest his soul in peace,* Jack quickly added. W.T. had died late last fall, leaving the ranch to Destry instead of Carson.

"Carson's doing okay, right?" Jack asked as they walked toward the big house her father had built.

"He's not gambling and he's paying back what he owes," she said. "But I worry about him. I think he's restless."

"He just needs a good woman," Margaret said, and smiled at Jack as he and Destry reached the kitchen. "Welcome back." Margaret had been W. T. Grant's closest friend as well as the cook and housekeeper. When he'd died, he'd left the house to her, since Destry preferred to live in the old homestead down the road, until her upcoming wedding to Rylan West.

Rylan was in the process of getting a home built for them. The W Bar G and the West Ranch, where Rylan worked with his father, adjoined, so they were building on a site in the middle.

"You two aren't trying to line Carson up, are you?" Jack asked, seeing that they were.

"Lisa Anne Clausen has had a crush on him since grade school," Destry said and crossed her fingers. "They'd be good together."

Jack shook his head. "I'm not sure Carson is ready. Just saying…"

Carson seemed to be doing fine, though, Jack thought as he drove toward Beartooth and his cabin. It made him proud that his friend was finally taking responsibility for himself and his actions. It was his gambling and the murder charge that had made W. T. Grant cut his son from the will. Carson got to live in the big house as long as he was employed. Fortunately, he seemed to have taken to ranching after years of fighting it.

The long days on the W Bar G had also kept Jack out of trouble and away from the Branding Iron Café. Which meant he hadn't seen Kate LaFond again. But he hadn't stopped thinking about her. As he pulled up in front of his cabin, it was early, but he was tired and couldn't wait to lie down and put his boots up.

The knock at his door what seemed to be only a few minutes later brought him out of a deep sleep. For a moment, he didn't know where he was. He'd come into the cabin and collapsed on the bed still fully dressed after the long day in the saddle.

He rose now and padded to the door, thinking Carson must have stopped by for some reason.

When he saw the sheriff darkening his doorway, Jack felt that old, familiar fear he'd grown up with. The law at your door was never a good thing.

"Sheriff Curry," he said, fighting to fully wake up. Whatever the sheriff wanted, Jack figured he needed his wits about him. "Is there a problem?"

"Sorry if I woke you," the sheriff apologized.

"Been working spring roundup," he said, but figured the sheriff probably knew that. Sheriffs tended to keep track of ex-cons, and Frank Curry had watched him grow up so probably took a special interest.

"I heard you're on the W Bar G now." Frank pulled off his hat. "Just need a minute of your time, Jack. I've got something here I was hoping you might be able to help me with. Mind if I come in for a moment?"

Jack stepped back, wondering what the hell this

was about. He turned on another lamp and offered the sheriff a seat.

"I won't be staying that long. If you'd just take a look at this…" He pulled a plastic bag out of his jacket pocket. Inside was a coiled thin rope. Even from a distance, Jack could tell it was hitched out of horsehair. He'd watched enough of the inmates at Deer Lodge making everything from reins and ropes to belts and hatbands.

Hitching involved twisting three or four strands of dyed horsehair into what were known as pulls. The pulls were used with cotton cord and a wood or metal rod to hitch the horsehair in a circular pattern. A series of hitches created a variety of colorful patterns, most commonly diamonds and spirals.

What amazed Jack was how long it took—a couple of hours to do only an inch of hitching. When finished, the cord or rod was removed. The item was then soaked in water and clamped between two heavy plates of steel to dry.

A lot of the inmates sold what they made, getting as much as four to eight thousand dollars for bridles. Belts, hatbands and quirts were cheaper, because they were faster to make.

"Do you recognize the pattern?" the sheriff asked. "Is it one from Montana State Prison?"

Jack took the bag and held it under the lamplight. The colors were brighter and the pattern different from ones he'd seen in prison. "It's not from Deer Lodge," he said and handed it back. "At least it isn't like any I saw up there."

The sheriff nodded. He put the bag back in his pocket. "You do any hitching while you were up there?"

Jack laughed. "I was working the prison ranch, so I kept plenty busy. I've watched a lot of guys hitch, though. Takes more patience than I have."

"Well, thanks for your time." He started to leave, but stopped and turned. "Oh, by the way, while you were up at the state pen, did you happen to run across Cullen Ackermann?"

The infamous Ackermann. The sheriff had asked the question casually enough, but it still put Jack on guard. "I made a point of staying away from crazy old cons—especially that one."

Frank Curry nodded. "Was he still preaching revolution and the Armageddon of this country as we know it?"

Jack nodded, a little surprised by the sheriff's interest. But, then again, Cullen Ackermann was Beartooth's most infamous charismatic crazy, even though he'd never been considered a true local since he wasn't born here.

"I suppose he found an audience up there before he died," Frank said.

"He definitely had his followers in prison," Jack said. "Young, anti-government wannabe survivalists were big fans of his. A few of them bought into what he was selling." To fill the silence that followed, he added, "I think most of them were more interested in Ackermann's cache of gold he allegedly hid before he got sent up."

"That tale still circulating, huh?" The sheriff shook his head and looked as if he wanted to ask more, but apparently changed his mind. "Well, you have a nice night."

Jack followed him out onto the small porch in front of the cabin and watched until the patrol pickup headed toward Big Timber, then he went back inside. He hadn't asked where the sheriff had gotten the rope or why he wanted Jack's opinion on the hitching pattern. Nor had he asked about the dried blood that stained the horsehair in the evidence bag.

Jack had learned a long time ago not to ask questions where he didn't want to know the answers.

NETTIE WAS STOCKING groceries, trying to keep her mind off what the sheriff had shown her, when the girl came into the store. It had taken Nettie a few moments to get to her feet from down on her knees. Most of the time, she didn't feel her age—it was easy to tell herself that she didn't feel a day over thirty.

That was, until she tried to get up from where she'd been sitting on the floor and her body reminded her that she was hugging sixty. It was an odd feeling. Her life had always been ahead of her. Now most of it was behind her.

The girl had stopped just inside the door and turned to look out the front window. She was a skinny little thing with long, pale blond hair that fell most of the way down her back.

As if deep in thought, the girl didn't seem to hear

Nettie's approach. Which, of course, made Nettie wonder what she found so interesting out the window.

Looking past her, Nettie followed the girl's gaze to
where three men stood talking in front of the post office up the street. She recognized two local ranchers.
The third man was Sheriff Frank Curry.

"Can I help you?"

The girl jumped and spun around, eyes wide. She
was pretty, with big, dark eyes, and older than Nettie
had first thought, still somewhere in her late teens,
though.

"I'm sorry," Nettie said. "I didn't mean to startle
you." But she had, and badly.

It took a moment for the girl to catch her breath and
speak. "I'm here about the apartment?"

Nettie studied her. She'd hoped to get a man, prefer-
ably one who could watch the place. With her house on
the mountain behind the store, Nettie lived far enough
away that she wouldn't hear if the store was being bur-
glarized during the night. Last fall a grizzly had broken
the back window. Thankfully, something had scared
the bear away or it could have gotten in and made one
devil of a mess.

"I was hoping to rent it to a man," she said.

The girl's disappointment was almost palpable.
"It's just that there aren't any other places to stay in
Beartooth."

*That was because few people had any reason to
come here,* Nettie almost said. Big Timber was only
twenty miles away and had a lot more amenities.

Nettie glanced from the girl to her small, newer

model compact car parked in front of the store. "I would need first and last month's rent and a deposit." She named a number, a little higher than she'd originally planned to ask. She figured that would put an end to it.

"Okay," the girl said. "I have cash."

Cash? "How long were you thinking of renting the place?"

"I'm not sure. I'd be happy to pay for six months in advance if you'd consider me," she added quickly.

Six months? "Mind if I ask what brings you to Beartooth?"

The girl brushed a lock of hair back from her face and lifted her chin almost as if in defiance. "I'm applying to art school in the fall and I need somewhere to work on my portfolio."

It sounded reasonable. Even possibly true. So why did Nettie feel as though the girl had practiced it?

"I really would appreciate it if you would consider renting to me," she said, pleading in her tone.

All red flags. "Shouldn't you see the apartment first?"

"Yes, of course." The girl was visibly nervous, but Nettie reminded herself that she was young. This was probably her first apartment. No doubt her mother and father would be paying the rent and for her art school, as well. So Nettie wouldn't have to worry about bounced checks anyway.

"Come with me," she said. "There is a private entrance outside up the stairs, but you can also get to the apartment through here." She led the way, with each step telling herself to pass on this girl.

But curiosity had always been Nettie Benton's downfall. And there was something about this girl—and her desperation to live in Beartooth.

CHAPTER FOUR

SHERIFF FRANK CURRY had always prided himself on his patience. He was used to the state crime lab being backed up for weeks, if not months. Investigations took time. Some arrests weren't made for months and didn't go to trial for years. Justice moved slowly, as most of Montana wasn't automated. Things were done the way they'd been done for years, especially fingerprints.

Only a few cities in Montana had the electronic system. Otherwise, prints were taken the old-fashioned way and sent to the crime lab. He had no doubt that the victim's prints would be in the system, since he was betting the man had done prison time somewhere, possibly even Deer Lodge at some point. Which could explain how he had the photograph in his possession, if he'd crossed paths with Cullen Ackermann before his death.

"It looks like a map," Lynette had said of the faded marks on the back of the photo.

Maybe at one time it had been a map, but the drawings were indistinguishable now. Still, before he died Cullen could have given the photo and map to one of the boys. If any of the boys *had* survived. And if these marks on the photo were a map, was it to the fabled hidden gold?

Frank had learned to live with the slow pace investigations often took.

That was, until this one.

He couldn't help feeling anxious. He had to know what he was dealing with, starting with the dead man he had cooling his heels in the fridge down at the local mortuary.

It's that damned photograph. His gut instinct told him that the man on that slab at the morgue was connected to the Ackermanns. Maybe he'd made Cullen's acquaintance in prison. But why then was the rope, according to Jack, not one that was hitched at Montana State Prison, where Ackermann had been confined for the past thirty years?

Frank knew his fear ran much deeper than that. Hadn't he been afraid for years that Cullen Ackermann would release his vengeance on Beartooth, just as he'd promised all those years ago?

Cullen's dead. All the Ackermanns are dead.

Were they? He told himself that if any of the children had survived all those years ago, they would have turned up long before this. All four boys and the little girl had been presumed dead more than three decades ago. But the remains of only one of the boys had ever been found back up in the Crazies. Who was to say that one or more of them hadn't survived? And had just now turned up.

But if so, why *now?*

"Because their father died," he said to his empty office. "Cullen's death triggered whatever is going on."

He knew he was jumping to conclusions, which also

wasn't like him. But Assistant Coroner Charlie Brooks had estimated the dead man's age at somewhere around forty-five. The boys in the snapshot ranged in age from about twelve to seventeen. This photo had to have been taken about thirty years ago, which meant that the dead man could conceivably be one of the boys.

Frank felt as if a clock had started ticking the moment Cullen Ackermann died. He had to know who the dead man was. Or wasn't, he thought as he studied the photo again.

When he couldn't take it any longer, he picked up the phone and called a local artist he knew. "Have you ever done a sketch of a dead man?"

"You mean like a police artist's sketch?" his friend asked.

"Exactly."

NEWS OF THE BODY found by the river shot through the county like a high-powered rifle report. But since the dead man was found near the Yellowstone River twenty miles away and no one was missing from Beartooth, the news died down quickly.

That was until the sketch of the dead man came out Saturday in the weekly Big Timber newspaper asking if anyone could identify the man.

"Probably just some bum off the interstate," Jack heard people saying. He hadn't seen the paper. He'd been too busy on the W Bar G. Nor was he interested. All his attention Saturday morning at the café was on Kate LaFond.

"Some homeless guy. Or a hobo," he heard people saying.

He smiled to himself. Were there still hoboes who rode the rails?

The Branding Iron Café was packed this morning. Not because of the news about the dead man being found by the river a few days ago, but because the Sweetgrass County Spring Fair was this weekend in Big Timber.

Everyone looked forward to the fair. It was a sign that spring had finally arrived. The fair had everything from a rodeo, cattle auction and carnival, to arts-and-crafts booths and a swap meet. Plus it was a great excuse come spring to see everyone you hadn't seen over the winter.

Jack was finishing his coffee when Kate came by to refill his cup. It was the first time he'd been to the Branding Iron since he'd started work at the W Bar G. Since Destry had given everyone the day off to attend the fair, and he'd taken advantage of it, he decided to treat himself to breakfast. At least that was the story he told himself.

As Kate had done days before, she seemed to make a point of not looking at him. But when she came by to refill his cup, he pushed it closer to make her job easier and her fingers brushed his. She jerked back. Hot coffee sloshed onto the table and she let out an unladylike curse under her breath.

He reached for the napkins. "Here, let me—"

"I've got it," she snapped, her gaze coming up to meet his. In the alley, her eyes had appeared dark, like her hair. Now, though, he saw with delight that they were wide set and the color of good whiskey. Her hair was the same color, with strands of gold woven through it, and fell to just below her chin.

He drew back his fingers and watched as she snatched the handful of napkins from him and cleaned up the mess. The shock of her touch still warmed his blood. She, on the other hand, appeared to be fighting hard to hide her reaction.

As the café began to clear out, she hurried to ring up patrons at the till and help Bethany clean the tables. He watched her. The woman could flat-out move when the café was busy. He had to admire her work ethic and her efficiency. He guessed she'd waitressed before buying the cafe.

"Ever been to a branding?" Jack asked as Kate came by a second time to refill his coffee. She shook her head, not looking at him. "There's going to be a big one out at the W Bar G starting Monday. You should come. Get to know some of your neighbors, you know, socialize a little."

She raised her gaze to his again. He saw anger spark like a Fourth of July firecracker.

"That's right, you don't need anyone." He softened his words with a grin. "Especially the likes of me, huh."

Some of the fire died back in her dark eyes. "Especially."

"I just thought you'd like to see some of the real Wild West before you leave Beartooth."

"Who says I'm leaving?" she challenged.

"Aren't you?"

She looked away for a moment, then said, "I suppose I could bring out some cinnamon rolls. I heard neighbors bring food."

His grin widened. "That would be nice and neighborly."

She let out an amused chuckle as she left his table. He watched her, too interested in her for his own good.

As she started to gather up dirty dishes from a large table, he saw her freeze. Curious, he watched as she picked up what appeared to be a folded piece of paper that had been stuck under the edge of a plate.

She turned her back as she unfolded the note to read it. He saw her shoulders slump. She grabbed the edge of the table as if suddenly needing the support. For just an instant, he almost went to her. But she quickly straightened, tucked the note into her apron pocket and picked up the dirty dishes.

Jack tried to remember who had been sitting at that particular table. He couldn't recall. He'd been too busy watching Kate to notice anyone else in the café.

So what could be in the note that would have had such an adverse effect on her? As she headed in his direction, she showed no sign of having been upset. He idly wondered where she'd learned to hide her feelings so well as she swept past him without a glance.

SHERIFF FRANK CURRY stepped out onto his porch. The morning was bright, the air brisk, the scent of the new spring growth on the breeze.

A member of the crow family who lived on his ranch called to him from the clothesline wire next to the house. A half dozen of the birds had gathered, only part of what he considered his extended family.

He'd made a habit of studying the crows and found them fascinating. This family had taken up residence on his ranch and included not only a mother, father and their "kids" but also some nephews, brothers and half brothers related to the mom and dad, he was guessing. Fifteen birds in all made up this little family.

Like some human families, the crows formed close nuclear families. Often the "kids" stayed around for more than five years. Sometimes the mother and family even adopted kids of unrelated neighbors.

The irony of crows easily forming a close-knit nuclear family unit, although he'd never been able to, didn't escape Frank. He'd been married once a long time ago, after Lynette had broken his heart. He'd thought he'd gotten Lynette out of his system. But in truth, he'd gotten married on the rebound, a terrible mistake that he hadn't had the sense to end even quicker than he had.

Poor Pam. She'd tried so hard to make him happy. Once she'd realized he was in love with Lynette, she'd turned his life into a living hell.

At least he'd been smart enough to end it, setting her free to find someone who loved her the way he loved Lynette. He doubted she would ever forgive him, though, not that he blamed her. Fortunately, she'd moved away after the divorce. He hadn't seen her since.

But he'd lost his chance to have a family of his own. There was only one woman he'd wanted and Lynette had married Bob Benton. He wondered if she regretted not having a family or if he was alone in that.

One of the crows cawed at him. He smiled as more of them lined up along the clothesline as if coming to tell him good-morning. "Good morning," he called back to them. After hours of studying the birds and their habits, he'd become somewhat of an expert on their behavior.

It was spring, so the birds had been busy building nests and courting. They were just like the cowboys and cowgirls who would be attending the spring fair today, he thought. They would preen, court and squabble, and there would be trouble. There always was.

He glanced at his watch and realized he had to get moving. He hoped he might see Lynette at the fair and mentally kicked himself for not inviting her. But he had to work, so he wouldn't have made a very good companion anyway.

As he drove toward Big Timber, he thought about asking Lynette out on a real date. What was he waiting for anyway?

TUCKER WILLIAMS HADN'T read a book since high school and seldom even glanced at the local newspaper. But his wife, Mary, read it every morning to see who had given birth and who'd gotten divorced, died or been arrested, then passed on the goings-on around the county to him whether he was interested or not. This morning was no different.

"Some guy got murdered down by the river," she said as she handed him a cup of coffee. She loved all those cop and forensic shows on television. "Didn't have any identification on him, so they did a sketch and are asking if anyone knows him." She turned the paper so he could see.

Tucker glanced at the sketch and let out a curse. "I saw him the other night. When I came out of the Range Rider, he was just getting out of his pickup. He asked me if I knew where he could find the woman who was running the café. I pointed him down the street...." He felt a chill.

"You were that close to him?" Mary asked, wide-eyed. "Then he ends up dead? You have to go to the sheriff."

There were a lot of things Tucker had to do in his life. Work was at the top of the list. Tucker had been working construction for Grayson Construction Company for years—until recently, when his boss, Grayson Brooks, lost his wife, Anna, to cancer. Grayson had sold his construction business for pennies on the dollar to Tucker and left town. Now that Tucker was the boss, he couldn't be late for work. "Maybe later."

"Tuck, you can't put this off. You might be the last person to see him alive—other than the killer."

"Or Kate LaFond at the café was," he said, and remembered seeing someone walking down the street that night as he'd driven past in his pickup. The cowboy had been right by the café—if he was the same person. Tucker hadn't been paying any attention, just anxious to get home before Mary started calling the bar for him.

"You have to call the sheriff and tell him what you know."

"I'm sure Kate's already told the sheriff—"

"Tucker? Call the sheriff. Has anyone seen Kate since that night? What if something has happened to her as well?"

He sighed. "I'm sure if the café hasn't been open someone would have noticed. But I'll call the sheriff if it will make you happy, all right?"

SHERIFF FRANK CURRY had spent the morning at his office researching online for information about horsehair hitching, and waiting to see if the photo in the newspaper generated any clues.

Until it did, all he had to go on was the murder weapon—the length of hitched horsehair rope found about the victim's neck.

Frank took out the evidence bag holding the horsehair rope. Could this length of hitched horsehair help him solve this murder? He sure hoped so.

Jack said he didn't think the pattern was from Montana State Prison. Frank finally understood what Jack had meant. Apparently there were only four prisons where this old Western art form was practiced still: Deer Lodge, Montana; Rawlins, Wyoming; Walla Walla, Washington; and Yuma, Arizona; and each had their own designs and colors. The painstaking art was popular in prisons, where inmates had nothing but time.

From the bright colors used in the rope, it sounded as if there was a good chance the rope had been made in the Yuma prison. The colors apparently were the result of the Mexican influence at the prison there.

So if it was true that each prison had its own designs and colors and no two hitched ropes were ever identical, then the rope found around the dead man's neck, along with his morgue photo, might be used to identify either him—or his killer.

Frank had just left a message for the Yuma warden when Tucker Williams walked into his office.

"You're sure it was the man in the sketch?" the sheriff asked after listening to what Tucker had to tell him.

"Positive. It was right behind the bar under that outside light, so I got a good look at him."

"And he was asking about Kate LaFond?"

"Not by name." He took off his hat and scratched his head as if trying to remember the conversation. "The man described her and said he'd heard she was running the café. Now that I think about it, I don't think he knew she owned it."

Frank nodded. "So you told him where he could find her."

"Yeah. I mean, I didn't think anything of it, you know?"

He could tell Tucker felt badly about that.

"Is she all right? Mary's worried."

"She's fine." But now that he thought about it, he had noticed a bruise on her cheek that she'd tried to cover with makeup the morning the body was found. "Thanks for calling and letting me know. I appreciate your help."

"I hope it helps."

"It does."

KATE COULDN'T WAIT until the café emptied out. She kept moving, afraid to stop, let alone reread the note in her apron pocket. She could feel Jack French's gaze on her. Had he seen her pick up the folded sheet of paper from the table?

She'd felt him watching her all morning. But she couldn't worry about that. She had much bigger worries than that long, tall cowboy. She had felt like such a fool when his fingers had brushed hers earlier. It had been a shock, like the time she'd gone swimming in the creek and had raced back to her father's travel trailer. The moment her bare, wet foot touched the metal trailer step, electricity had shot through her. She'd felt that same kind of jolt when Jack had brushed her hand.

With relief she saw that he was leaving. As he walked over to the cash register, Kate motioned to Bethany to take care of him. She busied herself cleaning the last table until she heard the bell over the front door jangle.

She'd been threatening to get rid of that damned bell, but like the Branding Iron, it was apparently part of a long tradition started by the former owner, Claude Durham.

"Where are you off to in such a hurry?" Kate asked Bethany as they both took off their aprons, dropping them in a bin next to the washing machine by the back door of the café.

"Seriously, you haven't heard? The Sweetgrass County Spring Fair is today and tomorrow. Everyone in three counties will be there. It's the biggest event of spring." Bethany was looking at her as if to say, *Do you live in a cave?* "Didn't you hear everyone talking about it this morning at breakfast?"

Kate had quit listening to the café chatter when she realized all anyone around this part of Montana talked about most of the time was cows, crops and weather. "Well, have fun," she said, shooing Bethany toward the front door.

"You should come."

"And leave Lou in charge of the café?" she asked, joking about the cook running the place. Lou was more reclusive than she was.

"I don't think you'd lose any money if you just shut down for the rest of the day. Everyone will be at the fair."

Kate nodded, actually tempted. She could definitely use an afternoon away from this place. And if everyone was going to be at the fair, this would be a great time to do some exploring on her own.

She watched Bethany drive off, seriously considering locking the door and putting out the Closed sign. Lou wouldn't mind having the afternoon off, she thought as she turned toward the kitchen to talk to him.

Behind her, the bell rang and a draft of cool spring air rushed in. She gave a silent curse and plastered on her welcoming smile as she turned.

"Hey, Kate," bellowed a large blond woman wearing a Western shirt and jeans with a pair of new red cowboy boots and a straw hat. In the woman's arms was a stack of brightly colored quilts.

Kate's smile broadened. Priscilla Farnsworth or Cilla, as everyone called her, was a breath of fresh air. Loud, full of life and with a laugh that was contagious, Cilla was a member of the Beartooth Quilting

Society. The group of women, ranging in age from thirty to eighty, came in every Thursday afternoon for pie and coffee. Often they would bring some of their latest quilts to show her.

Kate had been invited to attend one of their meetings when she'd first hit town. Cilla and Thelma Brooks had come into the café her first week one morning after rush to ask if she sewed, if she wanted to learn and if she would buy a raffle ticket for a quilt they were selling to raise money for the one-room schoolhouse down the road.

Both women had apologized for being so pushy. "It's just that we get so little new blood," Thelma had said, and Cilla had added with a laugh, "That makes us sound like vampires." That was when Kate had fallen for the woman's laugh. She'd bought a raffle ticket, said she didn't have time right now to quilt—maybe later.

"We quilt and talk and eat!" Cilla had said. "Lord, how we eat. But what's the point of getting together unless someone bakes something, right?"

Kate didn't sew and didn't have a clue about quilting, not that she told them that. Every woman in these parts sewed, gardened and canned—except for Kate.

"I had this great idea," Cilla said as she bustled in now and dropped the stack of quilts into an empty booth. "I was on my way to the fair and I just swung right in here. Now, if you hate this idea, just say so. You won't hurt my feelings. What do you think about us putting up a few of our quilts in the café?"

Kate opened her mouth, not sure what was going

to come out, but she didn't have to worry. Cilla didn't give her a chance to speak.

"Okay, you hate the idea. I just thought these walls could use some color. No offense. Oh, me and my big mouth. You probably had plans to change the paint color and now I've gone and—"

"No, I don't hate the idea," Kate said. And plans? Her life had been moving so fast that her only plan had been to get moved into the apartment upstairs and re-open the café. She'd needed the money and hadn't given a thought to sprucing up the place. If it had been good enough when Claude was alive, then she'd figured it was good enough now.

Also the Branding Iron was the only café in Beartooth, and she knew if it didn't open again quickly after his death, the townsfolk would start going down the road to Big Timber. They were creatures of habit. She didn't want their habit of hanging out at the Branding Iron to change.

"Why don't you show me what you brought?" she said, realizing the walls definitely could use a coat of fresh paint.

The women of the Beartooth Quilting Society had made the first and only friendly overture anyone had made toward her since she'd arrived in town. She knew only too well how these small communities were when it came to outsiders. Which was just fine. She preferred her privacy, and anyway, she wouldn't be staying long, now, would she? She thought of Jack French's comment earlier about her leaving. What was it Jack thought he knew?

"Aren't you worried that the quilts will smell like grease before long?" Kate asked, the scent of bacon permeating the air as she spoke.

"We'll rotate them in and out," Cilla said. "And we'll do all the hanging and taking down. You won't have to mess with any of it."

Kate considered the walls. "I *was* thinking about painting first." Well, she was *now*. "What color would you suggest?" That was something else she didn't have a clue about.

"A nice neutral. You know, I have some extra paint from when I did my downstairs. Why don't the girls and I swing by with it Monday after you close? It wouldn't take us any time at all."

"Cilla, that is such a generous offer, but—"

"Not at all. We're glad to do it. Now, come take a look at these quilts and see what you think."

Kate felt swept along, as if she'd fallen into the roaring creek that ran by town and was now on her way to the Gulf of Mexico via the Yellowstone, Missouri and Mississippi rivers.

"I think they'll do this place wonders, don't you?" Cilla said after she'd shown Kate an array of intricate and beautiful quilts.

"I love them all," Kate said. "And I appreciate you thinking of me."

Cilla smiled, a twinkle in her eye. "I can't imagine what brought you to Beartooth, but I'm glad you're here. I hope you plan to stay."

"Thank you," Kate said, and glanced toward the Beartooth General Store across the street. As usual,

Nettie Benton was watching from the front window, determined to find out the truth about her new neighbor. Kate feared Nettie wouldn't stop until she uncovered everything about her.

Kate remembered the note and felt a chill run the length of her spine. She'd put the note in her apron pocket and dropped the apron in the bin by the back door earlier when she'd been visiting with Bethany.

After waving goodbye to Cilla, Kate locked the door, flipped the sign in the window to Closed and told Lou to take the day off. The moment he left, she hurried to the bin with the aprons in it. As she pulled hers out and reached into the pocket, her heart took off at a gallop. Frantically she dug in one pocket, then the other.

The note was gone.

CHAPTER FIVE

KATE WAS FRANTICALLY DIGGING through the aprons in the bin, searching for the note, when she heard a vehicle drive up in front of the café. She ignored it and the knock at the front door. The Closed sign was up. The person would eventually take the hint and leave.

She tried to tell herself not to panic. She didn't need to find the note. She knew only too well what it had said. So why was she panicking?

Because she didn't want the note to fall into anyone else's hands.

With a jolt, she realized it probably already had.

"You must not have heard my knock."

Kate whirled around to find the sheriff standing in the back doorway. A large, broad-shouldered man in his fifties, he blocked out the sun.

"Lose something?" he asked. He was good-looking, even for a man his age. His blond hair had started to gray, but it wasn't noticeable except for a little in his thick, drooping mustache. He removed his Stetson as he opened the screen door and stepped into the back of the café, his gaze intent on her in a way that made her heart hammer even harder.

"My grocery order," she said as she picked up the

pile of towels and aprons she'd tossed on the floor in her search, and dropped them back into the hamper. "I thought I left it in my apron. Apparently, I left it somewhere else," Kate said, pulling herself together. "I thought I'd drop it off on my way to the fair."

She hadn't planned on going to the fair. Quite the contrary—she had other, more important things to do. But if the sheriff thought he was keeping her...

"I won't keep you long," he said, taking the hint. He stood, turning the brim of his Stetson in his fingers as he looked toward the dining room. "Mind if we have a seat?"

"What is this about?" she asked. She'd seen him go to the general store the other day before coming over for his usual morning cup of coffee. Had Nettie put some bug in his ear? Everyone in the county knew he had a crush on Nettie Benton. Not that anyone could understand what he saw in the nosy old woman.

"Just need to have a little chat with you," the sheriff said as he took a seat in one of the booths.

Kate tried to imagine what Nettie could have told him. It would be just like Nettie to fill his ear with some nonsense or other. Or even shades of the truth, which could be worse.

"Can I get you a cup of coffee?"

"No thanks, Ms. LaFond. I don't want to keep you from the fair."

She nodded. Bracing herself, she joined him in the booth, trying hard to hide how nervous he was making her. First the note, and now whatever this was.

"Have you seen this morning's newspaper?" he asked.

She hadn't had a chance and said as much.

He pulled a copy from his jacket pocket and shoved it across the table at her. "If you don't mind taking a look."

She flattened the newspaper, the sketch on page one practically leaping off the page at her—along with the headline: Do You Know This Man? Kate knew the sheriff couldn't have missed her startled reaction.

"Have you ever seen this man before?" he asked.

Kate suspected he already knew the answer. The moment she'd seen the sketch, she'd given herself away. Not that it mattered. She couldn't lie. Jack French had not only seen her with the dead man, he'd also punched him and bloodied the man's nose.

"He's *dead?*" She didn't have to fake her surprise or the break in her voice.

"He was murdered."

She leaned back against the booth seat and tried to catch her breath. *"Murdered?"* She'd heard some of the locals talking about a hobo who'd been found down by the Yellowstone River, but that was more than twenty miles away. There'd been no mention of *murder*.

The sheriff sat across from her, waiting—and watching her with that same intensity she'd noticed when he'd walked in. "How do you know the man?"

"I don't know him. I'd never seen him before he accosted me the other night in the alley beside the café. Fortunately, Jack came along—"

"Jack?"

"Jack French. He ran him off."

"And then what happened?"

"Nothing. The man left, I went upstairs to bed and Jack went on down the street."

"You say the man *accosted* you?"

"I had gone for a run. He was in the alley by my apartment stairs. I thought he was drunk, because he obviously had me confused with someone else."

"What did he say to you?"

"I don't even remember." But she feared Jack would, and would tell the sheriff. "Like I said, I thought he was drunk. He wasn't making any sense. I'd never seen him before in my life."

"Did you see what he was driving?"

She shook her head. "Maybe Jack did. It sounded like a truck when he took off, but I could be wrong."

"Jack just happened to be walking by?"

"It was the first time I'd seen him, as well. It wasn't until the next morning that I learned who he was and that he'd just gotten out of prison." Why had she said that? She felt a stab of guilt for even bringing it up.

"Did Jack seem to know the man?"

"No. Jack just came to my defense, I guess, when he heard the commotion. He hit the man and ran him off."

"This was after the man hit *you*."

It wasn't a question, but she nodded anyway and touched her cheek. "He slapped me when I told him to leave me alone or else."

"Or else?"

"I like to think I can take care of myself," she said, even more shaken as she realized that she and Jack might have been the last two people to see the man alive. Except for the killer. "I wasn't very appreciative when Jack came to my rescue. I was too shaken by the encounter with the man," she added, trying to cover for whatever Jack would tell the sheriff. "Now, though…"

He nodded as if thinking the same thing she was— that she'd been lucky. She glanced at the sketch of the dead man on the front page of the paper again and shuddered. She didn't even want to think about who might have murdered him. Or why, because she feared the killer would be coming for her next.

The sheriff rolled up his newspaper and stuffed it into his pocket again. "If you think of anything else, please give me a call."

"I'd be happy to. Like I said, I'm sure the man had me confused with someone else." If only that were true, she thought.

After the sheriff left, she went upstairs and got the gun she kept hidden in the apartment. Claude had warned her. Apparently it was time to start carrying it.

I KNEW YOUR MOTHER.

That was the first thing Claude Durham said to her. Kate looked up to find a fiftysomething man standing next to her at the Nevada café where she'd been working, just outside Vegas.

At the time, she'd been standing at the pass-through waiting for her last order of the day to come up so she could leave. She'd been killing time, gossiping with Connie, the older waitress she worked with at the small dive of a café out in the middle of the desert.

"That's quite the pickup line," she said to the man. Her feet hurt and she was too tired for whatever he was selling. Not only that, he was also too old for her.

He gave her an impatient look. "You sure that's the way you want to do this?"

She gave him a second glance. He was pale, balding. What little hair he had was short and gray. He had a belly on him and he was sweating profusely.

He's sick, she'd thought. "Look, mister—"

"I don't have a lot of time, so let's cut to the chase," he interrupted. "If we have to do this here, fine. I knew your mother in Beartooth." When she didn't respond, he added, "Montana. Where you were born."

"My mother never was in Montana."

"Not your adoptive mother, your real mother, your birth mother."

"Meg was my real mother."

"Good. I'm glad to hear it. Too bad she didn't live longer—maybe she could have taught you to be nicer to your elders. I would have thought your adoptive father, Harvey, could have done better with you than he obviously did."

"How is it you know so much about my life?" she demanded.

He ignored the question. "They told you that you were adopted, didn't they?" He didn't wait for an answer. "Did they tell you how they came to raise you in the first place?"

A sinking feeling hit in the pit of her stomach. "What do you mean?"

"What did they tell you about your real...your birth parents?"

She'd asked a few times when she was younger. Her parents had hemmed and hawed. She'd quit asking. "What was there to tell? Obviously my birth mother didn't want me. She might not have even known who my father was."

His pale face colored with a flush of anger that surprised her. "That's bullshit," he snapped. "Your mother was a saint. She knew exactly who your father was and she loved you more than you—"

"Then why didn't she raise me?"

"She died when you were eighteen months old."

His words stopped her cold. It took her a moment before she asked, "What about my father?"

"That's why I'm here. To tell you. Now, do you want to do this here, or can you tell your boss you're done so we can get out of here?" He didn't wait for an answer, but made his way out to an old pickup parked outside.

Her order came up.

"I'll get that for you," Connie said.

"Thanks." Her hands were trembling as she took off her apron, tossed it into a booth, went outside to open the passenger-side door of the man's truck, but didn't get in.

"You look like hell." She wasn't sure why she said it. Maybe just because it was the truth and it seemed they were about to talk truths.

He laughed, a sick smoker's cough following it. "I'll make this quick," he said when he finally quit coughing. "I'm dying."

"So you decided to look me up and tell me...what?"

"Get in the truck."

"First, tell me who you are and why you're the one bringing me this news."

He looked out the pickup's sand-pitted windshield at the café. "What are you doing working in a dump like this? I've been watching you for the past couple of days. You're a damned good waitress. You could do better."

Anger rushed like a familiar drug through her veins. She'd been told once by a psychologist that she used anger as her go-to defense mechanism. No kidding.

"Thanks for the concern." She started to slam the truck door, planning to walk away.

"Your mother gave me something to give to you, but I also have something I want you to have. Consider it your inheritance."

She studied him through the open door of the truck. "If you're going to try to tell me that you're my father or some—"

"Just get in and listen to what I have to say. I own a café in Beartooth...."

She didn't remember sliding into the pickup seat. She did remember telling him to go to hell.

NETTIE'S NEW RENTER was an enigma. While she looked sweet and innocent, there was an edge to her that told a different story. When Nettie had shown her the apartment, the girl had gone straight to the window that overlooked the paved street running through town. To the southeast, the highway went to Big Timber. To the north, it turned to gravel just out of town before breaking off into dirt roads that turned to 4x4 trails as they headed up into the Crazies.

Beartooth was the end of the road, so to speak. Not the kind of place a young girl would want to hang out.

But that wasn't the only thing about the girl that bothered Nettie. There was something that seemed almost familiar.

I must be getting old. The other day, I was thinking that Kate LaFond reminded me of someone, she thought now.

She shook her head. Good thing Bob wasn't here. If she had voiced these suspicions around him, he would have shaken his head and told her she was losing her mind.

"So, what do you think of the apartment?" Nettie had asked the girl when she showed it to her.

She hadn't even turned from the window as she'd answered. "It's exactly what I was looking for."

Nettie had tried not to let the girl's lack of enthusiasm hurt her feelings. She had decorated the apartment and felt she'd done a remarkable job in making it homey and nice. But apparently her efforts had been wasted on the girl, who cared more about the view.

Curious again about what was so interesting outside, Nettie had moved up behind her to look out. The girl's gaze had seemed riveted on the Branding Iron. Or maybe it was the large table of local ranchers who met there every morning.

Nettie had tried to make out who was gathered there,

but someone inside the café had been blocking her view. With a start, she'd recognized that broad back.

Sheriff Frank Curry had stood with his back to the window, talking to the group of men. A moment later he'd stepped out of view.

The girl had turned then, clearly startled to find Nettie right behind her. "I'll take the apartment. That is, if you'll rent it to me. I hope you will." There had been that desperation in her tone again.

Nettie had told herself that it didn't matter why the girl was so set on renting the place. It wasn't as if anyone else had been around offering to rent it. Let the girl have it. She'd planned to require references but figured this was the girl's first apartment, so what was the point? Anyway, it would be her parents who would be footing the bill.

"I'll need your name, address and a phone number in case of an emergency," Nettie had said, handing the girl a piece of paper and a pen. She'd watched her quickly jot down the information, then pull out a wad of hundred-dollar bills.

"You did say you would take cash for first and last month's rent, plus six months' rent deposit, right?" the girl had asked, looking worried.

It must have been because of Nettie's surprised expression. "Sure, cash is great," she'd said as the girl had counted out bills and handed them over, along with her information.

"You sure you didn't rob a bank?" Nettie had asked in jest as she took the money.

"I cashed in one of my stocks."

One of her stocks? "Well, I hope you enjoy the apartment…." Nettie looked down at the sheet of paper the girl had handed her and read the name. "Tiffany Chandler."

"I will. It's *perfect*," the girl had said again before returning to the front window.

Nettie'd had a sneaking suspicion even then that it wasn't art—but someone in the café across the street—that had made the apartment so *perfect*.

AFTER HIS TALK with Kate, Frank stood for a few moments on the broken sidewalk. The spring sun felt warm and smelled of pine and water from the nearby creek.

He turned his face up to the warmth and closed his eyes, breathing in the familiar scents and enjoying the feel of the sun on his face. His mind, though, mulled over what he'd learned.

According to Tucker, the man had *described* Kate and known she was running the café. No mistaken identity. But the man apparently hadn't asked for her by name, so maybe he did have the wrong woman. Maybe.

As Frank opened his eyes, he was startled to see a face framed in the upstairs window of the general store. He felt a jolt, not used to seeing anyone up there, let alone a waif of a girl.

She looked ghostly, so pale, with straight blond hair that appeared almost white in the morning light. She was wearing a pale colored top that seemed to shimmer in the breeze from the open window. As if she'd spotted him watching her, she faded back from the window—gone in the blink of an eye, almost as if she'd never been there at all.

"Nettie's new renter," he said under his breath, surprised by the turn the girl had given him. Nettie had certainly rented the place quickly. It had only been the other day that he'd noticed the sign in the store window.

He thought about walking across the street to the store, but he didn't want Nettie thinking he was worried about her—or her new renter.

Also, he was anxious to talk to Jack French. He'd called out to the W Bar G and learned that Jack had the day off but had been out to the ranch and was on his way back into Beartooth.

He thought about when he'd questioned Jack about the horsehair hitched rope from the murder scene. Of course there was no reason Jack would connect the man he'd chased off down the alley the night before—with the murder weapon, right?

Jack had just driven up in front of his cabin when he saw the sheriff sitting in the shade of his porch.

He felt that old sinking feeling he always did at the sight of a lawman. Maybe that *too* was genetic.

While in prison he'd learned that crime and violence ran in some families. He knew he should feel lucky that it was only trouble that coursed through his DNA. But then maybe trouble was like a gateway drug, and violence was only one misstep away.

Either way, he had a sheriff sitting on his porch waiting for him.

He shut off the engine and climbed out of his pickup.

"Howdy, Sheriff," he said. "Glad to see you made yourself comfortable."

"I didn't think you'd mind."

"Nope, sure don't," Jack said as he climbed the steps. Too late, he thought about the note in his pocket, the one he'd sneaked out of Kate's discarded apron. If it was found on him— "Can I get you a cold one?"

He wasn't surprised when the sheriff shook his head. "Just need a few minutes of your time. The fair opens today. I would imagine that like everyone else in the county, you're headed there."

Jack nodded and leaned against the porch rail. He was too antsy to sit. He hadn't forgotten being hauled off to jail by the sheriff in the wee hours of the morning two years ago for something he hadn't done. He didn't need to remind himself that it could happen again. Innocent men really did get arrested sometimes and sent to prison.

"You want to take this inside?" he asked the sheriff.

"Out here is fine. It's such a beautiful day."

Wasn't it, though? Jack wanted to say, "Get on with it," but he held his tongue. The old Jack French wouldn't have been able to.

"I don't know if you've seen today's newspaper or not," the sheriff said and reached into his jacket pocket.

What the hell? Jack thought. *How long was this going to drag out?* He reached for the paper, unrolled it and stiffened as he glanced at the sketch of the man he'd seen the other night in the alley.

He could feel the sheriff's gaze on him. "Recognize him?"

Frank Curry wouldn't be sitting on his porch unless he knew that Jack did.

"This is the man who was bothering Kate LaFond a few nights ago in the alley by the café," Jack said, and he saw the sheriff sit up a little in the old rocker.

"I understand you hit him."

"Only after I heard him hit the woman. I didn't know who she was. It was my first night back and I really didn't want to get involved, but…" He shrugged.

"She said she wasn't very gracious about you coming to her rescue."

Jack smiled at that.

"You didn't know the man from prison?"

He thought of the hitched rope the sheriff had shown him with the blood on it. "Never seen him before in my life. This the man I heard was found down by the river?"

"Murdered," Frank said.

That didn't come as a surprise, given the blood on the rope.

"So you never crossed paths until a few nights ago," the sheriff said.

"Nope."

Frank got to his feet. "Remember that horsehair hitched rope I showed you? You said Montana State Prison's cons hadn't hitched it."

Jack waited.

"You were right. I checked. Seems only four prisons in the West are known for hitching horsehair. Deer Lodge, Montana; Yuma, Arizona; Walla Walla, Washington; and Rawlins, Wyoming. Each one has its own designs and colors. I'm thinking it might be from the Yuma prison. But I suspect you probably already knew that." He was eyeing Jack, waiting.

Jack shook his head. "Like I said, I never hitched in prison. Too busy working the ranch. It just didn't look like any pattern I'd seen up there."

The sheriff rubbed a hand over his square jaw. "You know I never figured you for rustling that bull. I always had the feeling there was more to it." His gaze locked with Jack's. "But if you're innocent as you said you were that night I arrested you, then I can't help but wonder who would do something like that to you and why."

Jack didn't move, didn't breathe. He'd realized as he was being dragged out of his house that morning two years ago that he'd been set up, but he'd saved his breath after his initial cry of innocence. When there is a world-class bull in your corral that doesn't belong to you and you've been pissing in the wind for much too long, well, you just have to figure that you've practically been asking for it.

"It cost you two years of your life, any way you look at it," the sheriff said. "That would make an innocent man pretty angry. Might even make him want to get retribution. 'Course there's no way to get back those years, no matter what a man was to do."

Jack held his tongue.

"I've always liked you, Jack," the sheriff said as he tipped his hat. "I'd like to see you stay out of trouble."

Jack let out the breath he'd been holding along with a chuckle. "Me, too, Sheriff. Me, too." Right now retribution was the furthest thing from his mind.

His thoughts were with Kate LaFond and her conversation with the man in the alley, the now dead man.

"I've been looking for you. I just didn't expect to find you here."

What had the dead man meant by that?

"Let go of me. I already told you. You have the wrong woman. But if you don't leave me alone—"

You'll end up dead?

Maybe it had been a case of mistaken identify, just as Kate had said. Or maybe not. His gut told him there was a whole lot more to it. Just as there was more to the woman herself.

He didn't dig the note out of his pocket until the sheriff had driven away. Earlier, he'd stopped by the post office to pick up his mail. Something had made him circle to the back of the café. Lou, the cook, had been out by the garage, smoking a cigarette.

Jack had stepped into the café kitchen without anyone seeing him. Kate was busy out front with Cilla, talking quilts. Jack had seen the worn aprons in the bin and on a hunch had looked in the pockets.

At the time, he'd just been curious after seeing Kate's first reaction to the note. Now with a growing feeling of dread he stared down at the block letters printed with a dull pencil on a half sheet of plain white paper.

One down. Two more to go, though. Better hurry, Kate. Ticktock.

Next to the words was a kidlike drawing that at first glance resembled a game of hangman. But if the rope the sheriff had shown him was what Jack thought it was—the murder weapon—then whatever Kate was running from... It had found her.

CHAPTER SIX

AFTER TALKING TO BOTH KATE LaFond and Jack French, the sheriff returned to his office. The Yuma prison warden had returned his call, asking for photos of the dead man and the rope used to kill him.

That done, Frank found himself at loose ends. All his deputies were at the fair, keeping the peace. With nothing to do but wait, he was reminded again of his promise to Lynette to find out more about Kate La-Fond. He'd always trusted her instincts—except when she'd married that fool, Bob Benton.

Frank shook his head. All these years later he was still mentally kicking himself for not storming that wedding and taking her hostage until she came to her senses.

But then Lynette wouldn't have the general store. She loved working in that store. He wouldn't have taken that away from her even if he could turn back the clock.

Things had a way of working out as they were supposed to, he thought with a smile. Bob was long gone and wouldn't be coming back.

He turned his attention to the new café owner. Kate LaFond was a mystery, Frank had to admit. On the surface, she seemed like a perfectly fine young woman, hardworking, likable. So what if she kept to herself? So what if she didn't want to share her past?

But Frank had a niggling feeling there was definitely more going on under the surface with the new owner of the Branding Iron.

He called a friend who was a local Realtor.

"I'm curious about the Branding Iron Café up in Beartooth," he said when his friend answered. "It sold so quickly after Claude died, I guess he must have had it listed long before then."

"It was never a multiple listing and I can't remember ever seeing it listed anywhere. You're sure it wasn't willed to the new owner?"

Frank had thought of that, but quickly kicked aside the idea. Seemed unlikely since the old bachelor had never had a family. At least not one Frank had ever heard about. And yet according to public records, Kate LaFond owned the Branding Iron.

Picking up his keys, he headed for his patrol truck. Ten minutes later, he was knocking at the door of Claude Durham's friend and local attorney Arnie Thorndike.

No one would ever take Thorndike for an attorney. Half the time he looked homeless. Like this morning, when he opened his door to find the sheriff standing on his stoop.

Barefoot, dressed in a pair of worn jeans and a flannel shirt that had seen better days, Thorndike raked a hand through his unruly head of blond hair and grinned.

"It's been too long since I've awakened to a sheriff on my doorstep," Arnie said. "Hell, I must be getting old. I'm not even going to put up a fight." He held out his wrists, pantomiming letting the sheriff put the cuffs on.

"This is a friendly visit," Frank said with a chuckle. Arnie Thorndike was an old hippie who'd caught the tail end of the "flower power" movement in California before returning to Beartooth and getting his law degree. "I need to ask you about Claude."

The grin left the man's weathered face. "Then I guess you'd better come in. I just made coffee."

"I need to know about Claude's will," Frank said as he followed Arnie into the cluttered kitchen. "He did leave a will, right?"

Thorndike dug out a couple of mismatched coffee mugs, filled both, then motioned the sheriff to a small room off the side of the cabin.

It wasn't until they were both seated in threadbare recliners, the morning sun coming through the dusty window, that Arnie spoke.

"I miss the hell out of Claude," he said and took a slurping sip of his coffee. He seemed to relax, his eyes misty. "There wasn't a day at the café that he didn't have some joke or story to share. Didn't matter if the story was true, Claude could spin a yarn like no one I've ever known."

"Did he have any family?" Frank asked.

"Not that I knew of."

"So he never married? I know he left Beartooth only a few times over the years, but he wasn't gone long. The café apparently was his family, his *entire* life." But

Frank had learned over the years of being a sheriff that even a man who appeared to have nothing to hide often had secrets. For all he knew, on those few occasions when Claude had left Beartooth for several months at a time, he had a family hidden away somewhere.

"Any idea where he went the few times he did leave Beartooth?" the sheriff asked. "Claude never seemed to want to talk about it."

"You know he wasn't all that healthy."

That was putting it mildly. Nettie over at the store used to nag Claude like crazy, telling him to quit eating off his own menu. It was no surprise when he'd dropped dead.

"Are you telling me that's why he left Beartooth those times? Because of his health?"

The attorney took a sip of his coffee. "I think he had a surgery or two."

"For his heart?"

Thorndike shrugged. "He didn't like talking about his medical problems."

"Or any personal ones," the sheriff said. "Which brings me back to his will, if he had one. I talked to a friend of mine who's a Realtor. He told me that, to his knowledge, the café was never listed for sale. So how is it that Kate LaFond ended up owning it?"

"Claude left it to her."

Frank couldn't have been more shocked. *"Why?"*

"He just did. It was clear he had his reasons. He didn't share them with me."

"What do you know about her?"

"Other than the fact that she is no Claude? The

woman doesn't tell dirty jokes or bitch about anything. The Branding Iron just isn't the same."

Frank took a sip of his coffee, pretending not to hear the break in Thorn's voice. The man had lost his best friend and was clearly struggling with that loss.

"Her coffee isn't as good either, but I'm adjusting," Thorndike said, lightening his tone and the mood. "If Claude wanted her to take over the place he loved, he must have had his reasons."

Frank nodded. But like Nettie, he was even more curious about Kate. What was the connection between Claude Durham, a confirmed cantankerous old bachelor, and Kate LaFond, a young woman no one knew anything about?

KATE HADN'T PLANNED to go to the Sweetgrass County Spring Fair. But after the sheriff's visit, she didn't feel she had a choice. She couldn't be sure he wasn't keeping an eye on her, and staying home—or worse, taking off for the hills—would only make her look more guilty. As if that was possible.

One down. Two more to go, though. Better hurry, Kate. Ticktock.

Who'd left her the note? Someone who knew what she was doing in Beartooth, that much was clear. *One down. Two more to go, though.* Did the writer, like the sheriff, suspect she'd killed the dead man found by the river? Or had the letter writer killed him?

She shuddered as she realized that the note had been taken while she'd been busy with Cilla. Maybe the letter writer had taken it back. But then that meant he'd been watching her and had seen her put it in the apron pocket and later deposit it in the bin.

She realized anyone who'd been in the busy café that morning could have stuck the note under a plate as they were leaving.

As she drove out of town, Beartooth, while darned close to a ghost town on its good days, felt eerily deserted. As much as she hated to admit it, she felt spooked and realized she was glad to be driving into Big Timber.

On the twenty-mile drive through rolling ranch and farmland, she could feel time slipping through her fingers, though. The author of the note was right. The clock was ticking. With winter over, the ground finally thawed and the equipment ready, there was nothing stopping her.

The thought made her laugh. Nothing stopping her? There were so many roadblocks thrown in her way.... She pulled into the fair's parking lot and killed the engine, pushing away the thought of two more men after her who might be out there right now, watching her and waiting.

She climbed out into the warm spring day, telling herself she could handle whatever was thrown at her. Or at least she hoped she could. She'd had a few curveballs thrown at her in her life, but nothing like this.

The spring fair was everything she'd heard it was. There were barns filled with prize-winning cows, pigs, horses, sheep, rabbits and even chickens. Other buildings held homemade clothing and baked goods, some sporting blue ribbons.

As she moved through the crowds—the men in their jeans, boots, fancy Western shirts and Stetson hats, the women just as duded out—she felt as if she must stand out like a sore thumb.

This was a world apart from where she'd grown up. Everything about Montana, especially Beartooth, felt alien to her and had since she'd arrived. She did what she could to blend in, even wearing boots and boot-cut jeans, Western shirts with snaps instead of buttons, and spending most Sunday mornings on a hard pew at church with the rest of the community.

She laughed at the regulars' jokes and kidding each morning. She'd learned to drive a stick-shift four-wheel-drive pickup as well as run a café. Last fall, she'd cut firewood for the coming winter and, once the blizzards hit, she'd shoveled snow and stoked the apartment woodstove just to keep warm as if she was a local.

Since moving to Beartooth, she'd done what she had to to survive.

But now with time running out, she felt discouraged. It had taken longer than she'd thought it would to get the café up and running and to settle into this new, strange life. But she couldn't afford to hire anyone to run the place for her.

Then winter had set in too soon. She hadn't gotten a feel of the land before the snow had started, the temperature dropping, the ground freezing, making finding what she'd come for impossible.

All she'd been able to do was bide her time. Get the lay of the land, as her father would have said. She thought of Harvey Logan, the only father she'd known.

He would have loved Montana. It was rich in history, with lots of stories of outlaws and gold miners, homesteaders and hard winters, along with buried treasure, strongboxes from robbed stages that were never found. Hidden miser's gold, nuggets the size of her fist, turning up when foundations were dug for one of the many towns that had sprung up overnight.

But what a hard life early settlers had faced. She thought of last winter and couldn't imagine how anyone had survived a hundred years ago without modern conveniences. She'd wanted to throw in the towel more times than she could count on those days when winter blizzards had rattled the café windows and whirled snow into icy drifts as the temperature plummeted.

She couldn't help but question if all of this was worth it.

At the thought, she drew on the granite-hard determination that had gotten her this far in life. She deserved to get what was coming to her—no matter what. One day it would all be worth it, she assured herself as she walked past tables of baked goods and handcrafts and women hawking their wares.

The sun beat down on her. She could hear shrieks coming from the carnival rides as she passed a line of canvas tents offering everything from tamales to tractor parts. The smell of cotton candy and corn dogs permeated the air, making her feel a little nauseous.

Kate started to turn back the way she'd come, having had enough. She knew she was still upset over the note and the sheriff's visit. She was pushing her way through the crowd when she saw him.

Jack French didn't appear to have seen her, though. At least she hoped he hadn't, as she quickly ducked into the nearest tent.

The tent was small and dark inside. She froze just inside the door. The strong scent of incense filled her nostrils. She blinked, surprised to find an old woman staring at her with the darkest eyes she'd ever seen.

The woman reached out her bejeweled hand.

It took Kate a moment to realize what she'd stumbled into. "Sorry, I didn't mean to come in here," she said, turning back toward the canvas door she'd just stepped through.

"There are no accidents," the old woman said in a voice as grating as a rusty hinge but strangely captivating. "Don't you want to know your future?"

She turned back to the woman, shaking her head as she smiled. "I believe in making my own future."

"Then you have nothing to fear, do you?" The elderly woman beckoned with gnarled fingers.

Kate knew that if she stepped back outside right now, there was a good chance of running into Jack, and it was cool in the tent. Even the scent of incense was better than that of fried food.

What the heck? Humor the old woman, pay her a few dollars. By then the cowboy would be gone and she could sneak out of the fair and back to Beartooth.

"Sit. Give me your hand."

Kate sat, taking in the dark velvet drapes that lined the small canvas tent. The old woman wore a caftan of equally dark jeweled colors. Her once dark hair was now splintered with lightning bolts of gray, but it was her dark eyes that held Kate's attention.

She gave the woman her hand, felt the icy-cold, thin skin as the gnarled hand closed around hers.

Kate was instantly startled by the alarm that flashed in the woman's black eyes. A rattled breath escaped the fortune-teller's lips. Horror contorted her features.

Kate tried to pull back her hand, but the woman's grip was like a vise.

"There is something dark. It's all around you," the seer said as if the words were being pried from her. "It's like a curse that has followed you since birth. I see a man, several men—" Her voice broke as the clawlike fingers released hers so quickly Kate's hand dropped to the small makeshift table. She felt the cool velvet of the table covering as she pushed away from the table and the crone's distressed look.

The old woman blinked, her eyes seeming to clear. She appeared upset to see Kate still there. Not half as upset as Kate, though.

"You could have just told me I was going to meet a tall, dark stranger who would fall madly in love with me," Kate snapped as she got to her feet. She hadn't even wanted to come in here. She certainly didn't need some dire fortune, let alone that accusing tone.

The woman shook her head. "You have already met him. He is tall. Not so dark."

Kate thought of Jack French with his blond hair and pale blue eyes.

"But the love affair is cursed because of the danger surrounding you."

"What kind of fortune-teller are you?" Kate demanded.

"I can only speak what I see."

"If you think I'm paying for that lousy fortune—"

"I don't want your money."

Insulted, Kate opened her purse, threw down a twenty and stalked out. Before the canvas curtain closed behind her, she saw the old woman cross herself.

Kate let the tent flap snap shut behind her as she stepped out into the sunlight, needing warmth to chase away the pall the old woman had cast over her.

But as she stepped into a shaft of warm, golden sunlight, she saw the man she'd been trying to avoid earlier. Jack French was leaning against one of the tent posts, clearly waiting for her.

"Bad news?" he asked. He wore a blue-checked shirt that brought out the blue in his eyes. His jeans, like his boots, looked as new as the Stetson cocked back on his blond head.

She glared at him and had the wild notion that he'd had something to do with what the old woman had told her. She knew she shouldn't let the cowboy or the fortune-teller upset her. Neither knew anything about her. But she had already been on edge from earlier.

"Were you listening to what she told me?" she snapped.

He shook his head. "Just saw you come out scowling," he said as he pushed off the tent post to join her.

Obviously she'd wasted her time trying to avoid him. He must have seen her duck into the tent.

"I thought fortune-tellers weren't supposed to tell you anything bad about the future," he said.

"She must not have read the fortune-teller manual. Or maybe she foresaw you waiting outside the tent for me."

He grinned at that and shoved back his hat. "So she *did* mention me?" He studied her a moment. The grin faded. "You really *are* upset. Over what some carnival charlatan told you? I thought you were smarter than that."

She knew her face gave her away. She *was* upset. It was foolish. Had she really let what the old woman said shake her composure? She was angry with herself for even stepping into the tent to begin with. Of course, that was all Jack's fault.

"Or are you upset over the sketch of the dead man in today's newspaper?" His eyes had narrowed, his gaze intent on her.

She unconsciously lifted her chin, bracing herself. "I was shocked."

"Uh-huh," he said, still studying her.

"As I told the sheriff, I'd never seen him before. The man obviously had the wrong woman." She wanted to bite her tongue. She didn't have to explain any of this to Jack French, especially since she could see that he didn't believe her.

"You know what I think?" he asked.

"No, and I don't care to. I've already told the sheriff everything I know." She started to walk off, but he grabbed her arm to stop her.

"I think you're in trouble and I stepped smack-dab into that trouble the first night I met you."

Kate thought about what the fortune-teller had said about the danger around her. Jack was in danger just being near her. Was that why she was so upset? Because what the old woman had told her was too close to the truth? Maybe especially for Jack? Wasn't that why she'd been furious with him the night he'd gone after the man in the alley, the now dead man?

"You shouldn't have butted in the other night," she said. "I didn't ask for your help or need it." She jerked free of his hold, hating that his touch rattled her. "As far as I'm concerned, that's the end of it."

"Is it? Let's hope the sheriff sees it that way—and whoever left you that note at breakfast."

Kate felt herself freeze. She opened her mouth and almost said, "You took the note?" But she caught herself in time. "I don't know what you're talking about," she managed to say.

"You never do." His gaze was hotter than the sun overhead. "Let's just hope you're right about being able to take care of yourself."

She walked away from him, but after a few steps she couldn't help glancing back. He stood watching her. The look in his blue eyes shook her more than his touch had.

JACK SWORE UNDER his breath as he watched Kate—or whatever her name was—walk away. Every instinct in him warned him to keep his distance from the woman. Whatever she was involved in, he wanted no part of it.

He looked around for his friend. If Carson had seen him talking to Kate, he'd feel the need to lecture him again about getting involved with the wrong women. Jack told himself he'd learned that lesson with Chantell Hyett, the judge's daughter. So why was his mind still on Kate LaFond?

Jack spotted Carson talking to Lisa Anne Clausen. Actually, Carson was nodding, and Lisa Anne was doing most of the talking. He had to smile to himself. When was Carson going to wake up and see what was right before his eyes? Lisa Anne was pretty and sweet and in love with him. She had been since grade school, Jack thought.

Carson just never seemed to notice. He'd been so in love with Ginny West that he hadn't looked at another girl. Now with Ginny's murder solved, maybe both Ginny and Carson could find some peace. He wanted his friend to start living again.

And Lisa Anne was just what Carson needed. Maybe Jack would have to help things along, he thought with a grin. Then he realized he was as bad as Destry and Margaret, wanting to play matchmaker.

As he started to walk toward Carson and Lisa, he nearly collided with Chantell Hyett, the woman he hadn't had the sense to stay clear of before his rustling arrest, which had cost him two years of his life.

"Jack," Chantell said in surprise. She was dressed in fancy Western wear, her long blond hair curling over one shoulder under her red cowboy hat.

The woman was beautiful, there was no getting around it. Tall, willowy, blue eyed, she was her daddy's princess. And she knew it and used her looks to get what she wanted. Not that she could have wanted for much.

"You're *out of prison?*" She seemed shocked to see him.

"I thought your father would have told you. It must have slipped his mind."

She smiled at his sarcasm. Judge Hyett wasn't about to tell her anything about Jack French. "You got out early."

No thanks to her father. "Good behavior."

She laughed at that, but quickly sobered. "I'm sorry I didn't write you more often. I wanted to come visit, but—"

"But you got a better offer," Jack said. "Understandable."

"It wasn't like that," she said, and pretended to pout. "You know how Daddy feels about *criminals.*"

He had his doubts that he would have been a criminal if it wasn't for her daddy, but he really didn't want to get into this with her, especially here at the fair.

"Well, it was nice seeing you," he said, although that wasn't entirely true. He tipped his hat and started to walk away. Seeing Chantell had brought back not only the reminder that he'd spent two years in prison for something he hadn't done, but also that old burning desire for vengeance.

"Jack," she called after him. "Give me a call sometime."

He nodded, but he wouldn't be calling. He was a changed man, he told himself as he kept walking.

He'd known what her father thought of him dating his daughter. But that hadn't stopped the old Jack French, who took dangerous chances.

The new Jack French didn't take unnecessary risks with women. That thought had barely surfaced when he spotted Kate LaFond climbing into her red pickup, and he felt a pull stronger than gravity.

"I'm a changed man," he said to himself as he started to turn way. A large, dark pickup with two men inside pulled out after her.

CHAPTER SEVEN

NETTIE HADN'T HEARD A PEEP out of her renter all day. Nor had she seen the little waif. She wondered if she should check on Tiffany. Surely she was planning to go to the spring fair.

Yesterday, she'd spotted her on the store's front porch, her sketchbook in her lap and her hand busy drawing. Nettie couldn't imagine what she was sketching—obviously something from memory, since she wasn't looking at anything but the sketch pad.

Dying to see what the girl was drawing, Nettie had gone out on the porch. Tiffany had been skittish as a new colt. She had hurriedly closed her sketchbook and took off like a shot.

What was she so afraid of? That Nettie would find fault with her work? Was the girl that insecure? Then how was she going to make it at art school?

All her instincts told her that Tiffany had lied about her reasons for wanting to rent the apartment over the store. Beartooth was twenty miles from Big Timber and even farther from the kind of shopping girls her age liked to do.

Nettie was mulling all this over as she straightened

canned goods on the middle aisle when she heard the creak of a floorboard behind her.

She spun around, startled to find the girl standing directly behind her. "Tiffany," she said, her hand over her thundering heart. "Don't sneak up on me like that. I'm an old woman. You'll kill me."

"Sorry, Mrs. Benton."

"And don't call me Mrs. Benton. That's my ex-husband's mother. Nettie will do just fine."

The girl nodded. She had her sketch pad under one arm and a large shoulder bag draped over the other. "I just wanted to let you know that the faucet in the bathroom upstairs is dripping. You said to tell you if there were any problems."

"Right. I'll fix it." Her heart rate was only starting to drop back to normal. What was it about this young woman that felt so...off? "Are you going to the fair?"

The girl nodded almost shyly.

"Well, you have a nice time and don't worry about the faucet. I'll see that it gets fixed," Nettie said as Tiffany left. She watched her drive away, headed down the road toward Big Timber in her cute little car, a girl who had everything. Or so it seemed.

Maybe she's just what she says she is. It was Bob's damned voice. Nettie wondered if she would ever get him out of her head.

Just like Kate LaFond is just a woman running a café.

Nettie harrumphed at that. Kate LaFond was a mystery, one that had consumed her since the day the young woman had shown up in Beartooth.

Kate had just appeared one day not long after the former owner, Claude Durham, died. She'd moved into the upstairs apartment and reopened the café only days after Claude's funeral, a funeral Kate hadn't attended.

Nettie couldn't imagine how the sale could have taken place so quickly. For that matter, she'd never even seen the café advertised for sale.

It was odd enough that a woman in her mid-thirties would be interested in a business in a near ghost town like Beartooth. Add to that the fact that no one seemed to know anything about her....

Kate had been living over the café and running the place now for months and no one knew any more about her than they had the day she'd shown up in town.

As far as Nettie could tell, and she'd been watching out the window, Kate hadn't made one friend or had any old ones visit.

Admittedly, Nettie wasn't one to make a lot of friends herself, but a woman Kate's age? Not only did she keep to herself, Nettie had also seen her digging in the middle of the night. Just last fall, she'd seen Kate sneaking around in the middle of the night with a shovel and later digging over by the old garage next to the café.

Just to fool with you, Nettie.

Bob might have been right—that one time, Nettie thought as she squinted through the dusty storefront window at the café across the street. When she'd done some sneaking and digging of her own, she'd found nothing buried in the garage or any sign that anything had been dug up. Worse, she'd been caught by a smirking Kate LaFond.

Now across the street inside the café, Kate looked up from a table she was serving to give Nettie one of those tight, knowing smirks.

Nettie quickly stepped back into the shadows, hating that she'd let the woman get to her. Kate LaFond was hiding something. Nettie felt it in her bones.

And now you suspect your renter has a secret as well? I worry about you sometimes, Nettie.

"Shut up, Bob," she said as she went to get the toolbox from the office to fix the leaky faucet—and get a peek at the apartment without the girl in it.

AFTER HIS VISIT with Arnie Thorndike, the sheriff returned to his office. He checked to see if he'd heard from the warden at the Yuma prison. No message.

He hadn't had much sleep since the discovery of the murdered man—and the photo—near the river. Common sense told him the two might not be connected. He could be wrong about the photo having been dropped by the dead man. He could be wrong about a lot of things.

Mostly he was trying not to let his imagination run away with him.

It had given him an eerie feeling to find a photo of a family that had, in effect, disappeared as if whisked off the earth thirty years ago. He'd known it was the Ackermann family the moment he'd put the magnifying glass to it. Nettie had, too. He'd been watching her face and had seen the instant she recognized the faces in the snapshot.

A photo like that didn't just blow into the weeds by the river without some connection. Not when there was a murdered man in the undergrowth only yards away.

With an exhausted reluctance, he drew out the evidence bag and held it under his desk lamp as he had done so many times since this case had begun.

The photograph was of a tall, gangly man. Next to him was a skinny woman holding a toddler. Around her were four boys, all with the same dour expression as their father, all in their teens or preteens.

The family was dressed in clothes most people would have thrown out. The children all looked dirty and underfed. The Ackermanns were a sad-looking bunch. Frank remembered as a boy only getting glimpses of the brothers—and only when he and his friends had braved going near the hollow where they lived.

Cullen Ackermann was an antigovernment survivalist who'd settled in the area after coming into some money. He'd bought a bunch of property up one of the canyons deep in the Crazies and proceeded to fence and post his property with Trespassers Will Be Shot signs.

Rumor around town was that Ackermann was growing marijuana and that's why the compound was heavily armed and even had booby traps and land mines for anyone stupid enough to step on his land.

Frank's father had been sheriff at the time. "I don't want you and your buddies going near that place. You understand?"

He had. He'd seen the young Ackermann boys, boys much younger than him at the time, carrying what looked like machine guns. And yet he and his friends had still gone up there a few times. They'd just never been brave enough to cross the fence.

Frank shifted his gaze from Cullen to the man's second wife. Teeny, as she was known, was much younger. Few people had ever seen her except for the day he'd brought her home. She homeschooled his children and never came into town, even on the occasional trips her husband made for supplies.

The Ackermanns had apparently grown and killed their own food, that self-sufficiency isolating them even further from the community. Not that the no-trespassing signs didn't keep locals at a distance. Whatever was going on up in that hollow, everyone figured it was none of their business and just left them alone.

But after some complaints about the boys running wild and getting into neighboring ranches' gardens and livestock, Frank's father had gone out there only to be met by an armed and angry Cullen Ackermann.

Cullen swore his boys had nothing to do with any stealing. Frank's father had said he'd be back if he had any more complaints. To most people, the Ackermanns were simply an oddity that few gave any thought to. That was until the day more than thirty years ago when Frank's father had come home with the news. Frank had been in his room and sneaked down the hallway to listen, knowing something was going on.

"We rushed the compound," he heard his father say. "One of my deputies was wounded, another practically had his leg cut off in a bear trap that damned fool Cullen had set."

"Did you find her?" his mother had asked in a whisper.

From where Frank stood, he couldn't see his father, but he heard him say, "She's alive, but just barely. She was locked in a root cellar dug into the mountain behind the house. Been there probably for years. It was horrible, Sadie."

"What about the Ackermann children?"

"They weren't there. Probably took off up into the mountains. We haven't been able to find them." His father sighed. "We should have stormed that compound sooner. I hate to even think what's been going on up there."

"Thank God Loralee Clark came to you when she did. I know you thought she was just being a nosy neighbor and talking crazy. What about the woman she called Teeny? Did you find her?"

He couldn't hear his father's answer, but he heard his mother begin to cry.

His father, as if sensing his presence, had looked over his shoulder and seen him standing there listening. "You go on now. This isn't for your ears."

He'd had no choice but to leave. But plenty of wild gossip circulated, sweeping through the community like any horror story. Then shame had stilled the voices. As a community, people blamed themselves for letting it happen right under their noses.

Frank didn't learn the full extent of what had happened until years later when he'd read his father's report. In it, he'd learned that Cullen's first wife had been kept prisoner in a hole dug back into the mountainside for years. She was so malnourished and in such bad shape she died shortly after she was freed.

Frank and his friends had sneaked up there to see the root cellar. It was more like a cave in the mountainside. It still gave him chills when he remembered what he'd glimpsed back in that hole.

Cullen's so-called second wife, only known as Teeny, had been killed by one of the booby traps on the property. Cullen had been arrested on numerous charges, including two counts of manslaughter and endangerment to children, after the deaths of the two women. He'd gone to prison on what became a life sentence when he died recently of cancer.

The county had seized the land for back taxes and brought in the military to remove what booby traps and land mines they could find. The property had never been put up for sale. Instead it remained fenced and posted against trespassing.

While Frank now knew the gruesome details of the day his father and his deputies had stormed what they called the Ackermann compound, one big mystery had never been solved.

What had happened to the children? He knew they had taken off up into the Crazies that day, because a year later the remains of one of the sons had been found at a deserted campsite. The bones were strewn across a wide area, leading them to believe animals had carried off the remains of the others or even buried them to eat later.

So, for over thirty years, the Ackermanns had been forgotten.

Until now, Frank thought as he stared at the photo.

His computer screen beeped letting him know he had a response from his earlier inquiry. He stared at the name on the screen, then grabbed his keys and hat and headed for his patrol pickup.

KATE COULDN'T SHAKE the feeling that she'd been followed. Not just this time, either. She watched her rearview mirror. Earlier she'd seen a pickup behind her as she'd left Beartooth, but when she'd looked again, it was gone.

"Just my imagination," she said, and concentrated on driving up a narrow dirt road that skirted the Crazies. After she'd left the fair, she'd dropped by the post office. Her infrared camera had arrived, along with a state-of-the-art metal detector. With the equipment in her hands and the clock now ticking, she had no excuse.

Her pickup rumbled over a narrow wooden bridge, the snow-fed creek below moving in a roar of high water. The land along the edge of the Crazy Mountains was lush with new spring growth. Pale green aspen leaves fluttered in the breeze against a backdrop of deep, dark green pines.

Miles out of Beartooth, on a narrow, obviously seldom-used road, she slowed as the fence came into view. Checking her mirror, she saw no one and yet she couldn't shake the feeling that she wasn't alone and hadn't been since she'd gotten to Beartooth.

The signs on the razor-wire fence had rusted with

the years, but the lettering was still clear enough. Danger. Live Ammunition Area. No Trespassing. In smaller letters were warnings of the legal penalties of crossing the fence onto the property.

Kate kept going up the road. She'd discovered another road that abutted the back part of the posted land. She headed there now, although she would have much preferred cutting the wire and driving up the weed-choked road into Ackermann Hollow, as Claude had called it.

While she'd never seen another vehicle on this particular road, she didn't doubt that one of the ranchers who lived farther out this way used this road occasionally and would notice a cut fence and report it.

She turned onto what locals would call a two-track. Tall weeds grew between two nearly indistinguishable tracks. They brushed the undercarriage of her pickup as she shifted down and bumped along through thick cottonwoods, until the trees opened to give her a view of the Crazies towering over her.

It always gave her the creeps coming here, but she steeled herself for what had to be done. At first she'd come armed only with a shovel and a map. Both had proved fruitless given the size of the hollow.

She slowed, checking her rearview mirror again. Dust billowed up behind her pickup, but the road was empty of any other vehicles. She was miles from Beartooth, completely alone.

And yet, as she pulled in so her pickup was hidden from the road behind a stand of pines, she couldn't shake the feeling that someone was watching.

Shoving away those thoughts, she slung the infra-red-camera bag over one shoulder, pulled her metal detector from behind the seat and strapped on her small digging tool. She could always come back for the shovel.

When she'd first gotten to town, she'd gone down to the county office and gotten maps of the area, saying she liked to explore.

"You don't want to explore anywhere in this area," the woman had warned her, pointing to the exact area she *did* want to explore in the worst way. "It's off-limits, for your own good. Some kind of government property they must have used for training purposes. Apparently they left land mines and booby traps behind."

Something like that, Kate thought now, as she eased through the hole she'd cut in the fence and headed for a spot she'd been wanting to check out. She knew it was like finding a needle in a haystack, but she wasn't giving up. What she was looking for was here—she could feel it.

Overhead, a hawk soared on a thermal. Nearby a squirrel chattered at her from a pine bough. Her boots crunched on the dirt as she walked along the edge of the crumbling rock foundation of what had once been an outbuilding of some sort.

Ahead she saw the house, barn and more outbuildings. They'd all weathered to a dull gray over the past thirty years. And while all were still standing, the years hadn't been kind to them. The hollow was reclaiming the land. Weeds grew high up all sides of the buildings.

Water leaked in the roofs, rotting the wood beneath. Critters had moved into each dwelling, making nests, chewing their way through the walls.

There was a desolation about the place she suspected had always been here, though. She avoided the buildings, keeping to the trees and a faint animal trail she'd found that headed higher up into the hollow.

The lower part of the land lay in foothills but quickly rose in a deep, fairly wide canyon with rock cliffs, towering pines and a meandering creek that any other time of the year ran slow and clear. Now the creek raged as snow still melted slowly in the shade along the north side of the cliffs.

She hadn't gone far when she found the spot she was looking for. She turned on the metal detector, anxious to get to work. It wasn't long until she realized the problem she was going to have using the metal detector. She was looking for a metal box and the area was littered with parts of old cars, food tins, nails and other junk.

Still her heart raced each time the device went off— like right now. She was getting a good, strong indication of something belowground. Turning off the metal detector, she grabbed her small digging tool and began to upend the earth around the spot.

Almost ready to go back to the pickup for the shovel, her tool struck something that sounded solid. She dug faster, realizing she was losing her light with the waning daylight. She unearthed enough of the object to see that it was an old vehicle bumper.

With growing disappointment along with aching muscles, she'd started to fill in the hole when she felt the skin prickle on the back of her neck. She spun around, half expecting to find someone standing behind her.

A breeze teased at the loose hair around her face. She brushed it back, staring downhill toward the road she'd come in on. No sign of anyone, but there were too many trees and buildings between her and the road where someone could hide.

A meadowlark sang from the spring grass nearby. The breeze sighed in the tall pines. Her heart began to settle down again, but one hand still gripped the gun in her jacket pocket.

Someone was out there, watching her. It *wasn't* her imagination.

SHERIFF FRANK CURRY was waiting for the new owner of the Branding Iron Café when she returned. He was surprised to see that her jeans and Western shirt were dirty, as if she'd been digging in a garden. But Kate didn't have a garden.

"Sheriff," she said when she saw him. "I didn't expect to see you twice in one day." She opened the back door of the café and he followed her inside. "Coffee?"

He shook his head and took the booth they'd shared earlier that morning. It had been a long day and Kate LaFond looked as tired as he felt.

"You get into the hog wrestling at the fair?" he asked, indicating her dirty attire.

"Just went for a hike," she said. "Took a little spill."

He didn't believe her, but he also didn't call her on it. "So you like running the café here in Beartooth?"

She smiled. "I doubt you were waiting for me in the heat of the day to ask me that."

He returned her smile. "I understand Claude Durham left you the café. I'm surprised. I didn't think you knew him."

"I'm surprised that you would be interested in my relationship with Claude."

"What kind of relationship was that?"

"Friends."

"So you'd been to Beartooth before Claude died."

"Sheriff, what is this about?"

"Your name isn't Kate LaFond."

"No, not legally, but I'm sure you know that. After Claude died and left me the café, I wanted a fresh start in Beartooth, so I chose a new name to go with it."

"How do I know you're this Melissa Logan, the woman Claude left the Branding Iron to in his will?"

She got up. He heard her go upstairs and listened to her footfalls moving through the apartment. A few minutes later, she returned and dropped on the table in front of him a Nevada driver's license in the name Melissa Logan. The photograph wasn't a great one, but there was no doubt the woman in it was the one now sitting in the booth across from him.

"You changed your hair color, too," he said. The woman in the photo was blonde, clearly not her natural color. "Most people don't change their appearance and name unless they have something to hide."

Kate laughed. "I'm not most women and neither is the woman who put you up to this. I notice Nettie has a new hairstyle and color herself. What do you think *she's* trying to hide?"

He smiled, her point well taken. "Under Montana law, you need to get a new driver's license," he said, handing back her old one. "You might want to see about changing your name legally. That is, if you think you're going to be Kate LaFond for a while."

"Sheriff, haven't you ever wanted to simply be someone else for a while?"

"Can't say I have." He got to his feet. The one thing he'd learned being a lawman was that changing a name didn't change a person—or their past. He had a body down at the morgue without a name. But even nameless the man's past was branded on him like one of his jailhouse tattoos.

Kate had a past, a murky one. It hadn't escaped his mind that the murdered man in the morgue hadn't just been looking for Kate. He'd found her—and now he was dead.

NETTIE FOUND THE apartment over the general store neat as a pin. She wasn't all that surprised. Tiffany hadn't brought enough personal items to make much of a mess. Nor did the girl seem like the disorganized, cluttered teenage type.

But as she glanced around, Nettie thought there was something almost *too* neat about the apartment. There was nothing personal in sight. No photographs. No books. No trinkets of any kind.

Tiffany seemed the kind of kid who would have brought with her a favorite stuffed animal. A collage of photos of her best friends. Or, being an artist, a favorite artwork.

The room looked exactly as it had the day Nettie had rented it to her—as if the girl wasn't planning to stay long.

Then why pay six months' rent?

Nettie shook her head at how human nature often astounded her, as she went into the bathroom and opened her toolbox. After she fixed the leaky faucet, she had a thought.

She walked back into the living room. Nothing about it looked lived-in. She noticed that the bedroom door was cracked partially open and realized she hadn't looked in there.

As the landlord she had the right to take a look, right? She stepped forward and slowly pushed on the door, not sure what she was afraid of finding.

The room looked much like the rest of the apartment—the same as the day it had been rented. The bed was made, the pillows lined up as neatly as if the bed hadn't been slept in.

Nettie moved to the closet. A jacket and a couple of shirts hung on hangers, but otherwise the closet was empty.

She checked the chest of drawers. A bare minimum of underwear, all very reserved for a girl of Tiffany's age, Nettie thought. No thongs, no lace, nothing sexy at all. It was as if this girl had been raised by monks.

Nettie had suspected Tiffany's coming to Beartooth had something to do with a boy. Now she wondered if the girl had ever even had a boyfriend.

As she closed the drawer, she looked around the bedroom. Nothing personal in here, either. It seemed strange. But then, there was something strange about this girl. Nettie remembered the bulging shoulder bag. Did the girl take everything of a personal nature with her each time she left?

As she started past the double bed, she noticed that the comforter was a little crooked. She started to straighten it when her fingers brushed against something.

Bending down, she saw the corner of a sheet of paper, thick like a page from a sketchbook, sticking out from between the mattress and box springs.

Carefully she lifted the mattress. A half dozen sketches lay on top of the box springs. Nettie reached for them, surprised that they weren't half bad. Also surprised that her renter might actually have been telling the truth about being an artist.

Told you so, Bob said in her head. *Just goes to show you that you should have more trust in people.*

Nettie wasn't listening. Her hands were shaking as she looked from one sketch to the next.

They were all of the same person, she realized, heart pounding. Each captured an age-weathered face. But each stroke of the pencil seemed to add not only years, but something more sinister. The harsh lines made the face seem…menacing to the point of evil.

Every sketch was of Sheriff Frank Curry.

CHAPTER EIGHT

IT WAS LATE BY THE TIME Jack reached Beartooth. He'd ridden a few carnival rides, feeling like a kid again, then had a couple of beers with Carson, though Carson had soda. As much fun as he'd had, seeing Chantell had left him angry and frustrated. He knew damned well her father had wanted to get him out of her life. But how far would the man have gone?

Jack feared he knew. The timing of the rustling and the two-year prison sentence was too convenient. Judge Hyett had always come off as a man who felt he was above the law.

But how could Jack ever prove that the judge had anything to do with framing him? Hyett had power in this county because he was hard on criminals. The only way Jack had a chance in hell of connecting him to this was to find out who had done the old man's dirty work. Judge Hyett was too smart to take a chance on any of this coming back on him. But who could the judge trust enough to frame Jack and never talk?

The thought hit Jack like a brick. *Someone coming up for a sentence from his bench.*

That was it. And if that person ever did tell the truth,

Hyett could simply deny it. It would be his word against a known criminal.

Jack pulled into the spot in front of the cabin and cut his lights. Darkness closed in around him. Not even starlight bled down through the thick pines. He sat for a moment, thinking about what he'd just figured out. It felt right.

But if nobody would believe the truth, then what was the point of his sticking his neck out in an attempt to find it? Once he started digging around in the past, the judge could get word of it. He already suspected how far the judge would go just to get rid of him for a couple of years. Imagine what he'd do to protect himself. Jack knew he could easily end up back in prison—or worse.

He rubbed his forehead under the brim of his Stetson as he looked out at the darkness. Through the pines he could make out a light in the distance. The Branding Iron Café.

The thought of Kate LaFond did nothing to improve his mood. All day, he'd been mentally kicking himself for taking the note. He had let himself get involved when it was the last thing he needed. She'd made it perfectly clear she didn't want or need his help. Whoever she was and whatever she was hiding, it wasn't his problem.

But he would love a cup of coffee and piece of peach pie—and while he was at it, he'd return her note. He could just hear what his friend Carson would have to say about this.

He climbed out of his truck, thinking that he and Kate were a lot alike. Tonight they had to be the two loneliest people in Beartooth. Everyone else was still in Big Timber either at the dance at the fair or one of the bars, partying. Beartooth tonight really was a ghost town.

Jack slammed his pickup door, glanced toward his empty cabin, then the café sign shining through the darkness. He recalled Kate's expression when she'd come out of the fortune-teller's booth. She hadn't looked just angry, she'd been scared. What the hell had that old woman inside the tent told her, anyway?

With a curse, he knew he wasn't going to get a lick of sleep for hours. The thought of peach pie drove him down the trail through the pines toward the café.

He was almost to the highway, still in the pines, when he heard a vehicle coming. He stopped in the blackness of the trees as a large, dark pickup rumbled past. It looked familiar, but he couldn't place it. There were dozens of trucks like it in rural Montana.

Trotting across the street in its wake, he was already talking himself out of knocking on Kate's door. But his boots seemed to have a mind of their own. The spring night air was brisk, the sky overhead a canopy of black velvet studded with rhinestones. A breeze stirred the nearby pines, emitting a comforting sigh. There was nothing like spring in Montana—unless it was summer, he thought with a smile.

The paved road through town was empty. Other than the truck he'd seen, there didn't seem to be a soul left. It gave him an eerie feeling, as if there'd been a disaster he'd only narrowly missed and now he was entirely alone on the planet.

He glanced toward the apartment window over

the café. A light was on. His stomach rumbled at the thought of pie, but he willed his boots to keep walking. At the alley, he glanced down it, recalling his first night home, the first time he'd laid eyes on Kate LaFond.

The sound of the earlier truck's engine broke the night's heavy silence. He saw the driver flip a U-turn down at the end of the road and start back in his direction. Instinctively, he stepped into the shadowed darkness at the mouth of the alley. The pickup rolled slowly up the street, the engine throbbing.

As the driver passed the café, he looked in the direction of the apartment upstairs.

Jack felt a chill run the length of his spine as he caught a glimpse of the two men in the cab. As the truck continued down the street, he saw that the back plate had been plastered over with fresh mud and realized where he'd seen the pickup before.

He let out a curse as the driver turned behind the post office and stopped. The truck's headlights went out. The engine died.

Jack waited for the sound of pickup doors opening. But all he could hear were the usual night sounds. An owl hooted somewhere close by, the breeze sighed in the pines across the road and closer he heard the steady thump of shoe soles. Someone was running toward him.

JACK TURNED AS a slim silhouette entered the alley and ran toward him. Like the first time he'd seen her, Kate LaFond was dressed in running gear. Over the sound of her sneaker soles pounding the hard earth, he heard another sound. Two pickup doors opened and slammed shut behind the post office nearby.

He realized Kate hadn't seen him in the dark alley. Nor had she heard the men coming. He grabbed her before she saw him and pulled her back against the rock wall, his hand cupping her mouth. She instantly began to fight him with a determination he'd only glimpsed in her before. Adding to that, she was stronger than she looked.

"It's me, Jack," he whispered in her ear. He let out a low groan as her instep connected with his ankle. But he managed to keep his grip on her.

She was breathing hard, but she quit fighting. A moment later, he heard her catch her breath. She'd heard them, too. Two men moving along the back of the café building. They stopped at the door to the café, tried the knob, one of them swore, then they came around the corner of the café and started up the stairs directly over his and Kate's heads.

All the fight had gone out of her, but he still held her, still cupped his hand over her mouth, but more gently, as they stood in the blackness of the shadow against the rock wall. He thought he could feel her heart thundering against his chest, but it could have been his own. The two men were directly above them now. One of them knocked on the apartment door, then waited a few seconds before knocking again. He tried the knob. Locked. The two looked at each other, clearly debating whether to break in. That's when Jack saw the handgun one man had drawn.

At the sound of a vehicle coming into town, the men quickly retreated down the stairs. A carload of kids drove past, stereo blaring, the music and their laughter trailing after them through the dark night. More cars were coming—the fair must be over. People would be coming home or heading to the Range Rider to party until closing time.

Jack realized he, too, was holding his breath. He didn't let it out until he heard the men get into their truck. The engine revved. A few moments later, the steady throb of the big motor died away as the truck left town. At least temporarily.

Kate was trembling in his arms. He turned her to face him as he stepped away from the wall. Fear and anger mixed into a deadly combination. "Who the hell were those men?"

"How would I know?" she demanded.

He shook his head, unable to contain his anger. "One of them had a gun. They would have broken into your apartment if that carload of kids hadn't come by when they did. They were looking for *you*."

"The real question is what *you're* doing here," she snapped.

"Saving your butt. Again. Please, don't thank me," he said as he took a step back from her, hands raised. "Lady, you're in trouble. You want to pretend you're not. Want to pretend you don't know what those men are after? Fine. Have it your way. Like you said, you can take care of yourself. Hell, one man is already dead. You figure you can handle two more? Maybe you can. Don't let me butt into your business." He turned and was halfway down the alley before she spoke.

"Jack. Wait."

He stopped, but he didn't turn. Looking up at the

night sky filled with stars, he told himself to keep walking. Hell, better yet, *run*.

She had followed him and touched his shoulder, her warm fingers like the jolt of a cattle prod. "I'm sorry. Thank you. I don't like needing anyone's help. I guess I've spent too many years alone, taking care of myself because there was no one else to do it. But I swear to you, I've never seen those two men before."

KATE WATCHED JACK turn slowly to look at her. He had the bluest eyes she'd ever seen. Right now they were like a cutting torch, flames of hot-blue light boring into her. She wasn't sure what she expected him to say, but it wasn't what came out of his mouth.

"Is there any peach pie left?"

She blinked and then laughed. She'd expected him to cross-examine her, demand to know what those men wanted. She was still shaking inside from the encounter. But was it from the close call with the two men? Or from being in Jack's arms in the darkness?

"As a matter of fact, there is a piece left."

"Coffee?"

"I could make some."

"That's why I came down here tonight. I had a sudden craving for peach pie and coffee."

"I'm glad you did." She tilted her head as she studied him in the dim light. He wasn't just good-looking. His cowboy charm was intoxicating. And he *had* saved her tonight. She'd had so much on her mind that she'd foolishly gone for her run without her gun. She wouldn't make that mistake again.

"Come on in," she said, a little afraid of where this might lead, but convinced she could handle it.

As she pulled her key and let them both in the back door of the café, her hands were shaking. She was sure Jack noticed. He noticed everything, but did he know how much *he* rattled her?

She turned on the lights and went to the coffee-maker. "I heard you just got out of prison," she said, hoping to steer the conversation away from her and what had happened tonight. "So you're a dangerous hombre, are you?"

He chuckled at that. "Yeah, that's me. A cattle-rustling fool. A prize bull ended up in my corral after a night at the bar."

"You stole it?"

"The judge thought so and sent me to prison for two years."

"I'm sorry," she said, glancing back at him.

He shrugged. "I worked the prison ranch, so it was pretty much like what I'd been doing all my life, spending my days on the back of a horse chasing cattle."

"A cowboy, huh." She wrinkled her nose.

"If you are so disdainful of cowboys, what are you doing in Beartooth?"

She started a pot of coffee and turned, expecting to see Jack in his usual booth or lounging against the counter behind her, waiting for an answer.

No Jack. But the inside door to her apartment was open.

Kate let out an oath and headed for the stairs. "The coffee is—" The rest of her words froze in her throat.

Jack was standing in the middle of the apartment's small living area. When she saw what he held in his hands, her heart dropped.

"You kept his hat."

Kate stared at the hat in Jack's hands. Why had she kept it? "It isn't what you think."

Jack laughed. "You have no idea what I'm thinking." He glanced at the hat in his hand. "The hatband is hitched out of horsehair in much the same pattern as the rope the sheriff showed me." His gaze came up to meet hers. "The same rope that was used to kill the man, I would imagine. But you wouldn't know anything about that, right?"

She said nothing. There was nothing she *could* say.

"Look, I already know your friend spent some time in prison. I've already narrowed it down to Yuma." He must have seen her skepticism. "It's the *hitched* horsehair. There are only four prisons I know of where inmates hitch. Walla Walla, Washington; Rawlins, Wyoming; Deer Lodge, Montana; and Yuma, Arizona."

"Yuma?" she asked, calling him on it.

"It's the colors and the pattern. Yuma has a Mexican influence—they hitch in a lot of bright colors. They also use a lot of pink." He tossed the hat to her.

She caught it effortlessly and glanced at the predominant pink color in the hatband before dropping it on the couch. Crossing her arms, she said, "What does that prove?"

"That the man who was accosting you in the alley the first night we met probably did time in the Yuma prison. If you didn't know him, then why keep the hat?

Because you expected him to come back? Or because you knew he would never be coming back for it? Either way, it proves to me that you knew him. Or at least knew what he wanted."

Kate let out a nervous laugh. "Based on a *hat?*" She shook her head and started to turn back toward the stairs. "Your pie and coffee are ready. If that's really why you came down here tonight."

He grabbed her arm, turning her to him and shoving her back against the wall to press her body there with his own. She didn't move, didn't breathe. Every instinct told her to push him away. She'd already let him get too close.

His fingers grazed her cheek as he brushed a lock of her hair back from her face. "Have you ever told the truth in your life?" he asked, though there was no accusation in his tone.

"It's never come up."

He smiled at that. He had the most amazing smile. Kate figured the devil smiled like that. Mischief danced in his liquid-blue eyes. Gold flecks flashed like sunshine on warm water, as if inviting her to come in for a dip.

The callused pads of his fingertips trailed down from her cheek to the corner of her mouth. This was no urban cowboy. He brushed his thumb across her bottom lip. His gaze followed it. At first she thought he didn't feel the uncontrollable shudder that moved through her. But when he glanced from her lips to her eyes again, he gave her a knowing grin.

She'd had enough of this, she told herself, and prying her hands between them, put her palms against his hard chest.

She opened her mouth to tell him his kind of cowboy charm didn't work on her, but when she parted her lips to speak, his mouth dropped to hers, robbing her of her breath and her senses.

He pressed her tighter against the wall, his body as hard and solid as the wall behind her. Even when she did come to her senses, cursing herself for playing with fire when it came to Jack French, she didn't break the kiss for what seemed a very long time. Had she ever been kissed like this? She made a halfhearted attempt to push him away, but it was like trying to dislodge an immovable object.

His hand moved from her hip to her waist, drawing her even closer. Her every instinct warned her to stop, but it felt so good and it had been so long since she'd felt—

Jack broke off the kiss with such suddenness that she stumbled against him.

That's when she felt his hand just below her rib cage, his warm fingers tracing—

"What the hell?" he demanded, and lifted the hem of her shirt. At the sight of her scar, he let out a curse. Clearly he had come to *his* senses. "What did you tangle with?"

She stepped back from him, jerking her shirt down and mentally kicking herself for letting him get too close. "It's nothing."

"Nothing?" He reached for her.

"Don't."

"Don't touch? Or don't ask how you got a scar like that?"

"Just don't." She turned her back to him.

"Kate, it just surprised me, that's all," he said softly as he came up behind her. "Was it an accident or some kind of surgery?"

"It's none of your business."

She swung back around to face him. "You should go."

"Everything is a secret with you, isn't it? Makes me wonder just how many secrets you have that you can't even tell me about a scar."

"Jack—"

"Don't bother. Whatever comes out of that beautiful mouth of yours will be a lie anyway. I forgot that you and the truth aren't on a first-name basis and that the last thing you want is me interfering in your life." He met her gaze, held it for a heart-stopping moment, then tipped his hat. "Good night, *Kate*." With that he walked out.

After he left, Kate moved to the full-length mirror on the bedroom door and, lifting her shirt, studied the scar. It was called a hockey-stick incision. Five inches at an angle just above her stomach, then seven inches back toward her right side. Twelve inches total and one hell of a scar.

Kate dropped her shirt, and stepping back in the living room, collapsed into a chair before putting her face in her hands. She hadn't cried. Not since Claude died.

When she went downstairs, she found that Jack had taken the last piece of peach pie and helped himself to a cup of coffee, leaving money to cover both on the counter.

She stood for a moment, fighting her warring emotions. Then, taking a deep breath, she went to the door, locked it and leaned against it. She knew it wouldn't be the last she heard of Jack French.

Or of the men who'd come looking for her tonight.

Shoving all thoughts of Jack and that kiss away, she concentrated on her bigger problems. Those men would be back—if she didn't do something.

Unlocking the door, she ran toward the Range Rider bar and the old-timey pay phone out back. It cost her fifty cents to make the call, giving the dispatcher what information she could about the two men.

"They were driving a truck." She could tell that by the sound of the engine. "A diesel, I think, because it was big, but it was too dark to tell what color or make. One of the men had a gun and they were trying to get into the Beartooth General Store."

She hadn't given her name, saying she was just passing through and didn't want to get involved because she was a woman traveling alone.

Kate hung up and walked back to her apartment over the café. Claude had been right. But it was getting more dangerous than even he had anticipated.

"Beartooth, Montana, is a little piece of heaven," Claude said.

She'd shown up at his door, telling him she was reconsidering his offer. It was a lie. She only wanted answers.

"Oh sure, the town won't look like much to you," he said. *She noticed how he seemed to have gotten some of his color back when he talked about the place. "Beartooth takes a while to get into your blood, into your soul. That's why I've added a provision with my gift."*

She objected, reminding him that she hadn't agreed to anything. But that didn't stop him.

"One full year. You have to run the café for one full year. Then if you still want to leave, well, I don't give a damn."

"Why do you care anyway? You'll be dead. What does it matter to you what I do with my life?"

He studied her, frowning. "I owe it to your mother. Your birth mother."

She scowled at that. "Why do you owe her anything? You still haven't told me what you have to do with all of this."

"I tried to help her, all right? I failed. I'll probably fail you, too. But damned if I'm not going to try." *He sounded out of breath and she noticed that he was perspiring heavily.*

"What about my biological father?" she had to ask.

"I think it is probably best if—" He started wheezing, all the color draining from his face. A moment later he was lying on the floor at her feet.

She'd come too far to quit now. She would just have to finish what she'd come to Beartooth for—and soon.

What she wouldn't do was let anyone stop her. Not

the two men who'd been looking for her earlier. And especially not Jack French.

It wasn't until later, when she'd gone up to her apartment, that she saw the note where Jack must have dropped it earlier. It lay on the couch, next to the dead man's hat.

CHAPTER NINE

"I NEED TO SEE YOU."

Frank sat up in bed, his gaze going to the clock on the night table as the phone rang. Not quite eight in the morning and on a Monday.

He rubbed a hand over his face. Because of the fair, he'd had two long days and nights. No wonder he felt as if he hadn't had any sleep. He barely had. He'd planned to sleep in this morning since he had the day off.

He'd listened to the messages left on his phone, but it had been too late to call Lynette last night. Seeing who was calling, he picked up the phone and said, "Lynette, if this is about Kate LaFond—"

"It's my new renter. There's something I need to show you. I think she might be dangerous." Lynette took a breath and then said, "Did you find out something about Kate?"

He let out a sigh, realizing there was no way he would be able to get back to sleep now. "I'll tell you when I see you. I'm on my way."

"Hurry. She could be back at any moment."

He hung up, swung his legs over the side of the bed and sat for a moment, head in hands, trying to wake up.

Her renter might be dangerous? He thought of the

girl he'd seen framed in the upstairs window over the store. She looked like a child. Why would Lynette think she was dangerous?

Pushing to his feet, he reminded himself as he dressed that he trusted her instincts. Lynette had been right about Kate LaFond—at least in her suspicions that there was something odd about how the young woman had come to own the café.

Kate had made it clear that Claude's reasons for leaving her the café were her business. He wondered what Lynette would make of that.

Lynette was waiting when he arrived at the Beartooth General Store. She appeared distressed—but even so, she was still beautiful. He loved the way she'd aged. He fought the urge to take her in his arms and tell her everything was going to be fine.

"Are you all right?" he asked, wishing now that he'd returned her calls last night even though it had been late.

"I'm worried about *you.*"

"Me?"

She reached behind the counter and thrust a handful of thick paper at him.

As he glanced down at the first sketch, he was surprised to see his own likeness. It wasn't half bad.

"Did you do these?" he asked.

She made a face at him that questioned his intelligence. "My *renter.* I found them hidden under her mattress."

"Lynette—"

"Don't bother lecturing me. I have every right to

check the apartment. In this case, she'd asked me to fix a leaky faucet. Look at the rest of the sketches," she said as she filled him in on what she knew of her renter.

He glanced at the second sketch. By the third one, he was frowning. A cold chill snaked up his spine as he thumbed through the rest and saw that they were all of him.

"You say she paid six months' in advance?"

"Cash. She says she's getting her portfolio ready for art school." He heard the disbelief in Lynette's tone. "The first day I rented the apartment to her, she seemed more interested in what was going on over at the café than the apartment. Guess who was standing outside that day in front of the café? *You.* Later she was staring out the window again, and I saw you talking to that group of ranchers at the front table."

"I'm sure there's an explanation," he said as he glanced again at the sketches.

"She makes you look like you're possessed by the devil," Lynette said, tapping one of the sketches.

Something like that, he thought. Each portrayed a malevolence in him that alarmed him.

"Where is she now?"

Lynette shook her head. "She said she was going to Bozeman." All her doubt was evident in her dour expression.

"You should put these back under her mattress where you found them."

"You aren't going to ignore this, are you?" she demanded, looking scared again.

"No, I'll talk to the girl."

Lynette seemed to relax a little. "I had a feeling the day she showed up here that I shouldn't rent her the apartment."

"Lynette, don't buy trouble. Like I said, I'm sure there's an explanation."

"For why she's stalking you? Did you notice in some of the sketches you're sitting at your dining room table on the ranch?"

He hadn't. He'd been too shocked by the way she'd drawn his eyes, the hard line of his jaw, the cruel twist of his mouth.

"Put these back, please, and don't say anything to her until I get a chance to talk to her, all right?"

Lynette nodded. "Just be careful. I have this awful feeling that she's dangerous."

It wasn't until he'd left, first checking around town for the car Lynette said the girl drove, then driving down the road toward Big Timber, watching for it, that he realized how worried Lynette had been for him. She hadn't even asked what he'd found out about Kate LaFond.

As KATE NEARED the W Bar G corrals, she wished she hadn't listened to Jack French. She'd never been to a branding and she wasn't sure she wanted to see one now as she heard a cacophony of mooing cows.

But as she pulled in, she spotted Bethany Reynolds, her waitress, standing near the barn where food had been laid out on several long tables. She couldn't very well leave now, she thought with a silent curse.

So she parked and got out, telling herself she wouldn't stay long.

As Kate put down the tray of cinnamon rolls she'd brought, she felt more ill at ease in this alien environment than she had when she'd arrived in Beartooth.

"Kate?" Bethany said excitedly. "I can't believe you actually came to a branding. Is this your first?"

She had to admit it was and Bethany began telling her everything that was going to happen as they walked out toward the corrals. The sound of bawling calves and cows grew louder—along with the strong smell of burning hide.

Kate had never given any thought to how cows were branded. She had no idea it was such a large, noisy operation.

"On branding day, the cutters split out cows with calves," Bethany explained. "In the old days, the ropers swung a loop over the calves, took a couple of dally welts around the saddle horn and dragged them over to the fire. There calf wrestlers flanked and flopped them so the brander could hit them with a hot iron. Bawling calves got an ear tag and a couple of shots to keep them healthy and then were released."

As they neared the corrals, Kate saw a sea of black calves being herded into smaller corrals, then into a wooden chute, where each one was pushed through an even smaller chute, though this one was made of metal.

"On the W Bar G, the calves are herded into a corral and from there sent one at a time into a chute, where they're prodded onto a calf table," Bethany was saying. "It's like a narrow chute that turns into a table when it's laid over. Each calf then gets a brand burned into its hide."

Once the calf was caught in the metal chute, it was just as Bethany said. The chute laid over on its side to became a table, the calf flopping loudly onto its side.

"See how the calf table holds the calf's head while a cowboy throws a loop around the calf's hind leg to hold him still," Bethany was saying.

Kate watched as Jack French pulled a branding iron from a makeshift oven, stepped to the calf and applied the smoking-hot iron. The calf let out a loud moo, the stench of burned hide and smoke rising in the air, and was quickly released.

She had to cover her mouth to keep from crying out. "Doesn't it hurt?"

"It's quick and they have a thicker hide than us."

Kate watched the calf run around the corral for a moment before joining the others, apparently unhurt.

"It's an honor to be chosen to do the actual branding," Bethany said, no doubt noticing Kate watching Jack work at one of three branding tables. "I'm still surprised that Destry chose Jack. It's not everyone she lets brand her cattle. You have to get the brand in the right spot and it has to be legible from a distance."

She had no idea there was so much involved.

"Brands are put on in one of three places usually—left or right shoulder, side, or left or right hip," Bethany explained. "Most of the newer brands require two to three branding irons because they are more than two letters or numbers. Takes more time."

"Why doesn't everyone have a two-letter brand?" Kate asked.

"They aren't available," she explained. "You have to apply for a brand or buy someone's who is no longer using it. Most people hang on to their brands. Having a two-letter brand usually shows that the ranch has been around for a while. W. T. Grant designed the W Bar G ranch brand."

Kate saw that the W Bar G's brand was WG with a bar over the two letters. She was mesmerized by how efficient Jack was at branding. Bethany whispered, "Here comes Chantell Hyett. Jack's old girlfriend."

Kate turned to see a tall, beautiful woman with long blond hair and blue eyes headed for them. The woman was dressed in Western attire and exuded confidence, looking as if she fit right in out here with the cows and the cowboys.

"You must be Kate," Chantell said, and gave her the once-over. She clearly didn't seem impressed with what she saw. "Jack mentioned you work at the café."

"She *owns* the cafe," Bethany said, coming to her defense.

"I'm sorry, Jack hasn't mentioned you," Kate said. "And you're…"

The blonde's nose went up in the air. "I'm his girlfriend, Chantell Hyett."

"I thought you two broke up after you dumped him when he went to prison," Bethany said.

Kate laid a hand on her arm. She could defend herself. "Well, there's Jack right over there," Kate said, pointing to him. "I assume that was where you were headed."

Chantell didn't give them a backward glance as she sauntered toward Jack, who was busy turning up the heat on the branding irons.

"What did Jack ever see in that woman?" Bethany said.

Kate knew that men often didn't see beyond a pretty face and a nice body. Chantell had both, she thought as she watched the woman stop next to Jack and lean toward him, saying something over the bawling of the calves about to be branded.

As Kate watched, she saw Chantell shoot a look in her direction, then grab Jack's shirt and pull him into a quick kiss. Some of the cowboys sitting along the corral fence began to hoot and holler.

Jack said something to Chantell, then looked in Kate's direction. Kate didn't watch to see Jack's reaction. Her own response was a painful ache in her stomach as she turned and said over her shoulder to Bethany, "I need to get back to the café."

In truth, she just needed distance. From Jack French, from Beartooth and from this horrible feeling of jealousy that clamped down on her heart like a vise.

She needed to dig, she thought as she climbed into her pickup, started the engine and headed for Ackermann Hollow.

JACK FRENCH HAD always believed that everything happened for a reason. Usually the reason was that the universe just wanted to see how bad it could make his life. At least that had been the old Jack's attitude.

At prison, he'd met too many men who thought it was bad luck that had put them there. He liked to think he was smarter than that, which meant admitting that it hadn't been just bad luck that he'd ended up in prison— but that he'd contributed through his don't-give-a-damn behavior.

He was thinking about that as he loaded up his pickup after the branding was over for the day.

"I finally remembered where I knew her from," Carson said, joining him.

Jack knew at once that he was referring to Kate La-Fond. He just didn't know if he wanted to hear this.

"She was going by the name Melissa Logan and working as a waitress at this place outside of Vegas called Pop's Oasis."

"Melissa Logan," Jack repeated. "You're sure?"

"Positive. There was this waitress named Connie. A friend of mine went out with her a few times. I just called down there a few moments ago. Connie remembered me, and guess what she told me?"

Jack shoved back his hat. "You aren't seriously going to make me guess, are you?"

"Connie said that some old man showed up one day, saying he knew Melissa's mother. Melissa quit a few days later. That was the last she heard from her."

"What old man?"

"Connie didn't know. But she did say that Melissa had seemed upset. When Connie asked, Melissa said she was about to take the biggest gamble of her life and to wish her luck."

"Strange," Jack said. "I wonder what all that was about?"

Carson scratched at the back of his neck. "I debated whether to tell you. But I figured you have a right to know what you're getting involved with."

Jack thought about denying that he was in any way involved with Kate LaFond's or Melissa Logan's life. But Carson didn't give him a chance.

"Let's meet later for a soda at the Range Rider?" his friend asked.

"Right now I just want to get cleaned up and off my feet," Jack said. "Give me a call later. You have my cell phone number."

Jack climbed into his pickup and started down the long road to Beartooth. "Melissa Logan," he repeated. "Kate LaFond. Who are you really?"

He knew he should stay clear of the woman either way. There was something about her that reminded him too much of himself—not a good thing.

And yet, he was drawn to her like a cowboy to the range. He'd known his share of women. None intrigued him the way Kate had the first time he'd laid eyes on her.

Jack couldn't get her out of his mind—or that scar he'd felt just below her rib cage. It was a good foot long in total and thick with scar tissue. A knife wound? Or some kind of surgery?

The woman had too many secrets. Any one of them could have made her dangerous.

He let out a frustrated curse. Wasn't his problem, he

told himself. *Just walk away. You have enough problems of your own.*

Judge Hyett came to mind, bringing with it an aching need for justice.

ON A HUNCH, the sheriff swung by his ranch. The place was more a hobby ranch, since he already had a full-time job. He raised a few cattle, a couple of pigs and enough chickens to keep himself and the staff at the sheriff's department in fresh eggs.

As he drove up the road toward his ranch, he felt his gut tighten. A small brightly colored compact car matching the description of the one Lynette had told him her renter drove was parked behind his barn. Even though he'd seen the sketch that definitely looked like him sitting at his kitchen table, he didn't want to believe the girl had been spying on him.

But apparently Lynette was right. The girl had taken an interest in him for some reason. Maybe it was a class project, he told himself as he pulled in, blocking the road that led out—just in case there was some reason she would need to make a run for it.

Getting out, he walked the last quarter mile through the tall, green spring grass, coming up behind her car. It was empty. He glanced around, wondering where she could be. He felt his chest tighten as he cleared the corner of the barn and saw that his front door was wide open. Well, that answered that question.

He thought about pulling his gun, but quickly rejected the idea when he thought about the young girl he'd glimpsed in the upstairs window over the store.

Whatever her story, he couldn't believe she meant him any harm.

As he stepped inside the front door, he stopped to listen. He heard something slam, like a drawer, and realized the noise had come from upstairs. Taking the stairs three at a time, he reached the landing and moved quietly down the hall toward his bedroom—the only room with a chest of drawers.

She had her back to the door and was just going through the bottom drawer when he saw her.

"Looking for anything in particular?" he asked.

He would have sworn she jumped a foot. She spun around, her eyes wide with fright, fear dominating her small, pale face. How could Lynette think, because of a few drawings, that this skinny little girl was dangerous?

"I don't believe we've met," he said.

She swallowed and pressed herself against the front of the bureau as if it was all that was holding her up.

"I'm Sheriff Frank Curry, but I have a feeling you already know that. I'm afraid I haven't had the privilege of meeting you, though." When all she did was stare, he said, "I'm going to need your name."

"Are you arresting me?" Her voice broke with each word.

"Should I?"

She straightened a little, defiance coming into those big blue eyes. "I haven't done anything."

"If you were looking for valuables—"

She scoffed at that idea. "I'm not a thief."

"But you did break into my house."

"You left your door unlocked."

"Not as an invitation for you to come in and go through my drawers. So if you're not a thief, then what were you looking for?"

She lifted her chin. It surprised him the amount of challenge she could put into one look. She was such a tiny thing, so young, so...innocent. "I was looking for a photograph of my mother."

He frowned. "Your mother?"

"You didn't even keep *one,* did you?"

"I'm sorry, but I don't—"

"My name is Tiffany *Chandler.*"

Chandler? He felt his eyes widen in surprise and alarm. His ex had taken back her maiden name of Chandler? "You're *Pam's* daughter?"

"She said you would deny me." Fury flashed in those blue eyes hotter than the coals of a branding fire.

"Deny you?"

"Deny that I'm your daughter."

CHAPTER TEN

FRANK STARED AT THE GIRL, too shocked to speak for a moment. His cell phone rang. He reached for it, never taking his eyes off the young woman standing in front of him. The call was from the dispatcher.

"I'm sorry, I have to go. There's been an accident. A semi rolled over on Highway 191 between Big Timber and Harlowton and is blocking the road on a blind curve. Can we talk later?"

"You don't believe I'm your daughter."

"I don't know what to believe. If this is true, then why didn't your mother tell me?" He saw her expression close like a steel trap.

"She said you would pretend you didn't know about me."

He fought back a curse. What had Pam told this girl? Lies, that was certain. "I have to go, but I will come by if it isn't too late so we can talk. You're staying in the apartment over the store, right?"

She didn't respond.

"I'm not denying anything, all right? This has been a shock—I don't know what to say."

She nodded slowly, but was clearly still angry.

"I will come by later or first thing in the morning,"

he said, and started to reach for her, to touch her shoulder, but she drew back.

"You'd better go," she said, and turned and walked away.

He followed her car as far as the highway. She turned toward Beartooth. He flipped on his lights and siren and headed north, his mind racing.

As he rushed toward the accident, he tried to remember those last few months with Pam, after spending almost eighteen years doing his damnedest to forget them.

Even now, the weeks before she moved out were a blur of arguments. She'd been more emotional than he'd ever seen her, but he hadn't thought anything of it at the time. Now he realized she could have been pregnant if the girl really was his.

Why hadn't Pam told him?

Or had she tried?

He had a sudden flash of Pam standing at the kitchen sink. She was wearing her favorite dress. The smell of roast beef was interlaced with the scent of her perfume.

It was years after that before he'd stopped smelling the sickly sweetness of that perfume. She'd quit wearing it after he'd told her he didn't like it. Had it been that night?

Candles. There'd been candles on the table and his favorite supper.

With a curse, he slapped his forehead. How could he have been so stupid? All the signs were there, but where was he?

Lynette. He'd been to see her at the store that day.

Probably stopped in for an orange soda and a candy bar. No doubt left there in a bad mood. He had seen that Lynette wasn't any happier in her marriage than he was in his. But at least Lynette had the store. He'd wanted children; Pam was always dragging her feet, saying she wasn't ready.

Had she planned to tell him that night that she was pregnant? She knew how badly he'd wanted a child. The nice dress, the candles on the table, his favorite dinner…

He couldn't remember anything else about the night except that she never lit the candles and he never ate the meal. They must have gotten into an argument. Pam was so jealous of Lynette it was like an obsession.

"I married *you*," he would snap at her.

"Only because you couldn't have her."

It was an old argument, one that got them nowhere.

"I love *you,* Pam. How many times do I have to say it?"

She'd never believed it, even though he *had* loved her. He just didn't love her the way he loved Lynette, the way he always would love Lynette, his first love.

A week after that night, he came home from work and Pam was gone. The divorce papers came a few weeks later. He didn't try to get her back. He just signed and mailed them. In truth, he'd been relieved. He couldn't live anymore with Pam's constant suspicions and accusations.

He'd always thought that if they'd had children, they would have made it. He would have loved Pam more than anything for giving him children. He'd thought children would give Pam what she needed as well—an anchor to him that would prove his love.

He hadn't realized how long he'd been driving until he saw the traffic backed up ahead. In Montana, miles were measured by hours or how many six-packs it took to get from one town to the next. Towns were few and far between in this part of the state, so it often took a lot of beer. Montana was new to the open-container law, not that some paid much attention.

That was one reason that crime in the state often involved alcohol and speeding. Murder was a rarity. But right now he would gladly murder Pam.

Ahead, he saw the overturned semi. Cursing how stupid he'd been about so many things, he slowed.

I have a daughter.

Was it true? Why would Pam have kept this from him all these years? Could she hate him that much? Apparently so, he thought as he pulled to the side of the road.

As he started to get out, his radio went off. A moment later, the dispatcher patched through a call from the warden at Yuma prison.

"You still need identification on that mug shot you sent me?" the warden asked.

Frank said he did. "So he was one of yours?"

"Up until two weeks ago, when he and his brother were released on some damned legal technicality. You say he was murdered? I'm not surprised. He was always in trouble while he was in. His name's Darrell Ackermann."

Ackermann? Frank's heart dropped. "You say he was released with his brother?"

"Gallen Ackermann. That photo you sent of the murder weapon? Gallen spent most of his time here hitchin' horsehair. I asked his cell mate. He says it's one of Gallen's ropes. He's another one headed for a violent end."

ONCE BACK IN TOWN after another frustrating day digging in all the wrong places, Kate hurriedly changed and went downstairs to the café. Fortunately, it wasn't busy yet. Bethany and Lou were handling things just fine, but even on a Monday night there would be a rush because of her weekly specials.

The special tonight was prime rib with a baked potato and a salad. She'd added it to the menu even though Claude's friend Arnie Thorndike had told her she was making a mistake.

"Claude never had weekly specials," the attorney told her.

"My Monday night specials are especially popular," Kate had said, annoyed that Arnie was butting into her business.

"That was what was nice about the Branding Iron," the older man said. "Claude kept it simple. People around here like simple."

She'd refused to argue with him even though she wanted to say, "What do you know about people around here? You live like a hermit. So if you don't like it, go back to your lair and leave me alone." But she didn't.

Instead she wondered why Claude had never mentioned Arnie Thorndike if they really had been best friends. It seemed odd, since Claude had told her about so many other people around Beartooth.

He'd warned her that Nettie would be trouble. She smiled now as she tied on her apron. Claude had certainly called that one right.

"She's incredibly nosy," he'd said. "Trust me, she'll try to find out everything about you or die trying. Best thing to do with her is put her off the scent as quickly as possible."

So why hadn't he mentioned Arnie Thorndike?

Because Arnie was merely annoying and not someone she had to worry about, she thought as the bell tinkled over the door and a half dozen ranchers and their wives came in.

The only other person Claude hadn't warned her about was Jack—and he'd turned out definitely to be someone she had reason to worry about.

"I THINK I KNOW who was behind framing me for the rustling charge," Jack said when he and Carson met at the Range Rider Monday evening.

Carson glanced over at him and then picked up his ginger ale to take a long drink.

"It's the only thing that makes any sense," Jack continued. He knew Carson thought the best thing he could do was to forget it. Jack couldn't have agreed more. But since when did he do the best thing for himself?

Kate LaFond came to mind. He pushed that thought away and continued. "I probably drank too much and had way too much fun in my young life and no doubt made some enemies I don't know about, but no one dislikes me enough to send me to prison for two years. No one but Judge Hyett."

Carson shook his head. "What are you saying?"

"Think about it. I was dating his precious daughter. He never made a secret of how he felt about that. Maybe he thought we were getting serious. Or maybe he just decided to nip it in the bud and get rid of me. What better way than sending me up on a rustling charge?"

Carson was still shaking his head. "Even if what you're saying was true—"

"I know. You can't imagine the judge stealing a prized bull in the middle of the night, right? So he got someone else to do his dirty work."

His friend looked as skeptical as Jack had originally felt when the idea had come to him. "Don't you see how perfect the judge had it? All he had to do was pick a couple of felons who would be coming before him for sentencing. He would make them a deal they couldn't refuse. And if they ever talked, it would be the judge's word against theirs."

"*Two* men who would keep this to themselves?"

"It would have taken two men to steal the bull and get him in my corral that night."

"A pretty dangerous thing for a judge to do." Carson took a sip of his ginger ale and continued, "He would be indebted to those men for life, always fearing that they could expose him at any time."

"It would be his word, a judge's, against theirs, plus he would have chosen men who wouldn't be believed.

Men who might have already had a brush with the law or would be afraid to stand up to him. Men who would have a lot to lose if this came out. Someone like—"

"Hitch McCray."

Jack laughed and nodded. "Exactly."

"Why would Hitch—"

"He'd been picked up for a couple of driving-while-under-the-influence charges before I went away. He's been in trouble since then. I heard something about him sideswiping a car outside the Range Rider and having a run-in with your sister out at her ranch."

Carson stared at him for a moment, then let out a curse. "You might be right."

Jack laughed. "Great. Not even you believed I was innocent."

"Come on, Jack, it wouldn't be the first time you had too much to drink and got into trouble."

Exactly. "I made it real easy for the judge, didn't I?"

"You're never going to be able to prove it, and if you go up against the Hangin' Judge—"

"Just let it go, right?" Jack asked.

Carson fell silent. "I know. You're a convicted felon and you lost two years of your life for something you didn't do. I'd be mad as hell."

Jack had to chuckle at that. "You lost eleven years because of something you didn't do."

"That was different. I loved Ginny. With her gone, I had nothing to lose. You on the other hand have a lot to lose. While any man in your boots would want to go after whoever was behind it, I'm just not sure you can get justice."

That was the hell of it and Jack knew it. "For the sake of argument, who would Hitch have gotten to help him?"

"One of his ranch hands?"

Jack shook his head. "It had to be someone of the judge's choosing. The two might not have even known each other. It would have been someone he could control if it all hit the fan. Also it would be someone coming up before the judge for sentencing. That should narrow it down."

"So if you're right, then what?" Carson asked.

He took a sip of his beer. "I haven't gotten that far yet."

"If he framed you the first time just to get you out of his daughter's life, imagine what he will do to keep this from coming out. Where are you going?" Carson demanded as Jack grabbed his hat and pushed off the bar stool to his feet.

"I need to find a computer."

"This time of the night?"

Fortunately, he'd seen one recently that he thought he might be able to use and kill two birds with one stone, so to speak.

"Jack, promise me you won't do anything…crazy."

Jack laughed. "Do I look like a man who would do anything crazy?" His laugh followed him out the door as he headed for Kate LaFond's.

"I NEED TO USE your computer."

Kate leaned into the door frame, wishing she hadn't opened the apartment door to him. A cold wind kicked up dust along the alley beneath the stairs. The temperature had dropped and she could tell a storm was blowing in.

"It's important," Jack said.

"Oh, well, then that's different."

He grinned. "Please? I know it's late, but I saw your light on...."

She moved aside to let him in, against her better judgment. Jack and his easygoing cowboy charm were deceptive. The man could worm his way into a woman's heart as well as her bed if she wasn't careful.

He seemed to think she owed him, and maybe she did. He'd crossed her path—saved her life, actually, when she was being honest about it. But she hated owing anyone, especially a man like Jack French.

"It's over there," she said, pointing to her laptop on the small dinette table. "Mind telling me what this is about?"

"I need to check on something." He glanced around her apartment. "I didn't notice last time I was here, but you're not much into decorating, are you?"

She bristled. "I haven't had a lot of time, not that it's any of your business."

He shot her a teasing grin as he sat down in front of the computer. "Like to keep things simple, do you?"

She ignored that as he began typing quickly on the computer keys. It surprised her to see that he knew what he was doing. Apparently, the cowboy hadn't spent all his time in the company of only horses and cows. She watched his large hands on the keys and remembered the feel of his callused fingertips on her skin and quickly turned away to finish what she'd been doing when he'd knocked on the door.

Claude had put a small stackable washer and dryer in a closet in the hallway. She pulled her clothes out of the dryer, listening to the steady click of the computer keys as she folded her still-warm clothes and headed for the bedroom to put them away.

She'd just opened the chest of drawers when she realized she no longer heard the clack of the computer keys.

Even more disturbing, she sensed Jack directly behind her. She dropped the stack of clean clothing in the drawer and shut it slowly before turning around to find him just inches away. Jack unnerved her in ways she didn't want to think about, especially with the two of them standing this close in her bedroom.

Kate tried not to react to his nearness or the fact that he had one of her lost-treasure magazines in his hands.

"Would you like a beer?" she asked as she stepped past him, heading for the small kitchen and putting distance between them. She opened the refrigerator, breathing in the cold air as she grabbed two beers and turned to find him watching her with amusement. The man knew the effect he had on her and enjoyed it.

She reminded herself of his kiss with Chantell at the branding. She wasn't the only one Jack French was busy charming.

"INTERESTING MAGAZINES," JACK said as she handed him a beer and took the magazine from him to toss it back in the pile on the table. "So you're into lost treasure, are you?"

She had seemed nervous moments before in the bedroom, but now her confidence had returned. "They were my father's. I couldn't part with them. I grew up on stories of lost mines, stagecoach caches and strongboxes full of gold, silver and coins."

"Your father was a *treasure hunter?* That must have been a fun childhood."

She smiled as she curled into one of the overstuffed chairs and took a sip of her beer. She relaxed now, as if she didn't even mind his company—as long as she could keep a few feet between them.

"Living in the back of a pickup camper, traveling around the country looking for lost mines and buried treasure does make an interesting childhood. It had its moments."

"Did he find anything exciting?" Jack asked as he turned one of the kitchen chairs around and straddled it to face her.

"He found rattlesnakes, rock slides and gully washers that finally took out the pickup and camper. He was killed in a rock slide looking for a lost mine."

"I'm sorry."

"Don't be. That's the way he would have wanted to go. He would have kept looking for buried treasure until he couldn't walk anymore. Not being able to chase the stories would have killed him in a much more tragic way. I guess if he had to go, I'm glad it was doing something he loved."

"I admire that kind of passion," Jack said.

She cocked her head at him, openly studying him. "You don't have it?"

He grinned. "I'm passionate about some things."

She shook her head at him in mock disgust. *"Women."*

"That's one," he admitted as he watched her get up and move across the room. She was lithe and graceful. He realized she moved like a cat—quiet, no wasted effort—and she had to be the only person in Beartooth who ran for exercise.

"Don't most lost treasures have some curse attached to them?" he asked.

Her laugh was musical. It made him smile.

"My father said he didn't believe in the curses, but by the end, after a lot of strange accidents, I suspect he became a believer."

"What about you?"

"We're all cursed in some way. It's like luck. I make my own."

"I don't know," he said with a shake of his head. "I think some of us are cursed when we're born. The only thing that keeps us going at all is a little good luck."

"*You* were cursed at birth?" she asked, sounding amused and suspicious. "That fortune-teller said I was, too. You sure you didn't have a hand in that?"

He shook his head and made an X over his heart. "Scout's honor."

"You were never a Boy Scout."

"No," he admitted. "Is that what upset you, what the fortune-teller told you about being cursed at birth?"

"We were talking about you. So you weren't born into a life of privilege?"

"My mother died when I was three." He didn't mention his inheritance he'd never touched. "My father never got over it. He was known for brawling and ending up in jail."

"I'm sorry."

"Sometimes I think from the get-go my story was already written. It's been hard trying to overcome my family legacy, not to mention my father's genes."

"I lost my mother, too, only my father had a little different approach. He sold everything and we hit the road in search of lost treasure. I guess it was *his* way of running away, like your father ran away by fighting."

"Sounds like our fathers were a lot alike." He met her gaze. "Makes me wonder what else you and I have in common."

She put down her beer and got to her feet. "Must be time for you to go."

"Was it something I said?"

"It's just that I know your type, Jack. This isn't my first rodeo."

"Mine, either. But there's something different about you. About us."

She tilted her head at him as if to say she wasn't buying a word of it. "I saw you with your girlfriend at the branding."

"Chantell isn't my girlfriend." He could see she didn't believe that, either. "The only reason she kissed me was to get a rise out of you. Did she?" He grinned. "Apparently she succeeded."

He finished his beer and got to his feet. As he passed her on the way to the door, he touched her shoulder. "Thanks for the beer and the conversation. This is the nicest time I've had in years. No bull."

He let himself out into the cold. It had started to snow. Nothing quite like spring in Montana. Eighty degrees one day and snowing the next. Huge, lacy flakes drifted down into the darkness. Several inches of the light, airy stuff had already fallen. It now blanketed everything, including his pickup.

"Why the devil did you come back here?" he asked himself as he tracked through the snow to his truck.

As he started to open the driver's door, he glanced up at the window of the upstairs apartment over the café. Kate had turned out the lights, but he could see her standing there, a dark shadow.

Something about it sent a chill up his spine. He brushed snow from the door handle and opened the door. Snow floated in the air, swept into the pickup and covered the seat. He brushed it off and climbed in.

The engine turned over with a low groan. The heater came on blowing ice-cold air. He turned it off and glanced through the falling snow again to the apartment window. It was empty.

KATE WATCHED JACK drive away. She couldn't believe it was snowing again. She had witnessed the land turn from a dull winter brown to vibrant green. Each day the fields turned a brighter green and blossomed with wildflowers.

The creek across from the café roared, snow fed

from the mountains and smelling of pine. Just this morning she'd awakened to the sound of birds singing and a fresh breeze stirring the new leaves of an old cottonwood next to her window.

Was this place growing on her? She scoffed at the idea. "I only have a few more months, Claude. Then no matter what, it's goodbye, Beartooth."

CHAPTER ELEVEN

"DON'T YOU DARE DIE."

As Claude Durham slowly opened his eyes, Kate got up from the chair beside his hospital bed and moved to him. He looked weak, but he'd gotten some of his color back.

"I thought you would be long gone," he mumbled, and closed his eyes again.

She wasn't about to admit that she'd spent the night in an uncomfortable chair next to his bed. "You're the one who barged into my life. I wasn't leaving until you told me the truth."

"The truth?" His smile was wan. So was the soft chuckle he emitted. He opened his eyes again. "I already told you. I'm dying."

"I want to know about my mother." She met his gaze. "And my father."

His eyes fluttered closed again. "It's a long, not very flattering story."

"Since I've probably been fired from my job by now, I have a lot of time on my hands—and you owe me the truth, since you started this. Also, I doubt I could think less of you."

He smiled at that, no doubt seeing through the lie. It

was a while before he finally began to speak, though. Still keeping his eyes closed, he said, "I had an older brother. He ran away when he was fifteen. Our father drank. Our mother finally ran him off and remarried a man named Bruce Durham. Bruce was fine. We were living on a ranch down in Wyoming. Bruce adopted me and my younger brother, Everett. But Bruce didn't last long. My mother had a few problems of her own, and social services finally took Everett away. I was old enough, seventeen by then, that I took off. I lost track of Everett. Because I was good sized for my age, I went to work on a Wyoming oil rig and saved every dime I made."

"Fascinating, but what does any of that have to do with Beartooth?"

He opened his eyes. "My mother was born there. She used to tell stories about growing up on the edge of the Crazies. I had this idea that it was Shangri-la. When I finally had enough money that I could buy an old pickup, I headed there. I got a job working in the kitchen at the Branding Iron Café."

"So that's how you ended up with the café," she said, more to herself than to him. "And my mother? Where does she come into your life story?"

"Months went by before I heard about some crazy survivalist who had holed up in an isolated hollow deep in the mountains outside town. His name was Cullen Ackermann."

She took a guess. "Your older brother?"

Claude nodded. "He no doubt remembered our mother's stories, too. My brother had always been a bully. I wasn't looking forward to seeing him. I was enjoying my job at the café and I wanted to put that old life behind me. Fortunately, he hardly ever came to town. When I finally ran into him, he didn't recognize me. I was so relieved, I left it that way. Over time, I was able to buy out the former owner of the café. By then Cullen had become even more reclusive and fanatical. Then the rumors started about him having a young, beautiful second wife."

Kate felt a start, knowing even before she said it. *"My mother."*

"Her name was Katherina, but everyone called her Teeny. She was a tiny young thing, all right. I had no idea how Cullen got her to marry him—he was much older than her and already had four nearly grown boys. I later learned that he tricked her. She didn't know what she was getting into, since he found her out in Washington and brought her back here. She hadn't seen what a lunatic he was."

He took a shaky breath and continued. *"But it didn't take long before she realized her mistake in marrying him, let alone letting him take all her money. Teeny came from a wealthy family. It also wasn't long before she came to realize Cullen was getting more paranoid, more violent, and so were her four stepsons."*

Claude coughed and stopped for a few moments.

Kate's heart was in her throat. *"He was violent with my mother?"*

"Not in the way you think. He patrolled his land up the hollow armed with every kind of weapon you could imagine. He wouldn't let anyone on the property and

he wouldn't let Teeny or the children leave. Teeny was homeschooling his boys best she could. She was a virtual prisoner, since they raised all their own food and killed what animals they needed for food, and the only person allowed to go into town was Cullen."

Claude stopped again, and she could see that this was the hard part of his story. "My brother had booby-trapped the whole area and had his boys standing guard ready to shoot to kill. But I kept hearing stories about Teeny and I became more curious about her."

"Curious enough to go up there even though it was armed like a fortress?"

He smiled and nodded. "I used to be a lot braver than I am now."

"DID YOU FIND a computer?" Carson asked with a grin when he and Jack took a break from the branding the next day.

"As a matter of fact, I did." His friend shook his head as Jack added, "Kate was very obliging and let me use hers."

"I'll bet."

"Just as I suspected, Hitch McCray was set to go before Judge Hyett two weeks after I was arrested for rustling."

"You said it would take at least two men to pull off stealing that bull."

Jack nodded. He'd found several names he recognized. He figured it wouldn't be easy for a man with a conscience to frame an innocent man—unless he already knew Jack, knew about his family legacy of getting in trouble, and had a lot to lose. Jack had been far from innocent on numerous occasions. Everyone in the county expected the worst from him. The rustling charge had proven them all right.

It wasn't until he'd found a name he hadn't expected that Jack knew he'd struck pay dirt.

"Cody West," he said, and saw his friend's shock. Rylan West's younger brother had been arrested just three weeks before Jack had been awakened to find a prized bull in his backyard and the sheriff reading him his rights.

"Cody's arrest was for a minor in possession of alcohol and driving under the influence. He'd probably been busted at a kegger down by the river," he told Carson, who knew as he did that kids had partied down there for years. Probably Judge Hyett had too when he was young.

But for years, Hyett had been making a name for himself by busting up keggers and getting tough on drinking teens. He always pointed to the decrease in automobile accidents by young drivers and took all the credit.

"Cody got off with a slap on the hand," Jack told his friend. "The other kids didn't fare as well."

Carson shook his head. "I can't believe Taylor West would let his youngest son make such a deal with Judge Hyett. You know Taylor. He would have been furious with his son about the arrest and probably harder on him than anything the judge would have given him."

"True, but getting the sentence busted down to only a minor in possession? The kid made a deal with the judge knowing how furious his old man would be if he got a DUI on top of it." Taylor West was the kind of father every young man wished he'd had. Unless you ticked him off. Then Taylor could be tough as iron railroad spikes. "Cody would have been scared. I get how scary Judge Hyett can be."

"I hope that's true, because quite frankly, Jack, you're scaring *me*. Do I need to remind you how dangerous going after Hyett is? If you're right, the man has already committed a crime. As powerful as he is, who knows what he might do to get rid of you this time."

Having the judge drop the serious charges would have indebted both Hitch and Cody to the judge. But indebted enough to help frame a man for rustling? That was the question. Jack was still trying to decide if he wanted the answer badly enough to go up against the judge.

I HAVE A DAUGHTER. It was Sheriff Frank Curry's first thought the next morning. He'd directed traffic until late in the evening, then gotten called out on another accident. He'd spent most of the time cursing Pam. Of course, he had a right to be angry. He'd lost seventeen years with his daughter.

If she's even my daughter.

If Pam hadn't bothered to tell me about the child all these years, then isn't there also the possibility Tiffany isn't mine? Maybe Tiffany had misunderstood her mother. Or maybe Pam had never told her who her father was and Tiffany had just concluded that it had to be him.

He had to talk to Pam.

But in the meantime, he needed to see Tiffany again.

Tuesday after work, Frank found her in the apartment over the store. Beartooth General Store was closed for the day, so Lynette wasn't around, something he was grateful for as he climbed the stairs and tapped on the apartment door.

Tiffany didn't answer the door right away, but all the lights were on and her car was parked out front, so he knew she was home.

When she did open the door, he saw that she'd been crying.

"Are you all right?" he asked, alarmed.

"What do you think?" With that, she turned and went deeper into the apartment.

He followed her, closing the door behind him. She stood with her back to him, looking out the window. He realized she'd probably been watching for him when he'd driven up, growing more irritated with him by the minute because he hadn't come back last evening.

"I'm sorry I had to take off like that yesterday. I had to work today or I would have come out sooner." The truth was, he'd needed time to think—and also to try to track down Pam. All the thinking in the world hadn't helped. Nor had he been able to find Pam. He'd realized that she could have remarried, changed her name, moved out of the country.

He couldn't jeopardize his job by searching too deeply for her without probable cause. Unfortunately, finding out he had a daughter wasn't enough.

"You didn't have to come by now if you didn't want to," Tiffany said, hurt dripping from each word.

His heart went out to her. She was the true victim here. Hesitantly, he touched her shoulder. She flinched, but turned to look at him.

"I want to get to know you," he said. "If I'd known about you sooner—"

"What would you have done?" she demanded.

"I would have never let your mother leave."

His words seemed to help, but he knew if he said the wrong thing, she would be off again, angry and upset with him.

As he searched for what to say to his daughter, he felt as if he was tiptoeing through a minefield. He looked around the small apartment, surprised how nicely Lynette had fixed it up. It was a side of her he'd never seen. He felt that old tug on his heartstrings. There were so many sides to her he'd never seen.

"So you like to draw." It seemed a safe thing to say, but she instantly made a face. "Tiffany, give me a break. I don't know anything about you. Why don't you try to help me out here?"

She moved past him to sit, legs crossed on an over-stuffed chair. He followed and sat down on the edge of the couch, his hat in his hands.

"I've never ridden a horse. Do you have horses?"

He smiled and nodded, finally feeling on familiar ground. All young girls loved horses, right? "I have a half dozen horses. Would you like to learn to ride?"

"Is it hard?"

"No, I have a gentle mare that you would like. I can teach you."

"Mother said you were a cowboy sheriff."

He chuckled at that. "I guess that's true. I ride and raise a few cattle, along with being sheriff. What else did your mother tell you about me?"

She must have picked up the edge in his voice. "You didn't love her."

"That's not true. Look, I need to talk to your mother. Can you give me her number?"

"No."

"No, you don't have it. Or no, you won't give it to me."

Tiffany scowled across the space at him. "This is between you and me."

"But there are things that only your mother can answer."

Her eyes widened. "You don't believe I'm your daughter." Suddenly she was on her feet. "She said that's what you would say. Get out."

"Tiffany, I didn't say—"

"Get out!" She was crying again.

He got to his feet. "I'm sorry, but I'm angry at your mother for keeping you from me. I need to know why."

"Why?" she screamed. "Because you didn't love her or me. Because you divorced her."

She divorced me. Fortunately he only thought it and didn't say the words.

"I'm sorry that's what you believe, but it isn't true. I would have never let your mother go if I'd known about you. Never."

She stopped crying and brushed angrily at her tears.

"I'm taking tomorrow off. Why don't you come out to the ranch about ten? Wear jeans and boots if you have them. If you don't, we'll get you a pair. You'll need them when you ride. You'll like my mare Princess, and she'll like you."

Tiffany swallowed. She looked even more like a child than she had before. So small and skinny, so young even for seventeen. He wanted to take her in his arms and hold her and never let her go. He couldn't bear how much she'd been hurt. He wanted to kill Pam with his bare hands.

He walked to the door and turned to look back at her. With a smile, he said, "I really do want to get to know you. There's no better place to visit than on the back of a horse."

On the way to Big Timber, he forced his thoughts away from Pam and Tiffany to his job. He had a dead Ackermann on a slab at the local mortuary and at least one more in the wind. As he pulled into the sheriff's department parking lot, he latched on to a stray thought and, like grabbing a loose thread, he pulled, knowing that with one phone call the whole scenario could unravel.

Walking into his office, he closed the door and grabbed his phone. His heart was pounding as the warden at Montana State Prison came on the line.

"I need to know if Cullen Ackermann had any visitors the week before he died," Frank said.

"I can check."

"I'll hold, if you don't mind."

The warden was gone long enough that Frank was questioning his theory.

Finally the warden came back on the line. "I don't know if you were old enough to remember, but when Cullen Ackermann was sent up, he was bombarded by the media and every crackpot that crawled out of the woods. He loved the attention. But as the years went by, he didn't want any visitors. In the end, he had only two he agreed to see."

Frank held his breath as the warden read off the names.

"Cecil Ackermann." *Another* son. That meant that three of the sons had survived, two of them now at large. Frank swore under his breath, his suspicions confirmed.

"The other visitor was a man named Claude Durham."

Frank let out a surprised sound, unable to contain his shock. Why in the hell would Claude go see Cullen Ackermann? "One other question, Warden. I understand Ackermann bragged about his buried treasure."

The warden chuckled. "Said he married a young woman with money, turned it all into gold and buried it. Carried around an old photograph of his family—at least he said it was his family—with a map on the back of where the gold was buried. He showed it to me once. I couldn't make heads or tails out of it. Anyone who looked at the so-called map knew he was a lunatic. It was nothing more than a bunch of chicken scratches."

Frank thought of the photograph he'd found. So Cullen had given it to one of his sons. Cecil. He thanked the warden and hung up, sitting for a long moment just staring at nothing. His mind whirled. Another thread ran from Cullen to Claude to Darrell Ackermann to Kate LaFond. Why, he had no idea.

Picking up the phone, he called the Branding Iron, only to learn that Kate had taken the rest of the day off and was last seen driving north out of town.

CHAPTER TWELVE

IT WAS LATE AFTERNOON by the time Jack loaded his pickup and drove toward his family homestead. He knew why he'd been putting it off. This was where he'd been living when the sheriff had arrested him.

At the time, he hadn't been sure what hurt the most, being dragged off in handcuffs after seeing the bull in his corral or realizing that he'd been set up by one of his neighbors. He had no doubt it was someone he knew.

At the time, he hadn't suspected Judge Hyett. It wasn't until his sentencing that Jack noticed Chantell wasn't in the courtroom. He shouldn't have been surprised. Her father had never made a secret of the fact that he thought his daughter could do a whole lot better than Jack French, and Chantell was her daddy's girl.

He tried to shove away the thought, telling himself it was enough to know who'd set him up—and why. He was a changed man, Jack reminded himself now. Well, at least he was trying to change. He'd known the first time he'd asked Chantell out what her father the judge was like. But that was back when he rode bulls and took crazy chances.

Jack was almost at the turnoff to the French place

when he saw a flash of red in the distance. Earlier, when he'd driven by the café, he'd seen that Kate's pickup was gone.

He'd come down a seldom-used road today, taking a longer way to his family's ranch because he didn't want to run into anyone he knew. In this part of the country, if the other driver recognized your rig, he would feel he had to stop, put down his window and visit for a while.

Slowing to turn down the road, he saw the red truck turn at the edge of the old Ackermann place and head west toward the hollow.

Swearing, Jack sped up, heading in the same direction the pickup had gone. He told himself it probably wasn't even Kate. But somehow he knew better. What would she be doing going up that hollow, though?

When he reached the turnoff he could still see tracks through the tall weeds that had taken over the old road. He drove a little farther, parked in a grove of cottonwoods just off the main road and took off walking.

As he did, the land rose sharply from the valley floor toward the high, rugged peaks of the Crazies. He hadn't gone far when he stopped to look back down the valley. He could see his family homestead in the distance. Even from here he could make out the old shotgun house with the dilapidated porch. The place needed a new roof. Hell, it needed to be torn down.

Before he'd left here in handcuffs, he had been living in a cabin out back that had once been a bunkhouse. It wasn't much to write home about either.

He shook his head now, wondering why he didn't just sell the place lock, stock and barrel to Hitch Mc-

Cray. *You've been talking about going down to Wy-oming and working on the Green River spread, to wrangle for a rancher who knows you and would hire you even though you are a felon. Why not do it? Why not put Beartooth and the past behind you?*

Yeah, why not? he asked himself as he began to walk again. Now that he was a felon, his options as far as real jobs went had certainly narrowed. He shoved the thought away, knowing that going down that path could lead to nothing but trouble.

The afternoon light was intense. A low sun washed the scene in eerie golden light. He worked his way through the tall grass, feeling the ever-present Crazies looming over him. Snow gleamed on the high peaks from the latest snowstorm, the icy scent coming down on the breeze. Down here the snow had melted by the afternoon.

He hadn't gone far when the trees became more dense. He spotted Kate's pickup parked back in them. No sign of her, though.

That's when he spotted where someone had cut the fence into the old Ackermann place. It didn't take much to figure out where Kate had gone. But why the hell would she? Surely she'd seen the signs on the fence. Surely she would know how dangerous it was.

That's when he heard a sound he recognized in an instant.

A shovel blade pinging off a rock. This land of gla-cial debris was riddled with rock just below the soil's surface.

Someone was digging on the other side of the fence.

KATE SWORE AS the shovel hit another rock. She stopped, leaned against the shovel and wiped her face with her shirtsleeve. Heat radiated off the stone foundation of the barn.

She eyed the hole she'd only started to dig. It wasn't here. In a few moments the sun would dip behind the tallest peak of the Crazy Mountains and shine like a keyhole down into a long golden slant through the pines. Like the clue to the Lost Dutchman Mine, she thought.

Right now the last of the day's sunshine was glaring off the side of the stone. She wished she'd brought water. With a sigh she took off her shirt, shedding down to just a tank top and jeans. She told herself she'd dig just a little farther to the west, then she had to get back to town because the quilt group was coming to paint tonight.

As she lifted the shovel and took a step in that direction, a shadow fell across the stone in front of her. The shovel came up with a jerk as, startled, she swung around, heart in her throat, ready to defend herself.

Jack French.

She groaned inwardly. He stood, hands in his jeans pockets, looking only mildly curious. She wasn't fooled for an instant.

"There are easier ways to get to China," he said.

Caught. A half dozen lies leaped to her lips, but he didn't give her a chance.

"I should have known the moment I saw all those lost-treasure magazines at your apartment," he said with a shake of his head. "This explains what you're doing in Beartooth. Has nothing to do with the café, does it?" He looked disappointed in her. "On top of that, you can't read. This whole land used to be riddled with booby traps and minefields. The military came in and got rid of most of them, but it's still dangerous and if there was any treasure here, believe me, it would have been found."

She leaned on her shovel and said nothing. What could she say? He wouldn't believe her even if she told him the truth. Then again, he just might. She thought about telling him everything, right there and then. Wouldn't it be to her advantage to have Jack on her side? He was from here. And as strong as he looked, she didn't doubt he could wield a shovel better than she could.

He looked at her as if waiting to see what nonsense she was going to come up with. The sun dipped behind the Crazies, the barn wall going dark, but banked heat still radiated off the stone base of the barn.

She could feel perspiration trickle down between her breasts. Jack's gaze left her face to brush over her tank top, making her shiver as if he'd touched her. She felt her nipples harden under those blue eyes. Worse, she felt desire spark and run red-hot through her veins.

What had she been thinking? Tell Jack everything? Trust this cowboy? Given the way he was looking at her—and the effect it was having on her—she couldn't imagine anything more dangerous.

"I think I'm through here," she said, grabbing the handle of her shovel and pushing what little earth she'd turned up back into the shallow hole.

"I doubt that." His voice sounded as rough as his thumb pad had been when he'd run it over her lip.

She saw her own need mirrored in his gaze and quickly looked away. As she walked past him, she feared he would touch her—and feared he wouldn't. It had been so long since any man had made her want like this.

Just the thought of his touch… When he didn't stop her, she closed her eyes for a moment, telling herself she'd just dodged a bullet.

But as she opened them and kept walking, she couldn't deny the ache inside her. She wanted Jack French and that made him all the more dangerous. She told herself she'd narrowly avoided a disaster by not baring her soul to him only moments ago. Kate knew that with Jack French, she'd be baring a whole lot more than her soul.

JACK STOOD NEXT to the barn, listening to the sound of Kate's pickup engine as she drove away. He cursed at how close he'd come just now. It had taken everything in him not to drag her into his arms. But he'd known that if he touched her just then, he wouldn't be able to stop.

He shoved away the image of the two of them, her back against the barn wall, him—

"What is wrong with you?" She wasn't the first woman who'd made him crazy. But she was the first who he'd felt such an attraction to that he couldn't seem to keep away from her.

With a curse, he realized that the old Jack would

have taken her right there against the barn wall. He wished now he had. Maybe then he could get her out of his system.

He recalled the look on her face when he'd come up on her, startling her. She'd turned with the shovel in her hands. Surprise and determination written all over her face. She'd been ready to defend herself. He counted himself lucky that he hadn't been whacked with a shovel blade upside his head.

Or worse, shot with the pistol he'd seen tucked into the waist of her jeans.

His thoughts, though, had been more on the way her tank top stuck to her perspiring skin than her hitting or shooting him. He didn't even want to think about the way her jeans hugged her long legs or cupped that amazing behind.

As he glanced around, he saw other places someone had been digging on the property. Kate. The fool woman. He kicked with his boot at the dirt she'd dislodged, sending a few clods flying into the air.

The woman was a damned treasure hunter. He shook his head as he recalled the stacks of treasure magazines he'd seen in her apartment. She'd bought into the legend of Ackermann's gold cache. Which meant he was right about what she was doing in Beartooth. And worse, she was going to be disappointed— and eventually would leave.

He started to turn to the road for the walk back to his pickup when he spotted something Kate had dropped in her hurry to escape. He reached down at the edge of the barn foundation and picked up a single glove, knocked off the dust and pocketed it.

That was when he noticed something else Kate had dropped. Leaning down, he picked up a discolored scrap of paper and saw that it was freezer paper, the kind used to wrap meat.

"What the hell?" he said to himself as he unfolded it and saw what he was holding in his hands. One side was a slick, waxy surface. On the papery side, someone had drawn what looked like a map.

KATE DROVE BACK to town as if the devil himself was chasing after her. What she was running from, though, were her own feelings. Although she couldn't wait to get away from Jack.

He was going to ruin her plans. He'd already complicated them. She'd let him get too close and now he'd caught her digging in Ackermann Hollow.

She shoved down on the gas pedal as if she could outrun the crazy thought that had come to her. Why didn't she just give in to this mad desire? Jack French was the kind of cowboy who, once he got what he wanted, would hit the trail so fast all she'd see was his backside riding away.

The idea definitely had its appeal in more ways than one. She thought about the fortune-teller. It was true. Jack was in danger as long as he was around her. Better to cut those ties quickly, since it was only a matter of time before those men who'd come looking for her a few nights ago returned.

She couldn't shake the feeling that they *had* come

back. Only now they were waiting for her to do the dirty work for them.

Distracted with those thoughts, Kate was all the way back to town and parked behind the café before she realized that one of her gloves was missing. She reached for her long-sleeved shirt, which she'd discarded earlier when the day had gotten too hot.

Under it she saw the single glove and made a hurried search of the pickup cab only to realize she'd lost more than a glove. Suddenly panicked, she felt the open pocket of her shirt and realized it was empty.

Her heart lodged in her throat and for a moment she couldn't catch her breath. "No!" She searched the cab again, but it was fruitless.

The map must have fallen out when she'd grabbed up her shirt, which meant it was still out there by the old barn. She reached to start the truck and go back, but realized there wasn't time. The quilters would be here soon to start painting.

Unless she could call Cilla and get them to change the night.

Racing up the stairs, she hurried inside her apartment to the phone. She mentally kicked herself for being so careless and for letting Jack get to her yet again. As she started to look up Cilla's number, another thought slowed her movements.

What if Jack—

The sudden pounding on the door startled her. She hurriedly reached for her gun. With a curse, she realized that in her haste she'd left it in the pickup. Jack French was going to get her killed.

CHAPTER THIRTEEN

"Ms. LaFond?" Sheriff Frank Curry knocked again. He'd checked her pickup hood on the way in. It was still hot, the motor beneath it ticking softly. She hadn't been home long.

The door finally opened. Kate LaFond stood peering around the edge of it. Her hair was in disarray, her clothes dusty and the knees of her jeans were caked with fresh dirt.

"Did I catch you at a bad time?" he asked.

"I just got home from a hike and was about to climb into the shower."

"Looks like you took another spill," he said, motioning to the crusted dirt on her jeans.

She smiled. "You have to be half mountain goat to hike in the Crazies. Can this wait?"

"I'm afraid not," he said. "I won't keep you long." He stepped into the apartment, realizing it was the first time he'd ever been here. Claude hadn't been one to hold social get-togethers. He probably saw enough of people down in the café on a daily basis.

The apartment had the same overall footprint as the café, only this space had been divided into a small living room, kitchen, one bedroom and a bath, from what Frank could tell. The walls were bare, the rooms sparsely furnished. He got the feeling Kate wasn't planning to stay long. Or maybe she just hadn't gotten around to really settling in.

"Do you mind?" he asked, motioning to the small dinette set and the two chairs. He pulled out one and sat down.

She looked uncomfortable and nervously brushed a lock of her hair back from her face as she sat down. "If this is about the café again—"

"I suppose it might be, in a way," he said. "Here's my problem. A fisherman finds a murdered man down by the river about twenty miles from here. At first there doesn't seem to be any connection between the man and Beartooth or you. But then I find out that earlier the night before, the man had been asking about you outside the Range Rider."

He ticked off each point on his fingers, watching her expression.

"Then I find out that he not only crossed paths with you, but he also accosted you—I believe that was your word—even hit you, before Jack French heard the commotion and came to your rescue."

She started to say something, and he quickly continued, "Although you didn't feel you needed Jack's help at the time. You said you thought the man was drunk, confused, had the wrong woman, but the thing is, he described you to a local man here in town, who knew exactly who the stranger was asking about. The next morning, the stranger is dead."

"I told you that—"

"You'd never seen him before," Frank finished for her. "But the funny thing, as it turns out, is that you have a *connection* to him." He nodded. "The man's name was Darrell Ackermann. Ring any bells?"

"Should it?"

He smiled. "Darrell was released from prison in Yuma, Arizona, along with his brother Gallen. Most people in these parts thought the Ackermann boys were dead and had been for more than thirty years." He gave her a brief history of the Ackermann family right up until the day that his father along with county deputies tried to get into the place after a neighbor said a woman was being held on the property against her will.

"I don't see how—"

"I'm getting to the part where you come in," he assured her. "Cullen Ackermann was arrested that day. I won't get into all the gory details, but the four boys and a little girl disappeared. One of the boys' remains was found that next spring up in the mountains and it was believed that all had perished. That's why it was surprising to learn that the dead man was an Ackermann."

Kate leaned back in her chair as if realizing this was going to take a while. She folded her arms across her chest looking bored, but he suspected she also didn't want him to see that her hands were shaking.

"That's when it gets more interesting. Cullen Ackermann died in prison recently. You'll never guess who visited him in prison. His oldest son, Cecil, and of all people, Claude Durham."

If he was hoping for a reaction to this, he was sadly disappointed.

"See, this is my problem. Claude visits the prison, later dies, leaves you the café. Then out of the blue, one of the Ackermann boys returns to Beartooth and is looking for you—and ends up dead."

She shrugged. "That's a pretty flimsy connection, isn't it?"

"I think it might be clearer if we knew why Claude visited Ackermann in prison. You have any ideas?"

"Not a one since I barely knew Claude and I'd never seen the dead man before."

He studied her for a long moment. "Well, maybe you can help me with this. Saturday-night dispatch got a call from a woman using the pay phone behind the bar to say that she saw two men in a dark pickup truck trying to break into the Beartooth General Store and that one of the men had a gun. The woman refused to give her name. One of my deputies spotted the pickup and gave chase but lost it. I'm thinking that one or both of those men might be the two missing Ackermanns. I think they were in town not to break into the store, but to see you, and that you made that call."

Kate said nothing, as if determined to wait him out.

"Kate, I think you're in trouble and I want to help you. These Ackermann boys were dangerous when they were young. Now... I don't know why they're back here or what they want with you, but I suspect you do." He stopped to meet her gaze. "I suspect you're the reason they're here. Whatever it is they want, they won't rest until they get it. I've already got one murder on my hands—I don't want another one."

"Whatever these men might want, I promise I'll do

my best not to get murdered," she said, pushing back her chair and getting to her feet. "If that's all…"

He picked up his hat from where he'd set it on his knee and snugged it down on his head as he rose. "I don't want to see you get killed, either." He glanced at her arms. They were muscled from carrying heavy plates filled with food for what he guessed was a lot of years. Could she strangle a man?

"If you ever need my help—"

"I can take care of myself."

Frank met her eyes. "That's what worries me. I'd hate to have to arrest you for killing someone. If you haven't already."

KATE HAD BARELY closed the door behind the sheriff when there was another knock. Thinking it was Frank Curry with another accusation, she opened it, ready to tell him to either arrest her or leave her alone.

"I'm going out on a limb here," Jack said when Kate opened the door. He leaned into the frame, shoved back his cowboy hat and grinned at her. He couldn't have been more handsome—or more annoying. "Want to bet that this is what that man who's dead now was looking for?" He held up the map she'd lost.

She started to speak. He stopped her with one raised hand.

"I'll even go farther out on that limb to suggest that those two men with the guns were here for the same thing and that is also why the sheriff just paid you a visit," he said. "Convince me I'm wrong. Go ahead."

Kate glanced at the map in his hands. "I don't know what you're talking about."

"Then I guess we won't be needing this anymore." He started to tear it up.

"Stop!" she cried as she grabbed for the map.

"Not so fast," he said, pulling it back out of her reach. "Start talking or I'm calling the sheriff. He couldn't have gotten far. I would imagine he can be here in a matter of minutes. I think he might be interested in this map, the dead man's connection and where I found you today."

"Can you at least come in and close the door?"

"Not until you tell me what this is," he said, holding up the map.

"It's a map," she said, meeting his gaze with a dark, angry one.

"I can see that. A map for what?"

She shrugged, giving up lying since it was obvious he already knew. He just wanted her to admit it. "What else? Treasure."

"Ackermann's fabled buried gold?" He laughed. "I don't know where you got this, but it is nothing more than some crude drawings scribbled onto a piece of old freezer paper used to wrap meat. This piece even has the discolored places where tape had once been adhered. Whoever drew this map must have had elk steaks for dinner first." He scoffed. "Someone sold you a bill of goods if you really think this is a map to Ackermann's alleged hidden treasure."

"I don't care what you think," she snapped, taking it from him.

AS SHE TURNED HER BACK and walked into the room away from him, Jack stepped into the apartment, closing the door behind him. He stared at her slim back. By the set of her shoulders, he could see that she was upset.

He felt sorry for her, and more so for himself, because he didn't want to see her dreams crushed. Especially by him. Or worse, get herself killed.

"Did you know that they used to call Montana the Treasure State?" he asked. "You're not the first one who's come here chasing a legend. Hell, the first men who came to this country were in search of treasure. El Dorado, Sierra Madre and all were conveniently found and lost again."

"I really don't need a lecture."

He ignored the interruption. "All these lost-treasure stories have two things in common. Whoever found this amazing treasure was forced to leave it and was unable to return, usually because he was killed. But," he continued before she could interrupt, "the discoverer left behind clues, a map or journal—something so those fools after him could spend their lives searching for this mystical fortune. The second thing these lost treasures have in common is that there is always a curse attached to them. Didn't you learn anything from your father's example? This is just going to get you killed."

"Are you finished?" she asked, turning to look at him, arms crossed over her abundant chest. Her hair was windblown, as if she'd kept her pickup window down all the way back to town, and she still wore the tank top and dirty jeans. She couldn't have looked more sexy.

"You're wasting your time."

"It's my time to waste."

He studied her. "That's what brought you here. This lost treasure. It wasn't the café." He needed her to say it.

Kate looked away. "What if it is?"

Then it was just another reason not to get any more involved with this woman. "And that's what that man wanted. The dead one. He wanted the map."

She raised her gaze to his and locked eyes with him.

Jack let out a curse. "Why didn't you just give him the damned map if he wanted it so badly? It isn't worth the paper it's scratched on."

"Because it's *mine*. It was left to me."

He thought the map and a bunch of worthless old treasure magazines might have been all that she'd been left. Kate hadn't had an easy life. Was that something else they had in common?

But he quickly reminded himself that one man was already dead and Kate LaFond was in this up to her pretty little neck.

"Was it worth killing for?" he had to ask.

"I didn't kill anyone."

Why did everything out of her mouth sound like a lie? But what a mouth it was. He'd wanted to kiss her senseless from the first time she'd opened it.

Jack shook his head, mentally kicking himself for butting into her life that first night, let alone coming here now. "The sheriff has stopped by twice to talk to me about the murder."

"He talked to me, too."

"I know. You sent him after me."

"I had to tell the sheriff about the night in the alley. I couldn't chance that someone else had seen the three of us and already told him."

"So why didn't you tell Frank that you knew the man?"

"I *didn't* know him."

Jack made a disgusted sound and started for the door, but before he could get there, she grabbed his arm. "I didn't know him and I didn't kill him."

"But. He. Knew. You. He wanted the map." He could see her making up her mind whether to keep lying.

She nodded slowly and let go of him.

"How did he hear about it?"

"I don't know. Honestly," she said as he started to turn away again. "I thought no one knew but my father and I."

Jack rubbed a hand over his face before he looked at her again. "Okay, let's say that's true. But if your father had the map, then why didn't he go after the treasure?"

"He couldn't."

Jack laughed. "Or he was full of shit and knew the map was worthless."

She got that determined, obstinate and angry expression again.

He studied her angelic face, seeing the devil gleaming in her eyes. What was it about her that made him unable to stay away? "You'd better hope there is a treasure and that you find it, because you're going to need that money to keep your butt out of prison—that's if you don't get killed first." He turned for the door again.

"You know this country. You could help me."

He stopped and swore under his breath, his hand on the doorknob. Just a few more steps and he would have been through the door, out of this woman's life. At least that's what he told himself.

All the good sense he'd ever possessed told him not to turn around. *Just keep going. Don't look back.* It wasn't as if he didn't know what was coming.

"I'll split it with you. Seventy-thirty."

"Seventy-thirty?" he said, spinning around to look at her and knowing he was as lost as her treasure. He took a step toward her, eyes narrowed. She stood her ground, not even blinking as he closed the distance to stand over her.

"That map already has blood on it, and we both know more will be shed whether there really is a lost treasure or not," he said heatedly. "If you didn't kill that man, then whoever did will be coming after the map soon enough. I'd guess it was the two thugs from the other night. I'm surprised they haven't returned already. Unless they're waiting for you to find the gold, so they can take it from you."

"Sixty-forty," she said without batting an eye. She took a step closer. "I'm not used to asking anyone for help." She was just inches from him.

He saw what she planned to do even before she started to kiss him. He grabbed her shoulders and forced her back. With a curse, he reminded himself that he'd just spent two years in prison for getting involved with the wrong woman.

"Eleven years ago I lied to the sheriff to protect a

friend of mine," he said. "I'm not doing that again. And when we kiss, it isn't going to be as some sort of bribe."

Her dark eyes fired.

"Fifty-fifty or forget it." He didn't believe there was any buried treasure, but he couldn't stop himself. He had to see this through wherever it took him. "Like you said, *I* know the country."

Kate held his gaze for a long moment. "Fifty-fifty. But if you try to double-cross me—"

"I know what you do to men who cross you," he said, and held up his hand to stop her from professing her innocence again. "Also, insulting me isn't the way to begin a partnership."

She seemed to bite her tongue.

"But for the record, you're wrong about me," he said. "Maybe the other men you've known couldn't be trusted, but I'm not one of them."

Her expression said she'd believe that when she saw it.

"Shall we shake on it?" she said.

"Hell with that." He grabbed her and kissed her hard on the mouth. Just the taste of her stirred the banked fire inside him. Her lips parted, no doubt only in surprise. It didn't matter. He'd felt that slight tremor in her, almost an echo of the more powerful one that moved through him. She felt it, too. He broke the kiss, wanting more, but afraid of where it would take him.

She already had him right where she wanted him.

THE NEXT DAY, Frank had two horses saddled and was waiting for Tiffany when he got a call. His deputy

had information about the black pickup he'd chased
the other night.

"The truck was found abandoned down by Fishtail,"
the deputy said. "It had been stolen in Laramie, Wyoming, two days before it was seen leaving Beartooth.
I have the Billings cops seeing if they can turn up anything in the pickup, including a good set of prints."

Frank figured at least one of the men in that truck
could be the missing Gallen Ackermann.

"Thanks for letting me know," Frank said as he
watched his daughter park. She looked toward the two
horses he had saddled and ready to go. He'd been afraid
she wouldn't show and was relieved now as she got out
of her car. She saw that he was on the phone and made
a face as if expecting him to drop everything for her.
He reminded himself that she was young, very young,
even for her age.

The deputy was still talking, filling him in on
another case, when Frank finally interrupted him.
"Thanks for the information. I have to go. I'll check
in with you later." He hung up.

Tiffany was still looking at him, impatience and a
growing anger marring her pretty face.

"Sheriff business," he said as he walked toward her.
"Sorry. I'm turning off my phone so we won't be interrupted on our ride."

Her expression softened a little as she turned toward
the horses. "Which one is mine?"

"Princess," he said and walked over to the buckskin
mare. "She's very gentle. Come say hello."

Tiffany hesitated before slowly stepping to the horse.

He told her the dos and don'ts, then said, "Let me help you up on her. You can just sit up there and see how it feels," he added when he saw concern cross her features.

A stubborn resolve seemed to replace the concern. He wondered if she'd gotten that from him or her mother, as he helped her up into the saddle.

She gripped the saddle horn, white knuckled. The horse moved under her and she let out a startled sound. But after a moment she seemed to relax. She even took one hand off the saddle horn and stroked the mare's neck.

"When you're ready, I will lead you around the corral so you can get the feel of the horse's movements."

She nodded and he began to walk Princess slowly, all the time watching his daughter to make sure she was all right.

"How old were you when you first started riding a horse?"

He laughed. "Probably two. The first time I got bucked off, I was three."

Her eyes widened in alarm.

"It was my own fault. I wanted the horse to go faster and I took off my hat to swat the horse. The wind caught my hat and blew it right in front of the horse and spooked him. I got right back on, though."

She didn't look relieved by his story and he mentally kicked himself for telling it.

"So I would have learned to ride when I was two?" she asked.

He could see where she was headed with this. "Only if I was holding you in my lap."

Tears welled in her eyes, but she quickly looked away. "Aren't we going to ride anywhere?" she asked after a moment, her voice tight.

"You ready to take the reins?"

She reached for them and he explained how to get the horse to turn, how not to pull too hard, how to keep her balance.

Then he opened the corral gate, led his own horse out and swung up into the saddle.

"Do you ride a lot?" she asked as they started slowly down the road.

"Most days I try to get out. I enjoy using a horse rather than a four-wheeler to check the cattle I run. Much quieter," he said with a grin, but saw that it was wasted on her.

"Does your girlfriend ride with you?" she asked, an edge to her voice.

"I don't have a girlfriend."

She glanced over at him, eyes narrowed. "What about Lynette Johnson?"

He didn't let her see his surprise or his anger at her mother. What had Pam told this poor girl? "Like I said, I don't have a girlfriend."

Tiffany seemed to relax a little in the saddle. They rode in silence for a while. "So you have a lot of land?"

"Not much—a few hundred acres."

"That sounds like a lot. Are you rich?"

He laughed. "I'm a sheriff. Sheriffs don't make a lot of money."

"Then why do you do it?"

He shrugged. "I like what I do. Kind of like you. You like art. You'll probably never make a lot of money, but it won't matter as long as you love what you do."

She raised her chin and at that moment he saw her mother in her. "How do you know I won't make a lot of money with my art?"

He swore under his breath. "It's just that a lot of artists don't. You could be the exception."

Again they rode in silence. He wondered if he would ever be able to say the right thing to her, ever be able to have a close father-daughter relationship, or if it was too late because of all the lost years—and the lies.

Her questions about Lynette had unnerved him. Obviously her mother had told her things she shouldn't have. He thought of Pam and had to look away so Tiffany didn't see the fury boiling inside him.

After a while, Tiffany said she was tired and they headed back.

"You want to brush Princess down?" he asked as he helped his daughter from the saddle.

"No," she said. "I have things I have to do." She started toward her car without a backward glance.

"I hope you enjoyed the ride," he said after her. Pam apparently hadn't taught her any manners. All his ex had given their daughter was a hatred of her father.

At her car, Tiffany stopped and turned to look back at him. "Thank you for the ride."

He felt his heart well up inside him like a helium balloon. "You're welcome. Maybe you'd like to ride again sometime."

She didn't answer as she climbed into her car. He watched her drive away, his need to find her mother growing with each passing second.

But with the resources he'd been able to use, he hadn't had any luck locating Pam. It was as if she'd dropped off the face of the earth.

CHAPTER FOURTEEN

TRUE TO CILLA'S WORD, the entire quilt club showed up Tuesday evening, armed with gallons of paint, rags, drop cloths, brushes and rollers.

After Jack had left, a shaken Kate had showered and changed to hurry downstairs. She shoved tables and chairs into the center of the room and helped put drop cloths over the booths, as the women, dressed in dungarees, as they called them, went to work.

She worked with them, trying to distract herself from what had happened earlier upstairs. She couldn't help worrying that she'd made a pact with the devil. She didn't even want to think about the kiss or how it had affected her.

The quilters were a hardworking bunch, varying in age from early thirties to the oldest, Loralee Clark, who Kate would have guessed was over eighty.

Cilla introduced them quickly. "Don't worry, you'll never remember all the names until you get to know the women."

Kate had wondered why the elderly Loralee had bothered to come. She looked too old for this kind of labor. A petite woman with long, gray hair braided loosely down her back and piercing blue eyes, Loralee quickly went to work supervising the group. Once she had them all working, she asked Kate if she would make a pot of coffee, then reached into a large bag she'd brought with her and took out a half dozen plastic containers of food.

Kate saw that there were six desserts within the containers.

"For after the painting is done," Loralee announced.

Kate did whatever she could to help, but the women had clearly worked together before and made a quick job of painting the interior of the café.

"Do you like the color?" Cilla asked.

"I love it," Kate said without hesitation. She hated to think how long this job would have taken her alone. And the color was fine, a nice neutral, as Cilla had said.

When the work was done, the women cleaned up and all gathered at the large table that Kate had pushed by the front window.

Loralee brought out the desserts, while Kate provided the plates and silverware. She was about to pour the coffee when Cilla took the pot from her and insisted she sit down, even though Kate certainly hadn't worked that hard.

The moment Kate took a chair, she felt the older woman's keen blue eyes on her.

"Where do I know you from?" Loralee asked.

Kate shook her head, positive she and the elderly woman had never crossed paths before she'd come to Beartooth. "I just have one of those faces."

Loralee swatted that away with a wave of her hand. "I never forget a face. I just can't remember where I've seen you before and it's been bothering me all night. But it will come to me. It always does."

"Mother," her daughter Marian reprimanded. "Kate's not from around here, and you've only been outside the county a few times, years before Kate was even born, so I'm sure—"

"Pishposh," Loralee snapped.

The group fell silent as Marian gave Kate an apologetic smile.

Cilla changed the conversation to quilting and the rest of the evening the talk was of quilts, quilt patterns and an upcoming shop-hop.

Kate had never heard of a shop-hop but quickly learned that the women piled into cars and caravanned from one quilt shop to another, traveling all over their part of Montana.

"We'll come around to hang a few quilts on these walls this week," Cilla said. "I already have some in mind that will look beautiful in here."

It wasn't until the coffee and desserts were consumed that everyone readied to leave and Marian drew Kate aside.

"I'm sorry if my mother made you feel uncomfortable," she apologized. "She's starting to forget things and gets confused."

"Don't worry about it, really," Kate assured her. "Your mother is delightful."

"That's a word I've never heard to describe her," she joked.

Kate walked them all out. As Marian was starting

to pull away from the curb, her mother reached out the passenger side of the SUV and grabbed Kate's arm.

"I know you from somewhere," Loralee said with defiance. "I never forget a face. It will come to me."

She only released her hold on Kate when Marian started to drive away.

Kate stood at the edge of the road and watched the elderly woman squinting back at her in the side mirror. How long before Loralee figured it out?

Ticktock. Ticktock, Kate thought. Claude had warned her this might happen.

"As I ALREADY told you, I was curious about my brother's wife," Claude said. "I'd heard she was much younger than him. I couldn't help wondering what happened to his first wife. I guess I was wondering, too, how he'd gotten himself a young wife. I'd heard those boys of his were hellions."

"So your curiosity got the best of you," she said, trying to move his story along to the part she'd been waiting years to hear.

"It wasn't that simple. I didn't want to see my brother. He hadn't recognized me the one time we'd run into each other, but I didn't want to chance it should we cross paths again. The place was fortified with not only a wire fence, but also booby traps, and those sons of his were just itching to shoot someone."

She shook her head. "But all that didn't stop you."

Claude actually smiled, even though she knew he was in a lot of pain. "I found a spot where I could watch the place, and one day I got my first glimpse of

*her. I was astonished. Teeny was just as I had heard—
young and beautiful. That was the moment I knew I
had to try to save her."*

*Kate saw the pain in his expression. He hadn't saved
her. But he'd tried. "I'm guessing you met her."*

*He let out a sound, half laugh, half sob. "I didn't
dare try to get into the compound. I knew how crazy
my brother was, and from the local stories I heard, he
was getting worse with each passing day. Fortunately,
during huckleberry season, your mother ventured out
of her prison alone."*

Kate didn't know what to say. "The two of you—"

*"I hadn't planned to fall in love with her. I was much
too old for her. Not as old as Cullen, but still..." His
eyes took on a shine and for a few minutes, Claude
looked a third of a century younger.*

*"Something tells me you didn't plan on getting her
pregnant," she said. "That is what happened, isn't it?"*

*Behind her, the nurse came in, a new one on duty,
one Kate hadn't seen before.*

*"You can't be in here," the nurse said firmly. "Only
immediate family is allowed in here at this hour."*

*Kate looked to Claude. "Well? Am I immediate fam-
ily?"*

LORALEE CLARK MOVED to the sink and flushed the
pill her doctor had prescribed down the drain. Earlier, when her daughter had insisted she take it, she'd
palmed the pill. She'd become quite good at it, and
smiled as she turned on the disposal and ran water until
she was sure there was no more sign of it.

Her daughter meant well enough. But the pills made her groggy. She wasn't going to be one of those old women who dozed all day in a rocker until one day someone noticed she'd kicked the bucket.

No, she wasn't ready for a rocker, she thought as she left the kitchen and walked down the hall to her sewing room. Her husband, Maynard, had built the room large enough for her to have several quilting frames going at one time if she wanted.

Today there was only one set up at the center of the room. She moved to it, sat down and had to search a moment to find her needle where she'd left it stuck in the fabric. It worried her that her eyesight wasn't what it had been.

Marian kept trying to talk her into having that nice lady up at Fort Peck machine-quilt for her.

"Not as long as I can lift a needle," Loralee said now as she found her needle and began to make small, uniform stitches. She loved this part of quilting and had no intention of giving it up until she was forced.

But her mind wouldn't still as she worked. She kept thinking about Kate LaFond and where she'd seen the young woman before. It was driving her crazy, since she could feel the answer right on the edge of her memory.

The third time she stabbed her sewing needle into her finger, she pushed back from the frame in frustration. How could she concentrate on quilting, the one thing that gave her peace, when not only her daughter but also the entire quilt club thought she was losing her marbles?

Her old eyes were tired. She rubbed them, then straightened, realizing her back hurt, too. Getting old wasn't for weaklings, her mother used to say. Loralee couldn't have agreed more.

As she got up and wandered through the house, her thoughts, like vultures over roadkill, circled back to Kate LaFond.

Just this morning, Marian had put an arm around her and said, "Mom, you don't know Kate. She's not from around here. I've called Doc. He's going to give you a little something to relax you."

Knock her out was more like it. Loralee had shaken off her daughter's arm. She hated it when Marian talked to her as if she was feebleminded.

"I never forget a face," she'd snapped, knowing she should quit arguing. Marian had been talking lately about moving her into her house down by Big Timber, questioning if it was smart letting her mother live alone any longer.

"If you know her from somewhere, well, then I'm sure you'll remember, but in the meantime Doc is stopping by."

When she'd continued to argue that she knew what she knew, Marian had finally lost patience with her.

"Mom, you have to stop this. You made Kate uncomfortable staring at her like that. What does it matter if you know her or not from some other time and place?"

What did it matter?

Everyone thought she was getting senile. But it was more than proving that she wasn't. The moment she'd seen Kate she'd had this strange feeling of not just recognition but almost shock. Whatever she knew about the young woman, there was some bad memory attached to it.

She wasn't about to try to explain that to her daughter, even if she thought she could put the feeling into words and Marian would understand.

"You're going to drive us all crazy with this," her daughter had said as she'd left, soon after the doctor. "Let it drop, Mom."

Easier said than done, Loralee thought as she turned and walked back down the hall to where she kept her old photo albums. Her heart pounded with anticipation. Her every instinct told her the answer was in one of the boxes.

"WELL, CLAUDE? How immediate family am I?" Kate stood waiting at the foot of his hospital bed, all the time telling herself it didn't matter, when in truth it did.

Claude started to close his eyes again. But before Kate could turn away and leave the room as the nurse had ordered, he opened them again.

"She's my daughter," he said and looked over at the nurse. "She's my daughter and I need to talk to her."

The nurse gave Kate a disbelieving look and left in a little huff.

Kate didn't know what to say for fear he'd only said what he had so she wouldn't be forced to leave.

"I'm sorry I let you think you were only my niece," he said, his voice sounding hoarse. He motioned her closer to the bed.

"Is it true?"

Claude nodded. "I know you must be disappointed—"

"Then there is an even better chance that I'm a match."

He stared at her for a moment before shaking his head. "Forget about all that. It isn't why I found you."

"Yes, it was." That day at the café when she'd first met him, he'd offered her a deal. That was when she'd told him to go to hell.

His eyes filled. "It was why I found you back then. But not now."

"How do we find out if I'm a match?"

"I told you—"

"I'll ask the doctor. What is it you aren't telling me?"

He looked away.

"You don't really have a café."

"It's called the Branding Iron. It's nothing to write home about, but it has an apartment upstairs. It's the only café within twenty miles of Beartooth, so it does all right. You won't get rich on it, but you could be comfortable there." He smiled sadly. "It's all I have to offer you."

"I don't care about the café."

"I'm sorry to hear that," he said. "I'm rather fond of the place, but I can understand why you wouldn't be interested in going to an isolated, tiny town in Montana."

"That isn't what I meant. I'm not doing this for the café. I'm going to do the tests to find out if you're telling the truth and I really am your daughter. These tests *they run to see if my liver is compatible? They can also do a paternity test, so if you're lying to me—"*

"I'm not."

"Why don't you get some rest," she said. "I'll talk to the doctor and see how quickly we can get this done." She turned to leave.

"Kate—"

"My name is Melissa Logan," she said, turning back to him. It wasn't the first time he'd made that mistake.

"Sorry. It's what your mother called you. Her maiden name was Katherina LaFond so she named you Kate LaFond. You never went by Ackermann. As it turned out, your mother's marriage to Cullen was never legal. He hadn't divorced his first wife. But that's another story."

As she left his room, Kate didn't know what to feel. Claude Durham had come into her life uninvited and turned it upside down.

CHAPTER FIFTEEN

JACK FOUND HIMSELF at Kate's door early the next morning before she'd even had a chance to open the café.

She didn't look surprised to see him. As she handed him a cup of coffee, he asked for the map. She produced it without a word, sipping her own coffee as she watched him study it.

He couldn't help being skeptical about any lost treasure, especially this one. It was a wild-goose chase at best. At worst, there were men willing to kill for this worthless piece of paper.

"I can't make any sense of this at all," he said, turning to Kate.

She stepped closer as he spread the map on the table. As his fingers brushed over the faded drawings on the paper, her shoulder brushed his. He fought like hell to hide the electrical shock that charged through him.

"See, this is a stone building or foundation. There are trees and what could be a creek or road or maybe a trail that meanders past over here," she said. Clearly she'd studied these crude drawings at length. She actually believed there was something to this.

And so did the men after this map, Jack reminded himself. "How much gold?"

She shook her head. "No one knows. But a lot."

"Enough to kill for?"

Kate met his gaze.

He swore under his breath. "You're sure wherever this spot is, it's supposed to be on Ackermann land?"

She nodded.

Jack remembered a rumor he'd heard that Nettie had seen Kate digging in the middle of the night by the old garage next to the café. No doubt she had just been messing with nosy Nettie.

"How long have you been looking for it?"

"I wanted to start last fall, but since I didn't know the area, I didn't know where to look. Then winter hit, the ground froze.... I finally got enough money to order the equipment I needed."

"I'm going to have to think about this."

"Our partnership?" she asked, sounding worried as he headed for the door.

"No. That bargain was sealed," he said, unable not to grin at the memory of the kiss. "Fifty-fifty. I'm going to have to think about where this could be. According to this so-called map, it could be anywhere. Ackermann owned a lot of land and, as you know, it's posted because there could still be booby traps and land mines up there." He stopped at the door. "In the meantime, I think I'd better keep the map."

She started to object as he walked back over to her and picked it up from the table.

"You've studied it. I haven't. Don't worry, I won't lose it." He could tell she didn't want it out of her sight, but she nodded. He had his reasons. If those men came back, they'd have to keep her alive until they dealt with him.

Outside a pickup pulled up. "You'd better get the front door of the café opened. Looks like you have a customer already."

As he left, trotting down the outside stairs, he saw who the early-morning customer was. Hitch McCray.

Unfortunately, Hitch saw him.

"Nice night?" Hitch asked sarcastically as Jack walked between the two buildings to step out into the sunlight at the front of the café.

Don't do it. But he'd never been good at listening, even to his own advice. He walked up to Hitch and slugged him in the mouth.

STILL UNNERVED BY Jack's early-morning visit, Kate couldn't help wondering what she'd gotten herself into. But she'd found that life always came down to choices. She'd gotten into bed, so to speak, with Jack French. She was going to have to make the best of it.

She'd just gone downstairs to the café, opened the front door and put her apron on when Hitch McCray came in. He was her least favorite of the regulars. He was always hitting on her waitress, even though Bethany was married. Kate had seen him eyeing her, as well. He made her skin crawl.

"You're bleeding," she said in surprise, and grabbed a couple of napkins off a table so he could dab at his swelling lip. "What hap—" She stopped herself as she glanced out the front window and saw Jack heading up the road to his cabin. He was rubbing the knuckles of his right hand.

Kate had to hide a smile.

"That son of a bee. I'm going to sue your boyfriend," Hitch said. "But then again, what would be the point? He doesn't have anything. Just that run-down piece of ground no one wants—not even him. Jack's no good."

She started to come to Jack's defense, a mistake in so many ways.

"I guess you don't know he's two-timing you with his old girlfriend Chantell Hyett." Kate knew her expression betrayed her when Hitch laughed. "He didn't mention that, huh?"

"Jack and I aren't—"

"Right," Hitch said and took the menu out of her hand. "Just like he wasn't sneaking out of your apartment this morning." He leered at her. "I wasn't born yester—" The bell over the front door tinkled, cutting off the rest of his words.

Kate wanted to hit Hitch. She suspected a lot of people did, as the other regulars came in and sat down at the big table. A couple of them looked questioningly at Hitch, then at Kate, as if they thought she'd hit him. She smiled. Let them think what they wanted.

As she turned, she saw a skinny blond girl come in and realized she must be Tiffany, the girl who she'd heard was renting the apartment over the general store. The rumor going around town was that the girl was somehow related to the sheriff.

Tiffany slipped into the back booth. She glanced at the group of ranchers, who were now in a heated discussion of organic farming, then at Kate, and looked nervously down at her hands in her lap.

"Good morning," Kate said as she approached her table and set down a menu. "What can I get you?"

"Just some orange juice, a small glass, and maybe toast."

"You got it." She left the menu so the girl would have something to look at while she waited. She'd never seen such a nervous little thing. She wondered what nosy Nettie thought of her. Or if it was Nettie who was making her so nervous.

"Can I ask you a question?" the girl said when Kate brought her toast and orange juice.

"Sure."

"Do you know a woman named Lynette Johnson?"

NETTIE BENTON HADN'T seen Frank since showing him her renter's artwork. She hadn't talked to him since he'd called to drop the bombshell. Tiffany was his daughter. She'd hurried to the file where she kept the paperwork on her renter and checked the last name. Chandler.

Why hadn't she recognized the name? Because she hadn't been paying any attention and because it had been years since she'd even given Pamela Chandler a thought. Eighteen years, about, she thought.

She was worried about Frank on a lot of levels. Having a daughter he didn't know existed show up had been a shock. She'd heard his frustration and confusion when he'd called. He was probably still trying to make sense of everything. Such as, for instance, why Pam had kept this from him all these years.

If Tiffany really was his child.

It was no secret that Frank had wanted kids. She remembered him talking about filling up his house with the patter of little feet one day. Over the years, she'd often thought about how different her life would have been if she'd married Frank and filled his house with children.

Instead, she was childless. Bob, it had turned out, was infertile and she hadn't wanted to have his children anyway. Frank had a daughter, but a scary one. Nettie still shuddered when she thought of the sketches Tiffany had done of him. She'd sensed an edge to the girl that she now suspected was suppressed anger.

Her fear for Frank finally made her pick up the phone and call him.

"Lynette." He sounded as if he was glad to hear her voice.

"I was worried about you."

"There's nothing to worry about."

Nettie could have argued that. "How are things with your daughter?"

"We're doing the best we can, given that I didn't know she existed and her mother told her I didn't want her."

The bitterness in his voice surprised her because she'd never heard it before. If the same thing had happened to her, she would have been furious and a whole lot more than bitter. She would have been plotting revenge.

But Frank wasn't like her.

"So, have you talked to Pam?" She remembered

when he'd married Pamela Chandler. She'd been heart-broken that he'd married such a sniveling, weak woman and hadn't been surprised when the marriage hadn't lasted.

"I can't find her."

"But you're the sheriff. Surely you have resources—"

"Being sheriff doesn't allow me to use those re-sources for my own personal ends, and apparently Pam doesn't want to be found."

"I'll just bet she doesn't, after what she's done."

"Is Tiffany still in her apartment?" he asked.

"No, she left early this morning with her sketch pad." Nettie had to bite her tongue not to add, "She's probably stalking you as we speak."

"Okay," he said with a sigh. "Oh, there's my other line. I'm glad you called. Thanks for thinking of me."

"I always think of you," she said, but only after she was sure he'd hung up.

As she disconnected, she thought about Pamela Chandler. The woman had been so wrong for Frank. Pamela hated the ranch, didn't ride, didn't even eat beef.

Nettie had suspected, even though it had been years after her own marriage, that Frank had wed on the re-bound. He never seemed happy when he stopped in the store. The divorce and Pam's leaving seemed to free him. He'd perked up after that, even though he'd never married again.

Now she was sorry she hadn't been the one to give him a child. Tiffany could have been the daughter they raised together.

Just the thought choked her up and brought burning tears to her eyes. She hurriedly brushed them away.

She and Frank had made their beds all those years ago and now they had to sleep in them, alone and full of regrets.

For a while, she'd hoped that with Bob gone, she and Frank might finally have a second chance. But as Tiffany drove up in front of the store, Nettie watched her with a growing sense of loss. It was as if the girl had killed any hope of her and Frank finding their way back to each other again.

LORALEE CLARK WAS DUSTY, dirty and exhausted, but there was still one old box of photographs she hadn't gone through.

She was also hungry and wished she'd thought to eat something. But she couldn't stop now. Weary, she dragged the last box over to the rocker, and with much less enthusiasm than when she'd started, began to go through it.

The snapshot was at the bottom of the box. The moment she saw it, her pulse drummed in her ears. With trembling fingers she picked it up, torn between despair and a surge of self-satisfaction that made her want to snatch up the stupid cell phone, call her daughter and say, "I told you so."

She knew she recognized Kate LaFond. And now she knew why that memory came with such a sense of sorrow.

Kate LaFond looked just like her mother had when she was young.

Gripping the photo in her fingers, she went into the kitchen where the light was better. The trees now obscured her view of the hollow back into the Crazies.

But thirty-odd years ago, she'd been able to see the house's chimney from her kitchen window. Just as she'd been able to see Teeny the few times she had sneaked down to the house for a quick cup of coffee or just a short visit while Loralee hung clothes or washed windows.

It had been years since she'd thought about the people who lived up in that hollow. But she never forgot a face, she thought as she looked again at the photograph. She'd taken the snapshot the day the woman had stolen down while her husband had gone into town.

"I wanted to show you my baby girl," she'd said.

Loralee had stared down at the precious newborn. So tiny. So sweet. "She looks just like you. She has your heart-shaped face."

Teeny had beamed. She was smiling in the photo as she held her precious baby daughter out by the lilac hedge in Loralee's backyard. But the moment the photograph was snapped, Teeny had looked worried.

"My husband wouldn't like this," she'd said.

"Your husband will never see it. But years from now you might want to come take a look at it," Loralee had said right before she'd snapped the photo.

Loralee had forgotten about the roll of film and hadn't had it developed until over a year later. Too late for Teeny to see the photo.

CHAPTER SIXTEEN

WHEN THE RESULTS of the hospital tests came back, Kate walked down to Claude's room to find him lying in bed, staring up at the ceiling.

"I've been thinking," he said as she came into the room, closing the door behind her.

"Something new for you?"

He smiled at that and she could see he was feeling better.

"I have some good news," she said. "I'm not a match. I'm a perfect match." She saw his relief though he tried hard to hide it.

"I'm glad you're my daughter and that you now have no doubts about that, but I don't want you to do this. This is major surgery. I've already lived my life. You haven't. I won't take a chance with yours."

"I talked to the doctor. It's a piece of cake. You'll have to take anti-rejection pills, but he is very optimistic that because my liver is a perfect match, you won't reject it."

"Why are you doing this?" he asked, his voice small.

"For the café. What else could it be?"

He didn't say anything for a long moment. "I would think you would hate me for not showing up in your

life sooner. For waiting until I needed you before I told
you that I'm your father."

"Harvey Logan was my father."

He nodded. "I'm glad you had him."

She heard something in his voice and let out a sigh.
"That was your doing, too?"

Claude gave her a small smile. "I had to pull a few
strings but my best friend is a lawyer. I knew Harvey
and his wife, Meg, desperately wanted a baby and that
they were good people."

"You could have kept me."

He laughed at that. "An old sickly bachelor who
lived over a café in the middle of nowhere?" He shook
his head. "I did what I could for you. I had no idea
Meg would die so young or that that fool Harvey would
drag you around the country, looking for lost treasure.
I blame myself."

"Why would you?"

He laughed softly. "I was the one who got Harvey
hooked on it. There's so much I need to tell you." He
looked pale again and she could see he was fighting
exhaustion.

"First we'll get you well, then you can tell me everything," she said. "You can tell me about my mother
and why the two of you didn't run away together."

He nodded, his face seeming to age with sadness.

LORALEE CLARK STOOD for a long time looking out her
kitchen window and remembering the day Teeny Ackermann's life ended up in that hollow—and the horrible sense of guilt she'd felt.

The woman needed your help and the best you could do was take a picture of her and her baby girl?

She'd gone to the sheriff, hadn't she? She'd tried to save the poor girl. At least her daughter had survived, apparently.

If Kate LaFond really is the baby in the photo.

"She is," Loralee said to her empty house. Out the window, she saw something that made her squint. Lights up in that hollow. It wasn't the first time she'd seen them lately.

In that instant, she knew what she had to do. She looked around for her walking shoes as she tried to tell herself she'd done everything she could back then. Even thirty years ago, people kept their noses out of other people's marriages. She remembered mentioning Teeny to her husband, Maynard.

"I wouldn't go trying to forge a friendship. Not with Cull Ackermann's wife," he'd said, not looking up from his meal.

"I feel sorry for her. The way her husband treats her just makes me…"

His head jerked up, his soup spoon in hand, stilling the rest of her words. "It's none of your business what goes on up there, Loralee. That woman married him. You butt in and… Well, nothing good will come of it, I promise you that." He shook his head. "It's bad enough Cull bought that piece of land so close to ours, then putting up all those no-trespassing signs and him and his boys threatening anyone who comes near. He's armed those young boys and told them to shoot anyone who trespasses. You stay away from that place, you hear me? No telling what that fool and his kin will do."

Maynard had gone back to his soup, having said all he was going to say on the matter.

Loralee had never laid eyes on Cull Ackermann, but she'd glimpsed his boys on occasion—usually when one of them was stealing something from her garden.

The first time she'd caught them, she hollered out the window for them to skedaddle—just as she would to any young boys.

The two older boys had turned to look at her. Something in their dark eyes had sent a chill rattling through her. She'd just stood there feeling helpless while they ripped out some of her plants as they left.

She'd known then that they would be back. They'd scared her enough that she had no desire to run into their father. She'd started keeping a loaded shotgun by the back door.

But when they returned, she'd never threatened them with it. That was the second time in her life she'd felt like a coward. The first time was when she hadn't helped Teeny Ackermann and her baby daughter.

After Maynard's warning and her run-in with the Ackermann boys, she had broached the subject of her concern for Teeny to the Beartooth Quilting Society.

"Cull's wife made her choice when she married him and said 'till death do us part,'" one of the older women had said.

"If she's unhappy, then why didn't she take off a long time ago?" another said.

"I agree. Has she ever asked for your help?" another asked.

"I can tell she's scared of what he'd do," Loralee said. But she swore at that moment that if Teeny ever asked, she'd help her, no matter what anyone said.

"We all make compromises in marriage, some more than others," the elderly member had said. "I think this younger generation is much too quick to break their vows the minute things get tough. You have to admire a woman who makes the best of her situation."

And that was that, until of course the horrible day when all anyone was talking about was the Ackermanns. By that time, Teeny was already dead. No one regretted not helping the poor woman more than Loralee.

Swallowing the bitter taste of guilt, Loralee set out for Ackermann Hollow, armed with her old shotgun.

FRANK INVITED TIFFANY out again late that afternoon. She said she didn't want to go for a horseback ride.

"We can just talk, get to know each other," he suggested.

She hadn't jumped on that, but she did drive out. He'd made hamburgers on the grill, only to find out that she was a vegetarian. She picked at the salad he made her instead.

He had no idea how to reach his daughter—just that he desperately wanted to. Sometimes when he was around her, he had the feeling that she wanted to get to know him. He could feel her resisting him, though.

Maybe that's why he decided to tell her about his crows.

She'd thought he was joking at first. "You gave them names?"

He'd nodded and pointed to the telephone line where some of them had gathered. "At night they roost together to sleep." He told her about one time in Oklahoma when an estimated two million crows had roosted. "But tens of thousands of them roosting together isn't unusual. No one knows why they do this. It could be the wagon-train theory—you know, safety in numbers. Or maybe it's like a large sleepover where they stay up all night talking. Scientists have wondered where they exchange the important information, like where to migrate, where not to go and where to find abundant food. Maybe it's why they roost."

He thought of stories he'd heard about the passenger pigeon. Migrating flocks could darken the sky for hours as they passed. He would give anything to have seen that. None remained on earth, making him fear that the same could happen to the crows.

His crows. They were the only family he'd had—before Tiffany. He put out bird feed and scraps for them. He celebrated the births of the "kids" each year. He named them by their personalities and swore that he could distinguish one bird from another by their calls.

When he admitted this and told her about the one he named Billy the Kid after a deputy who used to work for him, Tiffany actually laughed.

"I saw a video about crows that drop nuts into traffic so the cars run over the nuts and crack them," she said, more animated than he'd seen her. "Then the birds wait until the light changes before they go out there to get the food." She smiled. "That's pretty smart, isn't it."

Frank returned his daughter's smile, feeling as close to her as he had since learning she was his child. "They're smart birds," he agreed. "They're a lot like humans. They have close-knit families and the kids play tag together. The breeding mother and father are the blackest and glossiest of the group. They're easy to spot because they stay close to each other." He pointed them out. "The father follows the mother wherever she goes, staking out his territory. If another male crow tries to horn in, he inserts himself between them." Strife and fighting among the birds, Frank had noticed, were highest during the spring.

When he looked over at Tiffany, he realized he'd said something wrong.

That spark of interest he'd seen in her had quickly extinguished. "Even crows understand family better than you do."

He realized belatedly what he'd said, but it was too late. "I'm sorry. I get carried away when I talk about the crows."

"They're just birds," she snapped.

Not to him. But he could see that she would never understand how special they were to him. Or care, for that matter.

"I didn't mean to upset you."

She shrugged and looked away. He caught a shine in her eyes. A moment later, she made an angry swipe at her tears. "You said you didn't know about me."

Her gaze was red-hot as it met his. "My mother said you knew. You were just glad to be rid of us both. So if you only have crows for family, it's your own fault."

Frank was glad he couldn't get his hands on Pam at that moment. It astonished him that she could hate him so much that she'd poisoned his own child against him. "I wanted children so, of course, I would have definitely wanted you if I'd known about you."

"You didn't want children with *my mother*," she challenged.

No. Toward the end he hadn't wanted to have children with her, so he said nothing rather than lie. He suspected she would have known it was a lie anyway. "I wish I'd known about you."

Speaking of lies, how many had Pam told this poor child?

"How about ice cream?" he suggested.

She shot him an angry look. "I'm not four. I need to get back to my apartment. I have work to do."

More sketches of the father she hated, he thought as he walked her to her car. His crows cawed at them from a telephone line, seeming upset. Tiffany shot them an irritated look before climbing into her car.

"I'm glad you came out to see me."

She responded by slamming the car door, starting the engine and taking off in a cloud of dust, leaving him afraid he might never see her again.

FEELING TIME SLIP like sand through her fingers, Kate couldn't help being anxious to get back into Ackermann Hollow. With Jack helping her, the search should go faster.

He was right about the map being unhelpfully generic. There were numerous places that looked like those on the map, too many to search in so little time. But she couldn't give up. Wouldn't.

Unfortunately, Bethany had called in sick this afternoon, so Kate had to work the evening shift at the café. It would be dark by nine, when she closed. Soon, though, it would stay daylight until almost ten. If she could wait that long.

"I NEED YOU TO MAKE sure this never falls into those thieving bastards' hands," Claude said. "I don't care what you do with the gold. Blow it all in Vegas. I just don't want any of my brother's descendants to have it. Promise me."

"Claude, if others haven't been able to find it, how do you expect me—"

"I know Cull. He'll hold on to the map as long as there is breath in his body. I heard he's sick. He'll try to find one of his boys to give the map to, probably his oldest, Cecil."

"I thought you said everyone believes his sons are dead."

Claude nodded. "Everyone doesn't know those boys like I do. The remains of only one was found. Those other three are alive somewhere. Count on it. And they'll come back to Beartooth. Either because Cull finally gave one of them the map. Or because they'll figure out that the only other person who knew was your mother. They'll come looking for the gold and if they don't find it, they'll come looking for you. It won't matter if you have the gold or not. You understand what I'm saying?"

SHE HADN'T REALLY understood back then. But she did now. She couldn't let the sons of the man who'd mistreated her mother get her mother's money. She had to find the gold first.

Jack. He was her only hope. He knew the country, he was smart and as wily as a fox.

She hated needing his help. It would mean spending more time around him. Which meant putting herself in danger in an even more frightening way. Jack was a heartbreaker. She didn't think for a moment that he would spare her heart.

She looked around the café. It was full this evening, alive with laughter and the sound of voices. She'd made a life for herself here. It wasn't a bad life. The gold only complicated things.

But as Claude had warned her, she'd have to deal with the Ackermann boys one way or the other. And his prediction had been right.

THE ACKERMANN PLACE was a good walk from Loralee's house. She had grabbed her sweater, determined to find out what was going on up there. At a spot near her property, she found a place in the fence where she could slide under.

She knew what her daughter would say if she saw

her sneaking up the hollow. As she walked, she could hear the whole conversation her daughter would be having with her right now.

"Mother, why in the world would you go up there, of all places?"

"Because I felt like it. Haven't you ever done anything just because you felt like it?"

"What's really going on, Mother?"

Loralee fingered the old photo she'd stuck in her sweater pocket. It was her proof that she wasn't senile. She wanted to shove it in front of Marian's face and say, "See? Now what do you have to say to your mother?"

Had the person Kate LaFond reminded her of been anyone but Teeny Ackermann, she couldn't have felt more satisfaction. She'd failed the woman and would never forget it.

She had to stop to catch her breath, having forgotten that the climb into the isolated hollow was mostly uphill. Between keeping her own house and her garden, she was in good shape for a woman her age. At least she'd thought so. But the walk up here had taken a lot of her energy. She wasn't as spry as she'd thought she was.

But she pressed onward, determined to make it to what was left of the house and outbuildings and find out what was going on up here.

It was cool and shaded in the hollow. She stepped over a piece of old barbed-wire fence that lay on the ground from where a tree had fallen on it, and moved through a stand of cottonwoods along the small creek. The silted water was running fast down from the mountains. Snow-fed, it seemed to throw off a cold breeze that made her hug herself.

Ahead, she spotted the stone corner of the foundation of the Ackermann house. Cull was said to have built it himself. Just like the old barn and outbuildings. Most still stood.

It surprised her. She'd have thought the land would have reclaimed everything over the past thirty years. As she moved, the tall spring grass whickered against her pant leg. The sound of it and the creek seemed so lonely she felt like crying.

Or was it the sight of the gaping hole, dug in the side of the mountain, that had once been a root cellar? And a prison for the first Mrs. Ackermann.

She felt a chill move through her and turned away. Her daughter would have been right. She was a fool to come up here. What had she hoped to accomplish by heaping on more guilt? Maybe more to the point, what was she going to do if she was right and someone was staying up here?

The house looked full of dirt and critters. No one in his right mind would be trying to live on this property. As she started to turn back, she was startled to see a man come out of the barn.

Strangling off her startled cry, she had the sense to step behind the trunk of a large cottonwood. But in her haste, she wrenched her ankle and almost fell, dropping the shotgun. It clanged on rock and she feared the noise had given her away. As she clung to the tree, the pain excruciating, she knew it could be the least of her problems if the man had seen or heard her.

She waited a few moments before peeking around the tree. The man was carrying a shovel, the blade dark with soil. He wore only jeans, his white chest bare except for a tapestry of dark tattoos.

Loralee held her breath as the man headed in her direction. It was his haircut that sent her already thundering pulse into overdrive. It was cut the same way all the Ackermann boys had worn theirs. A *buzz,* she thought it had been called thirty years ago. But maybe that was only in Montana.

What hair he had left was dark, just as she knew his eyes were—that bottomless black. Like a pit with no way out. He was tall and thin. Like his father, she thought with a shudder. His face was pockmarked and narrow as a ferret's. He moved stealthily, ghostlike, and she was reminded again of that brood of vegetable-stealing young'ns—now grown men. Which Ackermann was this one?

As he neared, she saw with relief that he had some kind of music device sticking out of his jeans pocket and those ear things stuck in each ear. She looked down at her shotgun only to find it had broken open, both shells having spilled out on the ground. Even if she could trust putting weight on her hurt ankle, she feared she would never be able to get the shotgun and reload it quickly enough.

When she looked up, he was within yards of her. All she could do was squeeze her eyes shut tight and pray he hadn't seen her. Her greatest fear was opening them to find him standing over her. Looking at her as he had thirty years ago before, when she'd chased him out of her garden only to find him back, ripping out her plants by the handfuls.

But when she opened her eyes, she saw to her weak-kneed relief that he was nowhere in sight. A few moments later, she heard what sounded like a four-wheeler start up over a rise to the north.

Loralee slumped to the ground, her good leg too weak to hold her as she listened to the four-wheeler drive away. Her heart was pounding so hard she couldn't think. She sat for a few long moments. Darkness was settling into the hollow. She couldn't stay here, because every instinct told her he would be back.

But she wasn't sure she could walk. Her ankle still hurt like the devil. She remembered the cell phone Marian had insisted she have and dug frantically in her pocket, praying she had cell service this far up the hollow. She'd never needed her daughter more than she did at this moment.

. But her pocket was empty. She'd left the cell phone at the house.

CHAPTER SEVENTEEN

IT WAS THE WEE HOURS of the night by the time Loralee reached the house. She'd used the shotgun like a crutch and still there'd been terrifying times when she'd thought she would never make it.

There's no fool like an old fool.

Was that a song? Or just a remarkably acute expression?

The cell phone wasn't the only thing she'd forgotten. When she'd left home, the day had been cool. She hadn't thought to bring water or even a candy bar.

She was famished and weak, her ankle hurt like the dickens and she would have given anything if someone had come along and offered her a ride.

But she lived miles from the nearest house, on a road that was seldom used. That was one reason Cull Ackermann had bought property out here, far to the north of town, hidden at the edge of the Crazies.

It made the trip into Big Timber thirty-five miles instead of twenty. Beartooth was closer, but not by much, since the road often drifted closed in the winter and was rutted and muddy most of the rest of the year. In the spring, it was sometimes impassable because of mud. By fall, the county would finally get around to grading it.

Loralee had always thought it was a darned good thing she wasn't like some women who thought they had to go into town all the time.

As she considered the way her thoughts kept straying, she wondered if she was suffering from hypothermia. With the sun long gone, the wind had come up and was now blowing a chill down from the mountains. At least it wasn't supposed to snow again. But this was Montana. She'd seen it snow any month of the year.

Cold and exhausted, stumbling along in the dark, she prayed she didn't encounter a grizzly. Or worse, that Ackermann boy.

When her house came into view, Loralee began to cry. She was glad there wasn't anyone around to see her. All her life, she'd prided herself on being strong and capable. Wasn't that what Maynard had said he loved about her?

Maybe she *was* getting senile. Maybe Marian was right. Maybe she should at least consider an apartment in Big Timber. Or even assisted living.

The thought stopped her tears. She straightened her back and limped to her front door. Had she left it wide open? She supposed so, since it had been nice earlier.

She pulled open the screen and stepped inside, never so glad to be home.

That's when she saw that someone had been here and whoever it was had torn up the place.

She thought about calling the sheriff. In fact, she planned to. But first she was too cold and hungry. She dropped her shotgun by the front door and stumbled into the kitchen. It wasn't quite as messed up, although someone had gone through her canisters. Her little bit of mad money she kept hidden in one of them was gone.

In the refrigerator, she took out the milk and saw that he'd gotten into her leftover fried chicken. Most of it was gone, but he'd left her a couple of pieces— probably the pieces he didn't like, she thought as she dropped into a chair at the table.

She drank half a quart of milk and ate the chicken before she felt better. Her ankle ached, but she knew it would be fine once she got off it.

As she glanced around the kitchen, she tried to assess what might be missing. Getting up, she limped to the drawer where she kept her mother's silverware.

It was still there. Relieved, she went back into the living room. A few things had been knocked over or taken off the wall. A lamp had been broken, as well as several picture frames. She'd never liked those pictures anyway.

The bathroom hadn't been disturbed, except he'd gone through her medicine cabinet and taken all the old pain pills she kept around should she need them. In the sewing room, she saw the sewing machine was still there. Thankfully he hadn't realized what a new model like that was worth.

In her bedroom, she found all the drawers in the bureau askew with some of her unmentionables on the floor. He must be desperate for money to go through an old woman's underwear drawer, she thought with an amused shake of her head.

That thought made her move to her jewelry box. To her surprise, nothing seemed to be missing. Maynard hadn't been the kind of husband who'd bought his wife diamonds or even gold. He might surprise her with a new tractor or even flowers a few times. Usually it was a box of candy and a note that said he loved her. That had been all she'd needed and more.

She tidied up her bedroom, but decided the rest of the house could wait, since she really needed to get off her bad ankle.

Everything could wait, she told herself. Just like calling the sheriff. No damage was done. She didn't keep much pin money in the house. Her purse was under a pile of new fabric she'd purchased, so the thief hadn't even gotten what little cash she carried.

And what could the sheriff do anyway? The thief was gone and it wasn't as if he'd left a calling card. Without proof of who'd done this, the sheriff couldn't do a darned thing.

She considered calling her daughter, but quickly decided it would only worry Marian and for no good reason.

Loralee was no fool. At least that's what she hoped people said after she was gone. She'd never been robbed in her life. Nor had she ever seen anyone slinking around the ranch house—other than those Ackermann boys.

It didn't take much to put two and two together and come up with who had been in her house, trying to steal from her.

"You must have been disappointed," she said out

loud. "And pretty angry that you got away with little more than loose change."

That's why he'd be back. Not for her money. He now knew she didn't keep much in the house. But he would be vindictive—just as he'd been as a boy. He would want to hurt someone. Loralee figured she'd just been lucky those boys hadn't had a chance to grow up in that hollow up the road, or they would have come back for her before now.

But she didn't expect him back tonight. He'd done his worst for now.

Exhausted, Loralee wanted only to go to bed and sleep. For the first time in her life, though, she locked both doors before she collapsed into a deep but troubled sleep.

BILLY WESTFALL LOOKED up to see the sheriff standing in his doorway. He blinked, thinking he was seeing things. He and Frank hadn't parted ways on the best of terms. Just the thought made him laugh. Frank Curry hadn't exactly fired the former deputy. He'd just refused to rehire him after Billy had made the bad decision to quit last fall.

"I know you didn't come to wish me good luck with my new business venture," Billy said. "If this is about my P.I. license…" He started to motion to the document he'd framed and put on the wall. The only thing on the wall. He hadn't had time to decorate yet.

The sheriff closed the door.

Billy slipped his hand into the top drawer, where he kept a spare handgun. His fingers closed around the grip as Frank Curry moved toward his desk. It wasn't that he was afraid of his former boss, but there'd been times when he was a deputy that the sheriff had looked as if he wanted to kill him.

He wasn't taking any chances, since the sheriff had one hell of a scowl on his face. "That's close enough," Billy said.

The sheriff stopped. He looked irritated. "Get your hand out of that drawer. In fact, I'd feel better if you stood up."

"What is it you want, Sheriff?" he demanded. "You can't just come in here and start—"

"Pamela Chandler Curry. I believe she's going by her maiden name again."

Billy freed his hand and leaned back in his chair. *"Your ex?"*

"I need you to find her."

It took him a minute because this was the last thing on earth he'd expected. Then he began to laugh. "You want to hire *me?*"

Frank made a distasteful face and glanced away as if this was hard on him.

Billy just bet it was. "All the time I was your deputy, you told me how undisciplined I was, how trigger-happy, basically how worthless I was, and how if it wasn't for my grandfather Bull you'd have fired me. Isn't that right?"

The sheriff scowled again. "Do you want the job or not?"

"Why *me?*"

"Isn't it obvious?"

"You think my grandfather knows where she is." Billy almost laughed as he realized Frank's real intent. Frank had always thought he had more pull with his grandfather than he did. But Billy wasn't about to let the sheriff know that.

"So you need *my* help," he said and smiled. "Why do you want to find her?"

"This was a bad idea." Frank started to turn to leave.

"I'll find her. Don't you want to know what I charge?" He rattled off his rate. The sheriff glanced around the office, his expression making it clear he wasn't impressed. Billy almost told him to forget it. But in truth he needed the money.

"Fine," Frank said and scribbled down his cell phone number on the scratch pad on the corner of his desk. "I don't want you talking to her. Just find her and call me right away. I don't want anyone else knowing about this."

"I'm going to need half my fee up front."

The sheriff looked as if he was thinking better of hiring him.

"I'll prove to you that you were wrong about me," Billy said quickly.

"We'll see." With that, Frank reached for his wallet, took out several large bills, tossed them on the desk and walked out.

KATE AND JACK had stolen a few hours to search the hollow since making their pact, but like this late afternoon, she could tell his heart wasn't in it. He didn't believe the gold was hidden here on the Ackermann property. And even though there had been no sign of any more Ackermanns, she could tell he was always on alert. Did he think she hadn't noticed the pistol he'd started carrying in his pack?

"Why are you doing this?" she asked him after another unsuccessful attempt to find the gold. She knew she should be touched that he wanted to protect her.

"What do you mean?" he asked as they were walking out of the hollow toward her pickup.

"Are you even really looking for the gold or just indulging me?" she demanded, feeling her anger rise.

"We're partners," he said calmly, looking at her as if surprised by her outburst.

She scoffed at that. "This is just like that first night we met. You think you're coming to my rescue. Well, I don't need your help if it's just about saving the damsel in distress."

He had stopped walking to stare at her. They stood in a stand of pines. The warm day had faded to a silver dusk. Deep shadows hunkered under the trees and a cool breeze blew down from the mountain peaks.

"You're the one who asked for my help," he reminded her.

She shook her head, hating that it was true. "Only because I thought—"

"Kate, what is this really about?"

"You don't believe the gold is here."

"But you do. So what is the problem? Why are you trying to push me away?"

She stared at him, realizing it was true. She'd picked this fight. She didn't want to need him. Worse, she didn't want to want him.

Since they'd made the pact, he seemed to be keeping his distance from her. Kate said as much to him now.

Jack laughed. "I thought that's what you wanted."

"It was. Is." Taking a deep breath, she let it out slowly and looked back toward the hollow.

"I know you're scared," he said quietly.

He had no idea how much he scared her. She liked her life to be an open, straight road. No surprises. Claude had put a huge bend in that road. She hated to think what Jack could do to it.

"I think they've been watching us."

Her gaze swung to his in surprise. She almost laughed. He thought the Ackermanns were her greatest fear?

"They're waiting for you to find the gold."

She thought he was probably right about that. "But since you don't think that it's going to happen... I need to get back," she said, and started past him.

He caught hold of her arm and turned her into him. "Why is it so hard for you to accept help?"

She shook her head and pulled free. "You're right. I was trying to push you away. I wish I hadn't involved you in this." She wished that she wasn't so aware of him on these trips into the hollow.

"I *am* involved." His gaze met hers and she felt a slow fire burn in her belly. Goose bumps rippled over her bare skin. She shivered, hugging herself against the growing desire she felt for him.

"You're just frustrated because we haven't found the gold," he said.

Yep, that was it, she thought as she dug a boot toe in the dirt.

Jack reached over and lifted her chin with his finger until they were eye to eye again. "Maybe one day you'll trust me enough to tell me about your scar."

She nodded, though she had her doubts. As she walked back to where they'd left her truck parked in the trees, she thought of Claude and the promise she'd made him.

How could she explain to Jack the tangled knot of emotions that came with this hollow? Or that even the sight of the hurriedly drawn map on a piece of used freezer paper brought her to tears? What did he know about loss? Or promises she feared she couldn't keep?

"I OWE YOU THE TRUTH," *Claude said a few weeks after the surgery. It would be a year before he recovered, but the doctor said everything had gone well. His body hadn't rejected the portion of liver she'd given him. Her recovery would be much shorter, just a few months, according to the doctor.*

"You owe me more than that," she joked, "but that's a start anyway."

"I'm sorry I have to be the one to tell you this."

"Shouldn't you have told me sooner that I have three violent, psychopathic, somewhat stepbrothers who are going to come looking for me?"

He met her gaze. "You were safe as long as Cullen Ackermann was alive. He's dying of cancer. He hasn't told his sons where the gold is buried yet or they would have already returned to Beartooth."

"You're that certain that three of the sons survived?"

He nodded.

"You told me my mother died soon after you got me out of there when I was eighteen months old. Why didn't she leave with me?" She swallowed. "Did he kill her?"

"Not in the way you're thinking, but he was responsible. She was killed by one of the booby traps he'd set up around his property to keep trespassers out. He went to prison for it. For that and what he did to his first wife, his legal wife."

"His first wife?" Kate wasn't sure she wanted to hear this.

"When the sheriff and his deputies stormed the place, they found Cullen's wife, the one he'd never divorced. He had her locked up in a hole in the side of the mountain. No one knows how long she'd been there, but I know your mother didn't know. The woman was in terrible shape and died shortly after she was rescued."

"Oh, my word," Kate said, feeling sick to her stomach.

"You see why I don't want this man or his whelps to get what was your mother's? They took enough from her."

She walked to the window, her back to him. "Let me get this straight. They think I know where this gold is?" She turned to look at him. "If I was eighteen months old when all this hit the fan, why would they..." Her words died off as he picked up a manila envelope and held it out to her. "What is that?"

He didn't answer.

She didn't want to know what was in that envelope and yet she stepped to him and took it, fingering the envelope for a moment before carefully opening it. It hadn't been sealed, the flap merely turned under. She suspected Claude had put whatever it was into the envelope for safekeeping—not her mother.

As she pulled out the faded, crinkled sheet of paper, she frowned. "It looks like a child's treasure map."

"I suspect it was the best your mother could do with what she had at her disposal. But you're right. It is a map."

She glanced up at him to make sure he wasn't kidding. "You can't be serious. This is a map to the gold hidden at the end of the rainbow?" She laughed. "You can't expect me to believe any of this. Why wouldn't your brother tell his sons where he buried this gold—if it exists?"

"Your mother's family had money. She'd just inherited it when her path crossed Cullen's. The money he turned into gold bullion is your inheritance. It doesn't belong to Cullen's boys. I promised your mother I would see that you got it."

"You didn't exactly beat a path to my door to get it to me, did you?"

"It wasn't safe."

"Safe. Like it is safe now?"

He looked away. "None of this is my doing, believe me."

"Why wouldn't they have found this gold by now? Surely they would have looked for it?"

"Ackermann Hollow, as it is now known, covers a lot of rough terrain. It would be like looking for a needle in a haystack without a map."

"Or with this map," she said, tossing it on the table. "If their father didn't give them the location, then why would they think I have it?" She saw Claude's expression. "What aren't you telling me?"

"Cullen. I saw him before he died in prison. He knows your mother made a map."

She felt a cold chill wind its way up her spine. "He told his sons?"

"He feels she betrayed him and wants revenge."

"She betrayed him?"

"It's his vengeance against her through you," Claude said.

She studied him for a long moment. "And against you. He knew I wasn't his, didn't he?"

He didn't answer. He didn't have to.

"I want nothing to do with any of this," she said, crossing her arms.

"I'm afraid you have no choice. Whether you decide to find the gold or not, they will come looking for you."

"I'll give them the map and good riddance."

"If that's what you want to do." He got to his feet, but she could see it was an effort. He still looked pale and sickly. "Cullen took your mother's money, kept her a prisoner and ultimately killed her. Now he is sending his rabid boys after you and the gold. Can you really just give it to them?"

She'd always been a fighter, but this was more than

she could handle. "I'd be a sitting duck in Beartooth,
Montana."

"If I could find you, then they can, too. At least
in Beartooth it would be on your own terms. At least
there, they'll probably wait until you find it for them
before they..."

"Kill me?" she asked, astonishment in her voice.
"Do you realize what you're asking me to do?"

"I'm just doing what I promised your mother."

She swore and stepped to the table to pick up the
map again. It couldn't have been more crudely drawn
as if her mother had been in a terrible hurry. She felt
her stomach roil at the thought of what her mother
had gone through to not only save her daughter, but
to try to get her this.

LORALEE WAS AT HER kitchen sink and just happened to
look up from the single plate and cup she was rinsing
after her breakfast, and there he was.

Used to seeing deer and elk and even an occasional
bear or two, she wasn't even startled at first.

Then he looked in her direction and she felt her
blood run cold. It was him. The oldest Ackermann.
Cecil, she'd heard him called.

Her grandmother's cherished china cup slipped from
her fingers. She hardly heard it shatter in the old white-
porcelain sink—or the plate beneath it crack and break
in two.

As if sleepwalking, she reached for the dish towel,
drying her hands as her gaze followed the man crossing her yard toward her back door.

Loralee had left the shotgun just inside the front door last night. She knew she would never reach it in time. At her age, just the force of firing both barrels would probably land her on her backside anyway.

She had another way of dealing with the critters that wandered into her backyard, one that had worked for her since she was a girl.

As she heard the back door splinter, she picked up the slingshot she kept by the screenless kitchen window and one of the round rocks she'd hauled up in a pail from the creek.

She'd sent grizzlies hightailing it with one good shot.

One good shot was what she needed now, she thought as she turned to see the man standing just feet away in the open doorway.

"Remember me?" he asked, amusement and malice in his tone. "Not going to chase me out of your vegetable patch this time."

Even if she hadn't seen the knife clutched in his hand, his expression told her everything she needed to know. She slipped the rock into the slingshot, never taking her eyes off the man. She could smell Cecil from where he stood, a potent mixture of sweat and rage.

The moment he moved, she lifted the slingshot, took aim and let the rock go.

As he left Westfall's office, Frank hated what he'd been forced to do, but there was only so much he could do on his own without jeopardizing his position as sheriff.

But had he really hired Billy the Kid Westfall? His reasons had made sense back at his ranch this morning. He couldn't do more than a cursory search for Pam because of his job. He needed someone without those limitations, and that was definitely Billy Westfall.

There was another good reason for hiring him, though, one that made even more sense. Billy's grandfather Bull was the one person Pam might have confided in. If anyone knew where she was now, it would be Bull Westfall.

When Pam had first come to Montana—before Frank had met her—she'd rented an apartment from Bull's sister Elizabeth. The Westfall family had adopted her, taking her under their wing, since she was a city girl lost in the wilds of Montana.

"Bull is like the father I never had," she often said. "He and Elizabeth were so kind to me."

"Before I came along," he would add for her.

Frank knew his talking to Bull would get him nowhere. Bull never liked him and no doubt still blamed him for his grandson leaving the sheriff's department.

But Bull might help Billy find Pam. Why was she hiding to begin with? It made no sense. Was she really that afraid of him? Or did she just want Tiffany to believe she was?

Frank swore under his breath. How convenient that Pam had disappeared and right when he had so many questions to ask her.

Billy had always been a loose cannon. If anyone could find Pam if she didn't want to be found, then it just might be Billy the Kid.

Frank hoped to hell he hadn't made a mistake. Not just in hiring Billy, but in looking for Pam. He was half-afraid Pam had reason to fear for her life if he found her.

He had just reached his patrol pickup when he got a call from dispatch.

"Loralee Clark says she has a dead man in her kitchen. She wants to know what you'd like her to do with him."

CHAPTER EIGHTEEN

JACK LOOKED UP and saw a dark-colored pickup coming up the road toward him. As it drew closer, he could hear the rumble of the motor and the missing tailpipe. His pulse jumped at the familiar sound as he recalled where he'd heard it only nights before.

The truck roared past in a cloud of dust, the driver keeping his foot to the gas pedal and his eyes straight ahead. Even if he hadn't recognized the sound of the truck, he would have known the man wasn't from around these parts. Everyone in the county gave a nod or raised a couple of fingers from the wheel when they passed another vehicle, especially out here on a dirt road.

He dropped over a rise, then turned around in the middle of the road and went after the truck. In truth, he didn't know what he was going to do. Maybe just see where the man was headed. Or get his license plate number. Anything more would be foolhardy at best if the man behind the wheel of that pickup was who he suspected he was.

Jack topped several rises. Ahead, all he could see was a cloud of dust. The road curved, dipped and finally rose again along the foothills of the Crazies. As he topped the next rise, he could see the road for several miles. It was empty.

He swore under his breath as he hit his brakes. Dust hung in the air, but there was no sign of the truck. Jack slammed his hand down on the steering wheel. The man must have turned off or circled back around.

The thought sent his heart racing. Circled back to town—or Ackermann Hollow?

Turning around, Jack took off toward Beartooth. Kate had said she was working late at the café. But what if things had slowed down and she'd decided to do some digging on her own this evening?

KATE LOOKED UP IN surprise as Jack stormed in the back door of the café. She'd just put the closed sign on the front door and locked it only minutes before and was heading upstairs to change.

"I was afraid you'd close early," he said.

"If you're hungry—"

"You weren't thinking of going to the hollow alone, were you?"

She put her hands on her hips. "We might be partners, but I can—"

"I just saw one of the Ackermanns. I think he's headed for the hollow."

Kate tried not to let him see how that news scared her. "You're sure it was an Ackermann?"

Jack swore. "It was one of those two men who paid you a visit not long ago. Does it really matter if they are Ackermanns or not?"

She didn't know why she was arguing with him. Maybe because she didn't want to believe they were back.

"Damn it, Kate. I'm telling you it was one of them. I passed him on the road. When I went after him, he—"

"Why would you go after him?" she demanded and pushed past him for the stairs to her apartment. "This is why I didn't want you involved."

He caught up with her before she reached the stairs. Grabbing her arm, he turned her to face him.

"Don't do this," he said, his voice breaking.

"I'm just going up to my apartment."

"You know what I mean. Let this go. No amount of gold is worth losing your life over."

She studied his handsome face, weakening at his touch, at the way he looked at her. Without thinking, she touched her palm to his cheek. His jaw was rough with a day's stubble, strong with determination. "I wish I could."

He shoved back his hat and his gaze locked with hers. "I can't protect you 24/7 and I can't stick around and see you get killed." She watched him reach into his jacket pocket and pull out the map.

She raised a brow, her heart sinking as he handed it to her. "Already running out on me, Jack? I thought it would be after we found the gold. I guess I underestimated you."

Letting out a growl, he grabbed her shoulders and pulled her to him. His kiss was an angry mix of frustration and passion. She opened her lips to his demanding mouth as he lifted her off her feet and pressed her against the café wall with his body.

She clung to him, unapologetic for the desire that rippled through her like a rogue wave. She wanted him, wanted him out of her system. She'd known he was a heartbreaker. She'd sworn he wasn't stealing hers the way he had that damned prize bull that had sent him to prison and yet when he ended the kiss and her feet hit the floor again, she felt something inside her break.

"I'll be out at my family's place in case you change your mind," he said, his voice sounding hoarse. "I'm getting the place ready to sell." With that he walked out.

SHERIFF FRANK CURRY RACED out to the Clark place, siren and lights blazing.

He found Loralee sitting on the porch, a double-barreled shotgun lying across her lap.

"Loralee?" Frank said as he climbed out of his patrol pickup.

"Sheriff."

"I understand there is a dead man on your kitchen floor?" he asked, glancing toward the house. "Did you shoot him?"

"Nope. Nailed him good with a rock and my slingshot. I'm a deadeye with that thing."

"Why don't you stay here and I'll go take a look," he suggested as he mounted the porch steps.

"Fine with me. I've seen enough of him and his."

Him and his? Frank pulled open the screen and stepped in. As he did, he drew his weapon and moved cautiously toward the kitchen.

The house was chock-full of things Loralee had collected during her lifetime. Knickknacks were everywhere. Those and quilts. They hung on the walls, off the backs of chairs and over the couch.

As he stepped into the large ranch-style kitchen, he couldn't help noticing how clean it was. So clean that the puddle of tracked blood on the floor jumped out at him. So did the fact that whoever had left the blood was no longer lying there.

The tracks in the blood headed for the back door. Frank followed the trail out the door and down the steps. From there the blood disappeared in the grass.

He glanced around the yard. Seeing no one, he went back to the front porch and Loralee.

"Well?" she demanded. "Are you going to arrest me?"

"There's no one in there." Frank saw fear seize her expression.

"He wasn't dead?" she cried.

"Apparently not. He left blood on your kitchen floor and a trail out your back door."

Loralee swore, shocking him. She clutched the shotgun tighter. "That means he'll be back."

"I think you'd best tell me what's going on, don't you?"

She nodded and he listened, even more shocked to hear what she had to tell him.

"You're sure it was one of the Ackermanns?" he asked when she'd finished.

"I never forget a face. I keep telling Marian that. I told her I recognized Kate LaFond." She scoffed. "She didn't believe me. Thought I was getting senile. Can't wait to see her face when I show her the proof I found."

"Excuse me. Kate LaFond?"

"She looks just like her mother," Loralee said emphatically.

If it wasn't for the blood and the male-sized tracks in Loralee's kitchen, Frank would have thought the woman *was* senile.

"I'm confused. What does this have to do with Kate LaFond?" Frank asked.

Loralee sighed and reached in her pocket to pull out a crumpled photograph. He was instantly reminded of the photo he'd found near the dead man's body.

He glanced at the snapshot of a woman holding a baby. He stared at the pretty young woman and the baby in her arms. The resemblance was undeniable.

"Who is this?" he asked Loralee.

"Teeny Ackermann."

Frank was already shaking his head. This couldn't be her. In the other photograph, Cullen's wife had been horribly thin, her face drawn, her hair looking as if it had been cut with dull scissors. There had been a vacant, despondent look in her eyes. Nothing like this happy, sweet-looking woman with the baby.

"I took that photograph," Loralee said. "It was about a year after Cullen married her and brought her back here to help raise his other woman's brood." She tsked, then added, "That baby she's holding? It's Kate LaFond. She can call herself anything she likes, but I'm telling you, that's her. Even you saw the resemblance."

Even me, he thought. "There is *some* resemblance," he said noncommittally.

Loralee humphed at that. "Like I said, I never forget a face. The minute I saw that cur, I knew it was the oldest Ackermann whelp. I caught him enough times stealing my vegetables from my garden. Thank my lucky stars those boys went away all those years ago. They scared me. I always knew that one especially would be back when he growed up. When I'd see him in my garden? That look he'd give me?" She shuddered and glanced toward the front door of her house. "I should have hit him harder."

Frank looked toward the hollow where the Ackermanns had lived. He had to hand it to Loralee for going up there alone. There were only a few places that he'd felt evil had holed up from some long-ago crime. That hollow was one of them.

"Lock up the house," Frank said. "I'll get one of my deputies to take you to your daughter's." He thought she'd put up a fight, but to his surprise, she didn't. "You can leave the shotgun here."

She looked skeptical.

"He won't come looking for you in Big Timber. But I'll have a deputy keep an eye on your daughter's place, just in case, until he's found."

While Loralee got together what she would need, Frank called for backup. He wasn't sure how badly the man had been bleeding. He hoped for enough blood to track him.

"Bring the dog," he told his deputy. "I want to find this man."

KATE HAD JUST TURNED onto one of the dirt roads that headed up into the Crazies when she spotted the sheriff's patrol pickup coming toward her.

She'd been upset after Jack left. He was probably right about the map being nothing more than fantasy. But Claude had believed it, and she needed to trust it, too. She felt she owed it to both her fathers—the one who had given her life—and the one who'd raised her. Both believed in lost treasure. Both had spent their lives looking for something they'd lost.

Just as she owed her mother after she'd risked her life to make the map and see that her daughter got it— and the gold.

She hoped the sheriff's patrol pickup kept going toward town. But luck wasn't with her. The pickup slowed, his window came down and he began to flag her over.

Her stomach roiled as she braked to a stop beside his truck.

"Afternoon, Sheriff. Is something wrong?" She didn't like the way he was looking at her, but she did her best not to show it.

"Why don't you pull your rig over and come join me," he said. "This is as good a place as any for what I have to tell you." He met her gaze and held it. "It's either that, or I can take you into Big Timber to my office. Whichever you prefer."

His words made her heart drop. "Like you said, this is as good a place as any to talk." Most everyone in these parts visited in the middle of the road anyway. It didn't seem strange to her in the least, knowing the sheriff.

By the time she'd pulled over and gotten out, she saw that the sheriff was standing on the other side of her truck, looking into the bed. She knew he'd seen the dirty shovel, but most rural Montanans carried a shovel to either clear a ditch on the ranch or dig their vehicle out of snow or mud.

They climbed into his patrol pickup and Kate braced herself, fearing what was to come.

The sheriff took off his Stetson and raked a hand through his hair before turning to look at her. "Something's happened."

She held her breath.

"A man broke into Loralee Clark's house yesterday evening. Fortunately, she wasn't home. But when he came back today, armed and threatening her, she fought back."

So this wasn't about her. "Is she all right?"

He nodded. "She thought she'd killed him, but she'd only wounded him. We're looking for him now."

"That's good, but what does that have to do with me?"

"Loralee says the man she wounded was Cecil Ackermann."

Kate let that sink in. Cecil. The oldest and possibly the most dangerous of the Ackermann boys. "I still don't see—"

"Kate, I need you to be honest with me. I let you give me a runaround the last time we talked, but things have changed now." He dropped a photograph on the seat between them.

SHERIFF FRANK CURRY watched the way Kate's hand trembled as she picked up the photo as if it was made of glass. He'd seen the change in her expression the moment her eyes lit on the two in the snapshot.

"Where did you get this?" she asked, her voice breaking with emotion. She wiped at her tears as she looked over at him.

"Loralee Clark. She apparently never forgets a face. She was so sure she knew you that she went through all her photos until she found this one."

Kate nodded.

"She said it was taken shortly after you were born." He couldn't help marveling at the resemblance of mother and daughter. Or the difference from this photo to the one taken eighteen months later of Teeny and her daughter.

"So you really are Teeny Ackermann's daughter," the sheriff said, unable to hide his surprise.

She didn't deny it.

"According to Loralee, your stepbrother is dangerous. If he's looking for you—"

"He's already found me."

Frank nodded. "You were the one who called in from the bar pay phone with the description of the pickup and the two men you said appeared to be armed and about to break into the general store."

She didn't deny that, either.

"Apparently after they eluded my deputy, they left for a while, but at least Cecil might have been hiding out on your father's old place."

"Cullen Ackermann wasn't my father."

He looked at her in surprise. "Oh?"

"Claude Durham was."

BILLY WESTFALL POSSESSED a handful of talents that had gotten him where he was in life. If he had to list those talents, he'd have to put good looks and charm at the top. His genes weren't far behind. He was blessed to have been born into the Westfall family.

He supposed some people wouldn't see that as a talent, but they would be wrong. Staying on the good side of his grandfather was a talent he'd acquired at a young age.

Bull Westfall not only had control of the family fortune, he also had the power. A former state senator, he also knew the right people. If anyone could get something done, it was Bull.

The Westfall ranch was thirty miles back up the Boulder River—fifty miles from Beartooth. The house sat in a wide basin of brilliant spring green.

As Billy turned down the road, several horses on the other side of the fence raced along with him, their manes blowing back in the wind.

He'd never come out here when he didn't appreciate the beauty of the spot or the grandeur. In a grove of trees stood the massive house, white-framed with a red metal roof and a wide, screened-in front porch that overlooked the river and the most fertile of Westfall land.

As he parked out front, he saw his grandfather riding in.

Bull Westfall was a short, stout man with huge, muscled shoulders that gave the impression of a bull. Thus the nickname.

Billy walked out across the yard to meet his grandfather. Shading his eyes, he tried to read what kind of mood Bull was in today. Bull cultivated a temper that apparently had something to do with his short stature.

Even at sixty-four, Bull wasn't one to back down from a fight. Not that anyone with a lick of sense was apt to start one with him.

"Nice day for a ride," Billy said as his grandfather swung down out of the saddle and handed the reins to one of the wranglers who'd run out to take them.

"William," Bull said as he strode toward the house.

Billy had gotten his nickname and his height and good looks from his mother's side of the family, bless her. Everyone had called him Billy from the time he could remember—except his grandfather. Even with his longer legs, though, he had to practically run to keep up with the older man.

"How's that new business?" Bull asked without looking at him as they entered the cool shade of the porch.

"Going great. That's why I stopped by. I'm working a case."

Bull pushed open the door to the house and stepped in, stopping just a few feet into the foyer to glance back at him. "A case, huh?"

His grandfather hadn't been happy when he'd quit being a deputy sheriff.

"I thought Frank Curry could teach you to be a man," Bull had said.

"I *am* a man. My own man. I don't need Frank Curry to teach me anything."

His grandfather had looked skeptical, but said, "I suppose you have to learn somehow. Maybe this P.I. business of yours isn't such a bad idea."

Billy couldn't have been happier at that moment to be his grandfather's favorite. "Does that mean you'll help me open my office?"

Bull was smart enough to know what Billy needed was an influx of money until he could get a few cases under his belt.

"Six months," his grandfather had said. "I'll give you six months, sink or swim."

Unfortunately, his six months had come and gone. As Billy followed his grandfather through the house, he suspected the old man thought he'd come out for more money.

The place was large and well furnished. The hardwood floors gleamed next to the huge river-rock fireplace. The furniture was soft leather, all in butterscotch, with rich wood tables and towering bookshelves. His grandfather loved to read.

"You're going to love it when I tell you who hired me," Billy said as he followed his grandfather into a kitchen better equipped than a four-star restaurant.

Bull poured himself a large glass of milk and took a long drink.

"Sheriff Frank Curry."

His grandfather slowly lowered his milk glass. "*Frank* hired you?"

Billy tried not to take offense. "I know. Pretty amazing since he never appreciated my potential."

His grandfather was studying him in a way that made Billy a little nervous. Had he already guessed what this was about? Belatedly, he realized he probably should have kept his client's name to himself.

"I could use your help with this one," Billy said. "I need to know if you've heard from Pamela Chandler. I'm sure she's kept in touch with you, or at least your sister."

Bull's expression didn't change. He lifted the glass to his lips again and drained it. "You wasted your gas driving all the way out here."

"Grandpa Bull, you have to help me," Billy said, hating the whining of his voice.

Bull met his gaze with a steely, stubborn one. "Even if I knew where Pam was—"

"If anyone knows where she is, you do."

"How many clients have you had so far?" The question took him off guard. So did the look in his grandfather's eye. He couldn't lie even though he wanted to.

"One," he said and rushed on quickly. "That's why it's so important that I find Pamela Chandler." He couldn't miss Bull's disappointed, sour expression. "I just opened my private-eye business. That's why I need your help. Once I get—"

"I'll do it."

He stared at his grandfather. "You mean it?" He broke into a big grin. "Thank you so much. I appreciate this so—"

"Don't grovel, William."

An hour later, Bull called Billy's office with Pamela Chandler's address and phone number.

WORD WAS OUT. The sheriff knew there would be no keeping a lid on this any longer. At least one Ackermann had been murdered and another was armed and on the loose. Residents would have to be warned.

Given the horror of the Ackermann history, people were bound to be scared.

With so little crime here, this kind of thing shook the foundation of everyone's lives. This would bring back the horror of what had happened over thirty years ago. The media would have a field day.

After he dropped Loralee off at her daughter's, he drove into Beartooth. Lynette was busy unloading a box of straw cowboy hats for the coming summer. She looked up when he walked in, the bell tinkling over his head.

He saw surprise, then pleasure light her face before worry knitted her brow. "Afternoon, Lynette," he said as he walked down the aisle to join her.

"What's happened?" she asked, sounding scared.

Could she read him that easily? Then she had to know how he felt about her. How he'd always felt about her. "Any chance you could put the closed sign out so we can talk undisturbed for a moment?"

She scurried past him to the front door, flipped the sign and locked the door before turning back to him. "Let's go into the office."

He nodded, thinking that was probably a good idea, even though the office still reminded him of the man

Lynette had married. Bob used to sit in there, going over the books, looking as dull as Frank suspected the man had been.

Lynette pulled the chair from behind the desk and sat down. So when he brought another chair in the room, they were facing each other, their knees nearly touching.

"If this is about Tiffany, I'm afraid she means you harm, Frank. I've already decided to give her back her money and send her packing."

He shook his head. "Please don't do that, Lynette. She's my *daughter*."

She swallowed and glanced away for a moment, but not before he'd seen the regret in her eyes. Like him, she must have wished for a child. Maybe even with him. "Is she? Is that what Pam told you? Or do you know it for a fact?"

"I haven't talked to Pam yet, but I suspect it's true. I'm trying to find her to see how it is that she didn't get around to telling me all these years. Apparently Tiffany was led to believe I didn't want her."

"Frank, I'm so sorry." She reached over to take his hand and squeeze it.

He held tight to it and gave her the rest of the news. "That man who was murdered down by the river? His name was Darrell Ackermann."

She let go of his hand and pressed both of hers against her heart. "Not—"

"One of Cullen's boys. Two of them were doing time down in Yuma and got out recently. Darrell and Gallen apparently headed for Montana. Loralee had one break into her place. She wounded him. We're searching for him now. She swears it was the oldest, Cecil."

"So they did survive." Lynette was shaking her head. "So two of them are still on the loose?"

"That is the assumption."

"Why have they come back now?"

"I'm not entirely sure." He didn't want to tell her about Kate LaFond, but he knew that by now Loralee had probably already told half the county. "Kate La-Fond is Teeny Ackermann's daughter."

Lynette's eyes widened. "With Cullen Ackermann."

He shook his head. "She says Claude Durham is her father."

NETTIE BENTON COULDN'T have been more shocked. "That's why Claude left her the café."

"Apparently."

"And the Ackermann boys have come back because of her?"

Frank seemed to hesitate only a heartbeat, but it was long enough for Nettie to put it together. "She's here for Cullen's gold."

The sheriff let out a laugh. "No one ever said you were slow on the draw, Lynette."

"The digging. She's been looking for it." Nettie frowned. "The whole bunch of them believes it really exists?"

"I'm assuming so. Lynette, I have more questions than I do answers at this point." He sounded so beat down, her heart went out to him.

She thought about Claude and the daughter no one

knew he had. At least he'd known of her. "So you really think Tiffany is your daughter?"

"The age is right, and looking back, yeah, I think it's possible," he said.

Nettie had never liked Pam Chandler. The woman had thought she was better than everyone—especially Nettie, of whom she was bitterly jealous. It was no surprise Pam could be vindictive, but to keep a daughter from Frank all these years… If Tiffany *really* was his daughter.

"Tiffany is angry, understandably, with me. She believes I abandoned her and her mother."

Nettie thought it was more than anger. "Are you sure you're safe? Really, Frank, after seeing those sketches she did of you—"

Someone banged at the back door, making them both start.

"Oh, I forgot," Nettie said. "I have another order being delivered this afternoon." She got to her feet and went to the back door to let the delivery man in.

"We'll talk soon," Frank said, his gaze lingering on her like a caress.

All she could do was nod as Frank went to the front door, flipped the sign to Open and unlocked the door. "Be careful," she called after him.

He turned and smiled back at her, but as he reached the porch steps, his gaze quickly moved up to the apartment over the store, even though Tiffany's car wasn't parked out front.

"Where do you want me to put these?" the delivery man asked, and Nettie showed him. When she looked again, she saw Frank across the street, talking to Arnie Thorndike in front of the café.

SHERIFF FRANK CURRY caught Arnie Thorndike coming out of the Branding Iron. The lawyer had a toothpick sticking out the corner of his mouth. An old straw hat covered most of his graying hair. As usual, he was dressed in a ragged flannel shirt, worn jeans and a pair of boots that should have been tossed in the trash miles ago.

"Got a moment?" Frank asked, and motioned to his patrol truck sitting down the block.

Arnie shrugged acceptance as if he had nothing better to do. He probably didn't.

"I've discovered some things about Claude Durham since the last time we talked," the sheriff said once they were seated in the pickup, windows down, a warm breeze blowing through.

"Claude?" Thorndike said. He looked tired, half-awake, as if he'd just eaten a large meal and had been on his way home for a nap.

"I know you feel a sense of loyalty to him even though he's gone."

"What's this about, Frank?"

"I asked you if you knew how Kate LaFond ended up with the café."

Thorndike nodded. "And I told you Claude left her the café. That he had his reasons."

"You failed to mention that one of his reasons was that she is his daughter. Is it true?"

"Claude didn't want anyone to know—for her sake, not his."

"Did he also not want anyone to know who her mother was?" When the lawyer didn't answer, Frank said, "So you know about Teeny Ackermann."

"And you know why Claude didn't want anyone to know," Thorndike snapped. "Can you imagine what the locals would have to say about her having any connection to the Ackermanns, let alone that her mother was married to Cullen?"

"Not legally," the sheriff pointed out.

"They lived as man and wife while Cullen's first wife was locked in a root cellar in the side of the mountain."

Frank didn't need to be reminded.

"Claude saved her," Thorndike said. "He got her out of here, set her up with a couple who was desperate for a child and kept an eye on her. He did right by her and in the end, she repaid him by giving him part of her liver."

"Why didn't you tell me this when we first talked?" Frank demanded.

"Because you were just fishing for information out of curiosity. I suspect now it's more serious. I heard that man found dead by the river was one of the Ackermann boys."

News traveled like the wild winds that came out of the Crazies, blowing through at gale force.

"I suppose you also knew Claude and Cullen were brothers." This time Frank saw surprise cross the lawyer's features. "So you *didn't* know? Claude never told you? Or Cullen? You were his lawyer, at least before he was arrested." Thorndike had just gotten out of law school about the time Cullen Ackermann had moved to the area. "So you worked for both of them but didn't know."

The lawyer chuckled and shook his head. "Neither of them ever mentioned it. They didn't look much alike and they certainly didn't act like brothers." He let out a laugh. "Hell, what am I saying? Claude knocked up Cullen's young wife. I guess they *did* act like brothers."

"Teeny wasn't legally married to Cullen, since he'd never gotten around to divorcing his first wife," Frank pointed out. "Not to mention she was being kept there like a prisoner."

"Cullen was a bastard. I can't say I'm sorry he's dead."

"You aren't going to tell me you don't know Cullen was growing pot up there in the hollow, are you?" Frank asked.

Thorndike just gave him an impatient look.

Frank shook his head. "I should warn you. Three of his sons apparently survived. That murdered man found down by the river? It was Darrell Ackermann, the younger of the surviving three. I don't see any reason they would bother you, even though you were their father's lawyer at one point. I assume he didn't leave them anything."

Thorndike shook his head, but he looked worried. "Those boys were more dangerous than Cullen."

"Cecil broke into Loralee Clark's place. When he

came back, she wounded him. We're still looking for him."

"And Gallen?"

The sheriff shook his head. "But I suspect he's around. Loralee said it looked like someone had been camping out up in the Ackermanns' old compound. When I checked it out, I found someone had been digging up there."

"Fools still believe their old man left behind a pot of gold." He shook his head. "I'm surprised they didn't get blown up or worse."

Frank thought about Kate's mother and the way she'd died up on that property, killed by one of the booby traps Cullen had built. "Is there anything else you want to tell me, Arnie?"

"You know more than I do."

He doubted that. Arnie Thorndike had always played his cards close to the vest. Then again, he was a lawyer, used to keeping people's secrets. "I just thought you might be the reason they're back—to collect their father's inheritance."

Thorndike laughed. "They come around me and they'll collect buckshot from my side-by-side shotgun."

CHAPTER NINETEEN

JACK FINISHED WORK EARLY and drove out to his family's old homestead. The last time, he'd gotten waylaid by Kate. At least that had been his excuse not to face the place that day.

Now he was determined to face a few things in his life—beginning with the old homestead, and ending with Kate LaFond and the bargain he'd made her.

The more he'd looked at the map, the more restless he had become. All his life he'd heard stories about Ackermann's gold. But he hadn't dreamed there was anything to them since he was a kid.

Kate believed it, though.

He mentally kicked himself as he admitted why he'd agreed to help her. It certainly wasn't for fifty percent of the gold. He didn't need the money. His mother's family had left him what he'd considered a small fortune. He'd never touched it.

So why agree to help Kate find gold he didn't even believe existed?

Because he had some crazy idea that he could protect her.

What a laugh. While she needed protecting, he had no idea how to keep her safe, short of kidnapping her.

That thought definitely had its appeal.

A brisk breeze blew down out of the Crazies. Overhead the sky was an incredible cloudless blue. Jack had always loved these days as a boy. Waking to the sound of birds chirping in the trees outside his bedroom window, the breeze restlessly stirring his curtains, the smell of coffee perking.

His father had brewed coffee on the stove in an old pot, refusing to buy one of those newfangled things that didn't know a damned thing about making coffee.

He thought of his father—a tall, weathered man with a quiet sadness in his blue eyes. Jack wondered if he'd ever really known his father, known the demons that haunted him.

Unconsciously, Jack slowed as the house came into view. It was a two-story, the windows blank, the once-white paint now grayed. Everything looked weathered as he pulled in, rolled to a stop and cut the engine.

He sat in the pickup for a moment before getting out and walking toward the house. The place had a worn feel about it, almost a comforting familiarity. Nearby, he could hear the steady whine of a windmill. As far as he could see to the east, the land had turned a vibrant green that appeared as smooth and lush as velvet.

Jack had never tired of this view. He'd forgotten what it was like to look across open land like this. There was something calming about it—unlike the view to the west.

The Crazies climbed skyward in the waning light of day. Rugged rock cliffs still clung to some of the light, but the dense pines were dark as the coming night.

Jack pushed open the front door. A musty, closed-up smell rushed out. Everything was covered with a thick layer of undisturbed dust. He was surprised that the local kids hadn't taken advantage of the fact that he'd been gone two years to use the house for parties, since he'd left the door unlocked. Then again, there were plenty of old barns and much cooler places to hold a kegger than the old French house.

The worn wood floors creaked under his feet as he moved like a ghost through the house. Memories assaulted him in every room, some actually good, others not so much.

He stood for a moment, looking into the deep shadows, remembering the night the sheriff had come to tell him that his father was dead.

He'd been seventeen, his birthday just weeks away.

"There's been an accident," Sheriff Frank Curry had said. "I'm sorry, Jack. Your father didn't make it."

Delbert French had been drinking, not wearing his seat belt, and the weather had been bad. Raining cats and dogs, his father would have said.

It wasn't until later that Jack had learned another vehicle had been involved. The sheriff had the paint color, so he knew it had been an older model blue pickup.

A half dozen people in Montana drove a pickup with that particular paint color. But only two lived in the area. One of the trucks had been abandoned for years and no longer ran.

The other one was owned by Ruth McCray. It was the one her son, Hitch, drove around the ranch. By the time the sheriff learned this, Hitch had already reported the pickup stolen.

Jack had always suspected that Frank Curry wasn't fooled. That like Jack, he had to suspect that Hitch had been behind the wheel that night. But the pickup had never turned up. Jack could only guess where it was now. In some deep ravine up in the mountains? Or at the bottom of Saddlestring Lake?

Either way, it was gone and even if Jack had found it, what would it prove? Hitch would stick to his story that it had been stolen.

Knowing the truth didn't always set you free, Jack thought now as he walked through the house to the back door. The back steps groaned under his weight and he had to wade through dried leaves from two past autumns.

As he walked toward the barn, a memory as bright as the afternoon flashed before him of playing in the hayloft one summer day. Maybe there were one or two good memories here, he thought as he stepped into the cool shade of the huge structure.

He surveyed the last of his inheritance. The house would definitely have to be razed and some of the outbuildings, too. The bunkhouse where he'd been staying when he was arrested was still in good shape.

The two rusted T's of the clothesline were still behind the house with several sagging lines still hanging between them. When he thought of his mother, he pictured her in a cotton-print dress, hanging clothes on the line behind the house. But he'd been so young, he wasn't sure that was even a memory.

Wind swayed the high grass in the pasture, undulating like waves. Looming over it all were the Crazies, snowcapped and pristine, looking cold and unforgiving.

For a moment, he stood merely breathing in the spring day, remembering how he used to feel about this land.

His cell phone rang.

"You didn't call," she said by way of greeting when Jack answered the phone without looking to see who was calling.

"*Chantell?* How did you get my number?"

"Carson. He was so sweet to give it to me. Don't be mad at him." She did her pouting sound that apparently worked so well for her.

"What do you want, Chantell?"

"You promised you would call me." He hadn't, but before he could argue the point, she continued. "It's not because of that woman who owns the Branding Iron, is it?" She scoffed at the idea. "I saw you talking to her at the fair. She's really not your type, Jack."

He gritted his teeth, surprised anything she would say could make him angry. Apparently her talking about Kate could. "Listen, Chantell—"

"Come on, Jack. You and I were good together."

"Too good together, if you ask your father."

She sighed. "You can't be angry at him for sending you to prison! Jack, he's a *judge.*"

"Even judges aren't above the law."

"What are you talking about?"

"I didn't steal that bull."

"Daddy says that's what they all say," she said, laughing.

"I was set up."

Her laugh died off into silence for a few moments. "Set up? By whom?"

The "whom" reminded him of her Ivy League college education. Jack had graduated from Montana State College, or Cow College as it was known.

"Your father."

This time the silence was much longer.

Then an impatient "Jack."

"I'm going to prove it and bust his ass." The moment the words were out, he knew that had been what he was going to do the whole time. He'd just been deluding himself if he'd thought he could let it go.

"That's crazy," she said, and he could tell she was wishing she hadn't called.

"Not really. He never liked you dating me, Chantell. Maybe he thought we were getting too serious. Or maybe he was just tired of seeing you date a saddle bum. Isn't that what he called me? Whatever the reason, he did it."

"He rustled a bull and put it in your barn to frame you? Jack, that's ludicrous."

Jack told himself to stop. If he really was going after the judge then he didn't want the judge knowing it. Nor did he want to show his hand by telling her how her father had done it. "He hired it done. Let's leave it at that."

"I'm sorry, Jack." Not sorry her father had framed

him. Not sorry he'd spent two years of his life behind bars for something he hadn't done.

Nope, she was just sorry she'd called. He could well imagine her saying to her friends, "Jack French used to be fun." Then making her sad face before she quickly got over it.

"Take care of yourself, Jack," she said and hung up.

He snapped his phone shut and climbed up to the hayloft to look out over this place where he'd grown up. The wind whistled past the eaves. An old rocker on the back porch of the house seemed to lean into the gale. He used to sit in that rocker at night, staring up at the Crazies, drinking beer and daydreaming about his future.

He hadn't daydreamed about his future in years.

At the sound of a vehicle coming up the road, he watched from the open door of the hayloft as a red pickup came roaring up into the yard in a cloud of dust.

"Kate?"

KATE CLIMBED OUT of the pickup as dust settled around it. She could see Jack silhouetted in the doorway of the barn hayloft. He was leaning against the doorjamb, that cocky way he had about him when he wasn't sure what was going to happen next.

She herself didn't know. All the way out here, she'd questioned what she was doing. For years she'd prided herself on not needing anyone else in her life. Then Claude had come into the café that day and turned her life upside down.

"Out sightseeing?" Jack asked as she climbed up

into the loft. It smelled warm like a summer day, the rich scent of dried hay in the air.

Jack narrowed his eyes, intelligence and curiosity at war with each other in all that blue, as she closed the distance between them.

"I was looking for you," she said, realizing how true that was, and not just today. Maybe she'd been looking for Jack French her whole life and just hadn't known it. The question was: What was she going to do about it now?

"Looking for me, huh? Well, it seems you've found me." He was waiting for her to make the first move, practically daring her to. Challenge shone in his eyes as she stopped just inches from him.

"Somethin' on your mind?" he asked, the low timbre of his voice like a caress across her skin.

Kate met his gaze. For the first time, she saw the flecks of gold in that sea of blue. His gaze invited her in for more than a quick dip.

She placed a palm on his chest, thought she felt his heart beating like a war drum beneath the cool feel of his Western shirt, but it could have been her own pulse she felt. All she'd thought about on the way out here was being in Jack's arms. She tried not to question it—didn't want to believe that she was running scared and had run to him out of fear.

But maybe that was easier to admit than her coming here out of a burning desire she was tired of fighting. Rocking forward onto the toes of her boots, she leaned into him to brush her lips across his.

His eyes locked with hers. "You sure you want to go down this trail?" he asked, his voice husky and low.

THE MOMENT SHE LOOKED into his eyes, Jack knew he was lost. He caught Kate's hand and dragged her to him as he drew back into the cool dark of the hayloft. Her soft, supple and lush body collided with his. He cupped her face in his hands, his gaze still locked with hers, and kissed her the way he'd been wanting to for too long.

Her lips opened to his, a soft moan escaping her mouth. He'd never wanted a woman the way he did her. This had been a long time coming, as if it had been written in the stars that they would end up here.

"Kate," he whispered as he drew back to look into that amazing face of hers. When his gaze lighted again on her eyes, he saw desire burning like an open flame that caught him up in its fire.

He swung her up into his arms and carried her over to a pile of hay. They both tumbled into it, tearing at each other's clothing in a need to free themselves of everything between them.

The snaps sung on her Western shirt as he jerked it open. He slipped the hook on the front of her bra, her full breasts filling his hands. He bent to run his tongue over the hard, dark pink points. She moaned beneath him, and he let out a groan of his own as his mouth returned to hers.

She rolled them both over so she was on top and pulled off his shirt, then pressed her warm palms to his chest, her eyes locked with his. He reached for the buttons on her jeans and she wiggled out of them. Her fingers went to the buttons of his jeans, and within pulse-pounding seconds they were both naked in a bed of their discarded clothing atop the hay pile.

They made love with a wild, uninhibited passion. Breathlessly collapsing in the bed of hay, Jack lay beside her. He couldn't take his eyes off her. She was so beautiful and so complicated. She'd given herself to him, but as intimate as they'd been, he realized he knew little more about her.

He ran a finger along her scar and felt her tense. Bending over, he traced it with kisses. A sound like a sob came from her, more powerful than any sound he'd ever heard. He thought his heart would burst.

She drew him up so they were at eye level again. She opened her lips, but then closed them again.

"You don't have to tell me," he whispered.

"I gave someone part of my liver."

He felt his eyes widen in surprise. "Whoa. That's amazing."

"It wasn't that big of a deal."

"Yes, it was. It must have been someone you cared an awful lot about."

She said nothing, but tears suddenly filled her eyes. He drew her to him, holding her.

"From the first time I met you, I've thought you were an incredible woman. You just keep surprising me."

"Don't, Jack." She drew away, turning her back to him as she picked up her shirt and shrugged it on.

"What's wrong?"

"I'm not the woman you think I am," she said, her back still to him.

"Kate." He touched her shoulder, pulling her down next to him. "I like whoever you are. But isn't it time you were honest with me?"

TEARS BLURRED HER EYES. Kate had told herself that she just needed to get Jack out of her system. She'd actually believed that once she gave herself to him, she could walk away. She willed herself not to cry, but Jack's passion and tenderness was her undoing. Just moments before, the way he'd touched her scar, lowering his head to gently kiss his way across her abdomen. A shudder of desire raced through her already heated blood. The man could be so tough and yet so gentle. So infuriating and yet so…lovable.

She pulled away from him. "There's something I need to tell you."

He propped himself up on one elbow. "I'm listening."

Kate licked her lips, tried to still her pounding heart. She knew she should have told him the moment she saw him. But confessing had been the last thing on her mind when she'd seen him in the hayloft door.

"This is about the dead man, isn't it?" he said.

She met his gaze and slowly nodded. "The sheriff identified the man. His name is Darrell Ackermann."

Jack stared at her. "*Ackermann?* A relative of Cullen Ackermann?" She could see him putting it all together. He let out a curse and sat up. "What are you telling me?"

"I didn't kill him over the gold, if that's what you're thinking," she said quickly.

"But that's what this is all about. The map. The gold." He shook his head. "I thought all the Ackermann boys were dead."

"Apparently three of them survived." She swallowed. "And the daughter."

His eyes widened. "Kate?"

"Darrell Ackermann was kind of my stepbrother."

Jack was shaking his head. "How is that possible?"

"I was born on the compound. My mother was the woman everyone calls Teeny Ackermann, only she and Cullen were never married and Cullen wasn't my father." She nodded at his confusion. "My father got me out right before the compound was stormed thirty years ago. He sent me to a couple he knew who desperately wanted a child. I was adopted but that's all I knew...until recently."

JACK DIDN'T KNOW what to think. He stared at her in disbelief as all the pieces of the puzzle that was Kate LaFond tried to fall into place in his head—but refused to fit.

"You said Cullen wasn't your father?"

She shook her head. "Claude Durham was."

Another piece of puzzle dropped into place. The café.

"And the scar?"

"I gave part of my liver to Claude. I was a perfect match. But it was too late. I couldn't save him."

"And he gave you his café and the map."

She nodded.

The pieces were coming together faster than the speed of light, making his head hurt. He thought about the note someone had left her at the café. Another chunk of puzzle slid in. "But now people know who you are."

"Loralee Clark recognized me. She knew my mother. She gave the sheriff a photograph of me when I was a baby. I look like my mother did when she was young. Apparently few people ever saw her, though, since Cullen Ackermann and his sons kept her a prisoner up in that hollow."

"But Loralee didn't leave you the note at the café, so someone else knows who you are and why you're here."

She nodded. "They think I can find the gold. One of them must have seen my mother making the map."

"That would be my guess. So what are you going to do about it?"

"I don't have a choice. I have to find the gold."

With a curse Jack got to his feet and pulled on his jeans. He heard her rise and follow him to the open door of the hayloft. He flinched when she put a hand on his bare back, and she withdrew it.

"I wanted to tell you—"

He spun on her. "How many secrets do you have? I feel as if I've just brushed the surface." He met her gaze. "Were you ever going to tell me the truth? Don't answer that. We both know the only reason you told me is that everyone else in the county must know by now." He swore again. "That's why you came out here, that's why you…" He motioned toward the hay where they'd lain entwined only minutes before.

"No, that's not true."

He brushed her protest aside. "All of this has only been about the gold."

"You're wrong, Jack." But her words lacked conviction and they both knew it.

"No, you're willing to risk everything for the gold, and anyone who gets in your way better look out." He shook his head. "Why can't you just be satisfied with what you have?"

"Because I'm not like you," she snapped. "I go after what I want." He saw that she regretted the words the moment they were out. But it was too late. He knew for certain now that she saw him as nothing but a saddle bum.

With a disgusted shake of his head, he stepped past her to finish dressing and then he climbed down from the hayloft and headed for his pickup.

"Jack—"

He didn't look back. He couldn't.

CHAPTER TWENTY

WHEN FRANK CALLED TIFFANY, to his surprise, she said she would like to ride later. So that afternoon he saddled their horses and the two of them had taken a long ride. She took to riding well and even smiled a few times.

He thought they might talk on the ride, but the afternoon was so beautiful and his attempts at conversation were met with sullenness, so he gave up and just enjoyed the ride.

Tiffany was a mystery to him. Her moods seemed to change in an instant. The things he thought would make her happy seldom did. And while she enjoyed the horseback ride, even though she didn't say it, as soon as it was over she wanted to go home.

"I thought we could go into Big Timber for pizza," he said.

"I don't like pizza." She said it as if he should have known that.

What kid didn't like pizza?

"We could get a burger. A tofu burger or one of those mushroom things that are supposed to taste like a burger," he added quickly, remembering that she was a vegetarian. Probably also her mother's idea, since Pam knew he raised beef.

Tiffany gave a hard shake of her head. "I'm tired. I want to go home."

"Where is home?" he asked.

She shot him a look that said she was too smart to fall for that.

"Is it so hard for you to understand that I want to talk to your mother?"

"You don't want to *talk* to her. You want to *yell* at her. Or maybe even arrest her."

"On what charge?"

She shrugged and looked away. "She doesn't want to talk to you."

"I'll bet."

"See," she said. "You do want to yell at her."

He let it drop. But it ate at him. He could understand Tiffany wanting to protect her mother. It was another thing for Pam not to have the guts to talk to him.

He thought of friends who'd gone through divorces. The kids often took the side of the mother. The fathers just got the blame, the bills and the attitude. Frank had often asked them why they didn't fight back, tell the kids what was really going on, but they'd just thrown their hands up and said, "What would be the point? My ex would turn it around to make me look like the bad guy. Even if she didn't, the kids wouldn't believe it. They feel sorry for their mother, protective, and believe me, my ex plays the helpless act like a pro."

Frank had seen that what usually happened was the ex-wife remarried, the kids came around and it all ended okay. So maybe he'd been right about keeping his mouth shut, just enjoying his daughter and letting bygones be bygones.

But just the thought of Pam getting away with what she'd done…

He wanted to tell Tiffany that he was a reasonable man and it was ridiculous for her mother to act as if he was dangerous.

But she might have a point.

AFTER HIS FIGHT with Kate, Jack drove back to town, parked outside his cabin and sat, too shaken to get out of his truck. The lovemaking had been incredible. He'd never felt anything near what he felt with Kate.

Which made it so much worse that she'd used him. All this had always been about the gold and nothing else. He thought again of her naked in his arms. Now he knew how far the woman would go to get what she wanted.

He couldn't face the empty cabin, and in the mood he was in there was a good chance he could find himself in trouble if he went down to the Range Rider. He could feel that brawling French blood of his just itching for a fight.

But he could no more keep his boots from heading down that hill to the bar than he could quit thinking about making love with Kate.

He'd made a point of avoiding the bar since he'd gotten out of prison, except on those few occasions when he had met with Carson. But this evening, he felt the need for the cool darkness of the bar, and a cold beer sounded good right now. And if anyone else in town was looking for a fight, then he would gladly oblige.

He wondered as he walked down to the bar if Kate had ever been honest with him about anything. Certainly not about him or what she was doing in Beartooth.

Jack cursed under his breath, wanting to forget about her for a while as he pushed open the door to the bar and stepped in. It took a moment for his eyes to adjust to the semidarkness of the cool bar. He was surprised the place was so empty until he realized the time.

The sun had gone down hours ago. It was dinnertime, which meant none of the men in the bar had a woman or a meal to go home to. Two wranglers sat at a table by the jukebox. The only other patron was at the bar.

With an oath, Jack recognized him. Hitch McCray.

Good sense told him to turn around and hightail it out of there. Hitch had probably spent most of the afternoon on that very stool. He'd be half drunk by now, and given the animosity between them…

"Howdy, Jack," Clete Reynolds called as he came out of the cooler with a case of beer and set it behind the bar.

"Clete," he said as he sauntered over to the bar, taking a seat four stools away from Hitch. The other times he'd been in the bar, Clete hadn't been working, so this was the first time they'd seen each other.

"Glad you're back," the bar owner said. "Heard you're working out at the W Bar G. What can I get you? It's on the house to welcome you home."

"Just a beer, thanks."

Clete opened him a cold one and set it on a bar napkin in front of him as the two wranglers in the corner said they'd have another round.

Clete went to serve them and Jack felt himself tense as Hitch slid off his stool, grabbed up his beer bottle and came down the bar to take the stool next to him.

"Clete acts like you've been away fighting for your country's freedom instead of in prison," Hitch said with a sneer. "He won't even let *me* run a tab, let alone buy me a drink."

Jack had heard that Hitch's mother had cut his allowance after his last drunk-driving arrest. Jack couldn't feel anything but contempt for a forty-year-old man who was still tied to his mother's apron strings. Add to that his suspicion that Hitch was responsible not only for his father's death, but also for setting him up on the rustling charge, and Jack felt a raging hatred for the man.

And his mother, Jack realized. Ruth McCray had to have covered for her son the night of the hit-and-run accident that killed Jack's father's. So she was just as culpable as her son.

"But, hell, you've got money. I just found out your mother left you a bundle. No wonder you wouldn't sell the place to me," Hitch said, turning on his stool to look at Jack. "You could at least buy me a drink."

The money was invested. That was one reason he hadn't touched it. The other reason was that he feared he'd do something stupid with it and disappoint his mother. So it had stayed invested and turned into more money than he knew what to do with. He wondered how Hitch had found out about his inheritance, not that it mattered.

"So are you going to buy me a drink or not?" Hitch demanded.

Jack's first impulse was to drag Hitch out behind the Range Rider and beat the hell out of him. But maybe he had changed more than he realized. He suddenly saw this moment as one of those crossroads in life where there's an opportunity to take the right fork. He'd come to a lot of forks in the road in his thirty-one years— and had often taken the wrong one.

As he looked over at Hitch, he knew this was another one of those times when he had the opportunity to go down a different road.

"Why not?" Jack said, and motioned to Clete as he returned to set one up for Hitch.

Clete looked surprised and concerned as he opened a beer and set it in front of Hitch. "I can't let him drive if he has any more to drink."

"Not to worry," Jack said as he picked up Hitch's keys from the bar where he'd dropped them when he'd sat down. "I'll see that Hitch gets home."

Hitch started to object, but Jack raised his beer bottle.

"To Hitch," he said and took a drink. "And who says I'm not interested in selling my place?"

Hitch seemed a little confused. He'd obviously come down the bar looking for trouble. He hadn't expected this. Fortunately, he'd already had enough to drink that it didn't take much persuading to get him to have more.

Three beers later, Hitch was slurring his words and having trouble staying on the bar stool.

"Best get you home," Jack said, taking Hitch's arm. "I'm as scared of your mother as you are."

Hitch tried to argue the point as Jack helped him out the back door of the bar. "Let's take your truck, Hitch. I'll see that you get it back tomorrow."

He poured Hitch into the passenger side of the truck and before he could get around to the driver's side, the cowboy was snoring.

Jack let Hitch sleep as he drove out of town. But at a literal fork in the road, Jack turned the opposite direction from the McCray ranch and headed toward Saddlestring Lake.

In the twilight, the pines were dark as the inside of a boot, the sky overhead a gleaming silver as Jack drove the ribbon of road deeper and deeper into the Crazies. He couldn't help being a little afraid of what he might do once they reached the spot he had in mind. But there was no turning back. This had been coming for a very long time.

The road climbed in a series of switchbacks up the side of a mountain before it opened on a high plateau. Jack slowed as the lake came into view. Saddlestring was one of those high mountain lakes set like a jewel in the rocks and pines. As if bottomless, the water was a dark, crystalline blue-green.

He stopped the pickup high above the lake next to a sheer rock cliff, and cut the engine.

"Time to wake up," he said to Hitch as he got out, and came around to the passenger side to drag the man from the truck.

BILLY PRACTICALLY JUMPED up and down he was so happy after his grandfather's call. He couldn't wait to see

Sheriff Frank Curry's face when he told him he'd found his ex-wife.

Still, he hated just turning it over to him without knowing why Frank would want to get hold of a woman he'd divorced almost eighteen years ago.

Billy rubbed a hand over his stubbled jaw as he caught his reflection in his office window. He had the looks of a movie star. Many women had told him that.

Maybe because of that, he'd always thought he'd been born to great things. Often it felt as if he'd been waiting around his whole life for those great things to begin.

As he studied himself in the glass, he realized how much he missed his deputy sheriff uniform—and the gun. He'd become quite proficient at quick drawing—another reason Frank Curry had threatened to fire him.

"You're going to shoot your damned leg off, Billy. Grow up."

He felt that bitter taste in his mouth at the memory of the way the sheriff had treated him, calling him Billy the Kid and making fun of him.

Billy looked down at the address and phone number he'd written on the tablet on his desk.

He'd been so excited to see Frank's face, but the thought of giving him what he wanted without first knowing why was just too great.

Frank had ordered him not to contact the woman. But Frank Curry wasn't his boss anymore, was he.

Billy picked up the phone and dialed the number. If Pam was hiding from her ex, she might not take a call from Montana. But if she saw *W. Westfall* on her caller ID—

"Hello, Bull?"

"Pam, it's Billy Westfall."

"Billy. I thought it was Bull calling."

He smiled to himself, pleased that it had worked just as he'd suspected it might. "I don't know if my grandfather told you when he called you…"

"I haven't talked to him. Why? Has something happened?"

He heard worry in her tone. "Bull's fine. It's about another matter."

"Oh?" It amazed him how much smugness she could put into one little word. Clearly she'd been waiting for a call from Frank and knew only too well why he was looking for her. That's why she'd made herself so hard to find.

"I opened my own private investigation business," Billy said. "Guess who one of my first clients is?"

"I'm afraid to." She was a terrible liar.

"Sheriff Frank Curry."

"I'm not sure why you would think I was interested in that, Billy," she said carefully.

He laughed. "Let's cut the crap, Pam. Give me one good reason not to turn this information over to him. Better yet, make that a thousand, in cash along with some information."

"What kind of information?"

"Tell me why he wants to find you so badly, while I tell you how to transfer that thousand dollars to my business account."

THE MOMENT KATE opened the door to her apartment, she froze. Her thoughts had been on Jack and what had happened between them earlier. She'd been filled with deep regret, especially about what she'd said to him right before he'd walked out.

"Why can't you just be satisfied with what you have?"

"Because I'm not like you," she'd snapped. *"I go after what I want."*

If only she could take back those words or the hurt she'd seen on his face, as if each word had been an arrow to his heart.

So deep in regret was she that it took her a moment to realize what she was seeing.

The place had been ransacked. Her treasure magazines were all over the room, many crushed under a boot heel, their covers dirty and torn.

Anger propelled her deeper into the apartment, even though she knew whoever had done this could still be inside. She hadn't gone but a couple of steps when the door, caught by the wind, slammed behind her, making her jump.

She froze again, listening, hearing nothing but her own pounding heart. Earlier she'd checked to see if Jack was at his cabin before going out to the French place looking for him. She'd changed clothes and when she did, she'd left behind her gun.

Kate wished she had it now as she checked each room. Fortunately, the apartment was small and there weren't a lot of places to hide.

The entire place had been gone through, but the intruder hadn't found the map, she thought with a wave of relief. She still had the map from when Jack had given it back to her earlier. The map was probably worthless, but it was all she had of her mother.

A thought zipped past at the speed of a bullet. Hurrying to her bedroom, she dug in her bureau drawer.

Her gun was gone.

"WHAT THE HELL?" Hitch cried as Jack dragged him to the edge of the cliff.

Jack watched fear sober him up some. "Here's the deal. I know you were the one who ran my father off the road that night years ago. You were driving that old blue truck of yours, weren't you? Probably half-drunk at the time."

Hitch wagged his head as he did his best to lean away from the cliff edge. "No, I told you, you're wrong. It wasn't me." Several rocks dislodged under his feet and careened down, eventually hitting far below like the echo of a rifle report.

"The truck wasn't stolen like you told the sheriff, was it? You were just covering for yourself. Does your mother know the truth? She must have helped you get rid of the pickup."

"It was stolen. I'm telling you the truth. Jack, you have to believe me."

"Just like you didn't put that bull in my corral?"

Hitch didn't answer and for a moment, Jack feared the fool had passed out. As it was, Hitch was having trouble staying on his feet.

But then, Hitch slowly raised his head. "It was just supposed to be a joke."

Jack felt his pulse take off like a rocket. He'd known it was something like this and yet he'd feared he would never know the truth. He'd known Hitch would be the perfect candidate for the job and yet he hadn't been sure until that moment.

"Who put you up to it?"

Hitch wagged his head again.

Jack gripped him tighter by the shirt collar and shoved him closer to the edge of the cliff. More rocks dislodged as Hitch fought to keep his footing. "Who put you up to it?"

"You can't *kill* me."

"You're so drunk that you could fall off this cliff. Everyone would just think you took a wrong turn."

"No, Clete knows you took my keys, saying you were going to give me a ride home."

"Clete also knows what an asshole you can be. All I have to do is tell him that I tried to drive you home, but you overpowered me and took your truck. How do you know I didn't call the sheriff before driving up here to tell him I saw you driving drunk again? That I tried to stop you but couldn't?"

Hitch looked more terrified than he had before.

"It makes sense," Jack said. "You probably drove up here to sober up before you saw your mother. I'll swear to all of it, just as you swore you had nothing to do with my father's death, unless you tell me the truth now."

When he didn't answer, Jack shoved him closer to the edge. A large chunk of earth broke off, rocks and dirt cascading down the cliff. Hitch began to scream as the earth under him gave way.

CHAPTER TWENTY-ONE

SHERIFF FRANK CURRY wasn't surprised when Billy Westfall called late that night. Bull Westfall had always given his grandson anything he wanted.

Frank had worried, though, that Bull might have lost contact with Pam. The call confirmed what he'd suspected. Bull Westfall had more power than pretty much anyone in the county. Except for maybe Judge Hyett.

"Frank, I need to see you," Billy said, sounding as cocky as he always had.

"Just give me the information and I'll send you a check."

"Stop by my office." Billy hung up.

Frank swore as he snapped off his phone. He'd put up with Billy the Kid Westfall while he was a deputy, but fortunately Billy had stepped over the line so far the last time that even his grandfather couldn't save his job for him.

Five minutes later, he walked into Billy's office. The punk had his boots up on his desk, leaning back in his chair and looking overconfident and overbearing.

"Get your gloating over with quickly. I need to get back to work," Frank said as he pulled out his checkbook, leaned on the corner of Billy's desk and began to write.

"I found her."

"I figured." He didn't look up as he filled in everything but the amount on the check.

"She told me something really interesting."

Frank stopped dead and slowly looked up. "I told you not to talk to her."

"That girl staying over the store. She's the daughter you've denied for seventeen years."

Frank considered himself a peaceful man. It took a lot to rile him. "Billy," he said between gritted teeth as he stepped around the desk to stand over the former deputy.

Taken by surprise, Billy tried to swing his boots off his desk to stand, but Frank was on him, holding his legs where they were as he tilted the former deputy's chair back until it was dangerously close to tipping over.

"I'm going to give you five seconds to give me the information," Frank said in a voice that brooked no argument. "Then I'm going to write you a check and walk out of here."

"Get off me," Billy cried.

"Are we clear on that, Billy?" Frank asked, ignoring him. "Because if I tilt your chair back any farther, I fear you might go out that second-story window. I doubt the fall will kill you, but I can only hope."

"You can't *threaten* me," he blustered, though it lacked much conviction.

"I'm not *threatening* you. I'm just trying to get out of this office with the least amount of bloodshed."

Billy visibly swallowed and reached for his desk.

Frank let go of him so he could sit up. Billy opened a file on the desk and pulled out a slip of paper with an address and a phone number.

Frank took it from his hand. "I changed my mind. Bill me." He started for the door.

"But I got you what you wanted."

He stopped and turned to look back at Billy. "I would imagine since you talked to her I won't be able to reach her at either the number or her address," Frank said, folding the note and putting it into his pocket. "If that's the case, then I won't be paying you, Billy, because you didn't do the job I asked of you. Consider this a learning experience. Your next client just might push you out that window."

"I'll take you to court."

"You do that," Frank said, and walked out.

AT FIRST, HITCH'S WORDS were indistinguishable from his screams. But when the words finally registered, Jack pulled Hitch back from the edge of the cliff.

Hitch collapsed on the ground.

"Tell me that again," Jack ordered.

Hitch gasped for breath. When he finally looked up, he was pale, sweating and at least partially sober. "My mother let me take the new pickup the night your father died. I wasn't even driving the old blue one. I swear. I went to a kegger down on the Yellowstone. It wasn't until the next morning that I went out to get into my old truck to get feed and it was gone. That's when my mother told me to call the sheriff and tell him that someone had stolen the truck. She said it must have been some kids who took it for a joy ride. We both thought it would turn up, probably wrecked."

"But it never did."

Hitch shook his head. "That's all I know. I swear."

"And the bull in my corral?"

Hitch looked down at his lap for a moment before he mumbled, "I didn't have a choice."

Those were the words Jack had heard through the man's screams as he'd dangled him at the edge of the cliff.

"Everyone has a choice, Hitch," Jack said.

"I couldn't get another DUI," he cried. "My mother was threatening to cut me off. I was going to lose the ranch, lose everything."

"So what did you do?" Jack asked.

"Judge Hyett offered me a deal," he said, crying now.

"And that deal?"

"I thought he just wanted to teach you a lesson," Hitch said. "He said you were dating his daughter, getting serious, that you needed a wake-up call before it was too late, that it was a little joke on you, bring you down to size."

Jack nodded. "And you'll swear on it to the sheriff, because if you renege, I'll see you at the bottom of this cliff one way or another."

Hitch nodded solemnly. "I'll tell the sheriff."

"Then let's go pick up Cody West so he can verify your story."

"You know about Cody, too?" Hitch asked in surprise.

"I do now."

FRANK DIDN'T CALL Pam's number. Not right away. He had little hope that she would answer when he did, so he was shocked when she picked up, since it was so late.

"Hello?"

Hearing her voice, he realized Tiffany was right. He didn't want to talk to her. He wanted to scream obscenities at her.

"Is that you, Frank?" she asked, as if she hadn't already known from caller ID. She'd obviously been waiting for his call.

He counted to ten before he said, "Why, Pam? Just tell me why." He heard the defeat in his voice and knew she did, too.

"I'm sorry, why what?"

"Stop. I know what you did. I can even guess why. But Pam, you knew how badly I wanted a child. Why did you have to do this?"

Silence filled the line and he thought for a moment she might have hung up.

"You lost all rights to me and the child I was carrying seventeen years ago." Her voice sounded brittle and merciless. He'd heard it before, but others only saw her innocent-looking face, the one she put on to hide what lay just below the surface—a heartless ability to be cruel and spiteful, to use an innocent child to get revenge.

"It was one thing to keep Tiffany from me out of spite, but to tell her lies about me? You know I never meant to hurt you."

"Oh, please."

"It's the truth. I tried, Pam."

"Yes," she agreed. "Don't you realize how much worse that made it? I saw you trying every day. You had to try so hard to love me, didn't you, Frank?" Her voice broke and he felt a stab of sympathy for her. He hadn't realized how much he'd hurt her. "Something that was so easy with Lynette was impossible with me. Was I that unlovable?"

"No." The sympathy he felt for her was overshadowed by the malevolence in what she'd done. "Pam, you did a horrible thing to your own daughter, and all in an attempt to hurt me, you've hurt her."

"Oh, please," she snapped. "She'll get over it. You will, too. I could have told her you died. I'm sure you've told her your side of it. So what real harm is done?"

Did she really not know how much harm she'd done to their child? "Do you hate me that much?"

Her laugh was like glass breaking. He felt a chill run through him. As a sheriff, he knew there was nothing more ugly or dangerous than a woman scorned.

"I'm sorry that you've spent the past eighteen years plotting misery," he said. "I doubt it has enriched your life or made you happy."

"You're wrong about that," she snapped. "I swore

when I left you that someday you would feel what I felt."

"Well, you've achieved what you set out to do. It must give you a real sense of accomplishment."

"It does. I just wish there was more I could have done to hurt you," she said. "She's your daughter now. I want nothing more to do with her."

"You can't mean that."

"I do. I told her if she left to go find her father not to bother coming back."

"Pam, how could you—" But he realized she'd already hung up.

Poor Tiffany. His heart broke at the thought of what she must be going through. He wadded-up Pam's phone number and address and threw it in the fire. He wouldn't look for her again, because he knew that if he found her, he couldn't trust himself not to kill her.

At the sound of a vehicle, he looked up to see Hitch McCray's pickup pull into his ranch yard. "What the devil does Hitch—" To his surprise, Jack French climbed out from behind the wheel. A moment later, Cody West got out of the passenger side, followed by a clearly half-drunk Hitch McCray.

SHERIFF FRANK CURRY listened as Jack related what he'd discovered about Judge Hyett. That Jack had been framed didn't come as a surprise. He'd suspected there were others involved and that Jack had covered for them. He'd even suspected the reason the judge had thrown the book at Jack had something to do with Hyett's only daughter.

That the judge had been involved caught him completely off guard. "Is this true?" he asked Hitch.

The man smelled like a brewery. It was apparent that he'd only recently sobered up. "I had to take the deal or do jail time," Hitch said. "My mother couldn't run the ranch alone."

Frank knew Hitch was more worried that his mother would disown him. Hitch needed to stay on his mother's good side if he ever hoped to get the family ranch. Everyone in the county knew that. Ruth McCray had bailed out her son two other times. This time could have been the last straw, and Hitch would have known that.

"What about you?" Frank asked Cody West. The kid was in his late teens, nice looking like the rest of the West men, and all cowboy.

"Yes, sir, I did help Mr. McCray take the bull and put it in Mr. French's corral. The judge led me to believe it was a prank. I never would have done it if I'd known Mr. French would be sent to prison."

"And after you realized that was the case?" Frank asked.

Cody West looked down at his boots and nervously turned the brim of his Stetson in his fingers. "I spoke to Judge Hyett, and he warned me to keep my trap shut or something like that could happen to me."

"So you kept quiet."

"I didn't want to, but it would have been my word against the judge's," Cody said. "Also, I didn't want my father to find out what I'd done."

"I'm going to need your statements," Frank said.

"I need all of it—what the judge told you, how this worked and everything that happened that night."

"Jack, it might be best if we left you out of this," he said. "Once this hits the fan, you can file a lawsuit for wrongful imprisonment if you're interested."

"I'm not," Jack said. "I just wanted to set the record straight."

Frank nodded. "Leave that to me."

"WHAT HAPPENS NOW?" Hitch asked after he and Cody had written down their statements and given them to Frank.

"There will be an investigation and complaint. Judge Hyett committed willful misconduct in office and violated the Canons of Judicial Ethics. He will have to face discipline from the Judicial Standards Commission, a regulatory committee under the auspices of the state supreme court."

"What will they do to him?" Cody asked.

"It depends," Frank said. "Public censure or suspension. Or they could force him to retire."

"He should have to go to prison like Jack did," Cody said.

The sheriff shook his head. "That won't happen. But Judge Hyett isn't fool enough to try something like this again—if they don't force him to retire."

Frank looked to Jack.

"It's enough," Jack said.

"I'd stay away from his daughter, though," the sheriff added. "Just to be on the safe side."

Jack laughed. "No problem there."

Frank thought about warning him away from Kate LaFond. But while he liked Jack—might have had a son his age if he and Lynette had stayed together—he couldn't save Jack French from himself.

But maybe this would help Jack turn things around. Frank sure hoped so.

He thought of his daughter, Tiffany, and wished there was something he could do to help her. He felt just as helpless when it came to her.

CODY PROMISED TO drive Hitch home after dropping Jack off at the bottom of the mountain below his cabin. "I'll see that he gets his truck back tomorrow," Cody said.

Both Cody and Hitch had had little to say after the three of them had left the sheriff's house. Both had confessed to what they'd done. The sheriff had made each of them put it in their own writing and sign and date it, telling them they would probably both be called to testify before a judicial committee at some point.

Now as Jack climbed the side of the mountain to his cabin, the sun was just coming up in the east. He'd thought he would feel better. His name would be cleared. He would no longer be a felon, but there was no getting back the two years it had cost him.

The sheriff had warned him that probably not much would happen to Judge Hyett. "Jack, there is a range of possible disciplinary actions that could be taken, private admonition to forced retirement. My guess, though, is if he has no other prior misconduct complaints, he will get public censure and that will be the extent of it."

"You're not telling me anything I didn't already figure."

The sheriff had laid a hand on his shoulder. "I'm sorry for what you've been through, Jack."

He was sorry, too. Sorry he didn't feel a sense of satisfaction; but what had taken place between him and Kate earlier weighed on him more than having just cleared his name.

All he could think about now was climbing into his bed and losing himself in the oblivion of exhausted sleep.

As he topped the hill on which his cabin was set, he saw the SUV parked behind his and swore under his breath. He was in no mood for this.

The moment she saw him, she climbed out of the SUV and started toward him. Clearly she hadn't had any more sleep than he had. He could smell perfume and alcohol on her, an all-too-familiar concoction.

"What the hell are you doing here, Chantell?" he said as he walked on past her. "I'm really not doing this right now."

"I've been waiting for you to come home. You have to talk to me." She followed him up on the porch and into the cabin. "Jack, my father was waiting up for me when I got home this morning. He said you're spreading lies about him."

He turned to look at her as he pulled off his boots and socks, then discarded his shirt. The rising sun silhouetted her in the cabin doorway. He realized how crushed she would be when she found out the truth about her father. Or maybe, like the judge, she'd deny it.

Either way, he figured she wouldn't be hanging around Big Timber after everything came out.

"Goodbye, Chantell," he said as he stepped to her and, taking her shoulders in his hands, moved her back until she was standing on the porch. "We won't be seeing each other again."

"No, Jack—" She threw her arms around his neck. "I know you wouldn't hurt me or my father." She pulled him down into a kiss.

He gently disengaged himself from her hold. "Don't come back here." He started to step back from the door when he saw Kate at the edge of the clearing.

KATE HAD AWAKENED before the sun rose after a night of restless sleep. She'd tried to talk herself out of going up to Jack's cabin before work. The best thing she could do was leave things as they were. Let Jack think all she cared about was the gold. It was the safest thing for him not to be involved with her. He'd made his ultimatum. Him or the gold. Was he afraid that looking for the gold would get her killed? Or more afraid of what could happen once she found it?

As the sheriff had warned her, there were still two Ackermanns hanging around the area. Why involve Jack further in this mess? She had been wrong to do it in the first place.

But all that good advice hadn't made her heart ache any less. She kept remembering the hurt she'd seen in his eyes. She couldn't leave things like this.

As the sun rose along the eastern horizon, she'd decided to walk up to his cabin. The day was already warm. A part of her thought she might come to her senses before she reached his door.

She'd just topped the hill when she saw Chantell back out of the cabin. Kate was too far away to hear what was being said, but there was no mistaking the way the woman wrapped her arms around Jack and pulled him down for a kiss before leaving.

Kate turned and fled back down the path toward the café. Her heart ached worse than it had before, and she cursed herself. It sure hadn't taken Jack long, had it? Or maybe he'd never stopped seeing Chantell, just as Hitch McCray had warned her.

She thought she heard him call her name, but she kept running. She'd wanted desperately for Jack to be different from other men she'd known, even though she'd known from the get-go what he was like.

Fool. At her pickup, she looked back. The highway was empty. Had she thought Jack would follow her? She'd seen him standing in the doorway as Chantell was leaving, his chest as bare as his feet and looking as if he'd just woken up—or had never been to sleep.

Furious with herself, she unlocked her pickup and slid behind the wheel. An instant later, the engine turned over and she took off in a hail of dirt and gravel.

She wanted to just keep going and never look back. Let the Ackermann boys find the gold—and her, if they were so determined. She didn't care anymore.

But even as she thought it, she knew she didn't want to spend the rest of her life waiting for one of them to suddenly appear when she least expected it. Nor did she have the funds to disappear the way she wanted.

No, it had to end here—just as Claude had said. On her terms. She had to find the gold, then she was out of here. No looking back. No regrets.

The thought brought a sob to the surface. She wiped angrily at her eyes as they filled with tears. This was why she hadn't wanted Jack's help, hadn't wanted to fall for his cowboy charm—because she'd known he would break her heart.

With everything she needed locked in the pickup overnight, she called Lou, told him that he and Bethany would have to handle the café today. Then she headed down the road toward Ackermann Hollow.

JACK SWORE WHEN he reached the café and saw that Kate's pickup was gone. He walked back up the trail, furious with himself, with Chantell and maybe especially with Kate.

She hadn't even given him a chance to explain. Hotheaded damned woman. If she had just given him a chance to pull on his boots and come after her...

At a sound, he looked up to find Chantell still standing on his cabin porch. "Haven't you done enough this morning?"

"It's not my fault if Kate got the wrong impression," she said, satisfaction written all over her face. "Jack, she's not like you and me. She'll want to get her lasso around your neck."

"While you just want to get your spurs into me."

"You always liked it before," she said, being coy.

"I told you. You're wasting your time," he said, moving past her. "I can't unring that bell. Just as your father can't, either."

"You're wrong about him. He swore to me—"

"Chantell, he lied to you. It's going to come out, and soon. You best be ready."

She looked at him as if confused. She was so used to getting her way on everything, apparently she'd never had to deal with *no* before. "Admit it, you miss me. After you fix this—"

"Chantell, find another challenge, okay?" He shook his head as she followed him into the cabin. "You had no interest in me until you thought I was interested in someone else, and throwing yourself at me won't save your father. Nothing you can do will."

"That's not true, Jack," she said, reaching for him as he grabbed his pickup keys.

"I can't make this any clearer. You and I were over a long time ago."

"I don't believe that."

"Believe it." He pushed past her.

"You aren't going after her."

"The hell I'm not."

KATE HADN'T GONE FAR when she realized she had taken the wrong turn. When she tried to turn around, she got stuck in a mud hole and couldn't get the pickup out.

Tired and heartsick, she sat down in the shade of a tree and cried until she couldn't cry anymore, then she fell asleep. It was late afternoon by the time she woke. She found a couple of old candy bars in the pickup's glove box, ate those and noticed that while she was sleeping the sun and wind had dried the mud hole she'd gotten stuck in.

The pickup came right out of it this time. Feeling as if her luck had changed and seeing that there was still a lot of light left in the day, she drove to Ackermann Hollow and hiked in, stopping near the house to look at the map. The paper had thinned and yellowed, quietly disintegrating before her eyes. She studied it as she had so many times before.

In her mother's haste, she hadn't marked north and south. Maybe she hadn't known which direction was north. With few or no unusual landmarks, the map was as Jack had said: worthless.

"The gold is here," Kate said to herself. Until she found it she wouldn't be free. Why couldn't Jack understand that?

What will you do with it if you find it?

She told herself she hadn't thought that far ahead. But in truth, she realized Jack might be right. Wasn't that why he thought she'd chosen gold over him already?

Shoving those thoughts away, she looked toward the mountains.

The lower part of the hollow lay in the foothills, but quickly rose in a deep, fairly wide canyon with rock cliffs, towering pines and a meandering creek that any other time of the year ran slow and clear. Now the creek raged, and snow still melted slowly in the shade along the north side of the cliffs.

Her mother's drawing showed the creek, several objects that could have been buildings or rocks or even stands of trees. As Kate looked up the hollow, she saw dozens of places where the gold could have been buried.

The first time she'd come up here, she'd tried to imagine her mother living here. Claude had only one photograph of Katherina "Teeny" LaFond.

Kate had seen the resemblance at once—just as Loralee Clark had seen it from the photograph she'd taken of Teeny.

"Cullen must have been charming to talk my mother into coming here," she said to the breeze as she stared down the mountainside at what had been the heart of Ackermann's compound.

"Or he lied through his teeth," she said. Feeling her anger fuel her, she continued toward the house. As it had been the first time she'd come up here, the day was eerily still. No breeze stirred the pine boughs or whispered in the new aspen leaves. A stark, blazing sun fingered its way down through the trees. As she walked through the shafts of heat toward the house, Kate cursed herself for falling for Jack.

The image of Chantell standing in his cabin doorway came back with a stab of pain that she tried to mask with anger. The pain won as she walked along the side of the house. She would go up into the mountains today, hoping it would be cooler at the higher altitude, to a spot she hadn't checked yet.

She stopped in the shade of the house to wipe perspiration from her brow and shifted the metal detector to her other hand. It was too late to have much time to dig, so she hadn't toted along the shovel. If she found something, she'd dig with the smaller tool strapped on her belt, marking the site for when she would come back later.

Looking up the mountainside, she almost changed her mind. Her disappointment in Jack had taken all the fight out of her. Even after sleeping a good portion of the day, she was suddenly tired and just wanted to go home, curl up in a ball and sleep for the rest of the week.

The café was hard enough work without spending all her free time climbing mountains and digging for treasure. The weight of it all lay heavy on her shoulders.

She took a step back toward her truck when the man came out of the shade beside the house.

CHAPTER TWENTY-TWO

KATE HAD BEEN SO LOST in thought that she hadn't sensed him waiting there for her. The moment he moved, she realized her mistake.

As he lunged for her, she swung the metal detector. It landed with only a glancing blow, which didn't slow him in the least.

He was good-sized and had the element of surprise on his side. He tackled her, driving her to the hard ground, knocking the breath out of her.

She hadn't had a chance to replace the gun that had been stolen from her apartment. But it wouldn't have done her any good if she had.

He was on top of her so quickly, she wouldn't have had time to use it. By now he would have taken it from her and used it on her instead.

"Shit. You look just like her."

She used his surprise to try to get him off her and almost succeeded, slamming him into the side of the house.

He let out a cry as his shoulder connected with the rock foundation of the house.

"Bitch." He spat the word at her as he grabbed her

wrists and straddled her in the dirt. His face was narrow, dark eyes close together, cheeks pockmarked.

"Get off me." She tried to buck him off with less success than the time before.

He let go of one of her wrists long enough to slap her, hard.

She went for his face with her free hand, only to have him crush her to the ground with his body as he grappled to get hold of her again.

She could smell his sour breath, feel it against her face. They were both breathing hard from the struggle.

"It's your fault I'm up here livin' like this," he said, spittle spraying her as he succeeded in securing her wrists again. "Cecil said we had to bide our time. Wait." He swore. "If she can't find it, then how the hell do you think we are goin' to find it?" The last was said in a way that she assumed mimicked the way Cecil spoke. "I told him you were probably just screwing with us."

She saw something change in his expression. Suddenly she feared even more for her life than she had before. "Gallen, right? I haven't been screwing with you," she said.

"I told him even if she really is looking for it, bet we could find it faster. We know this land. She don't."

Kate could tell he was trying to work this out in his own mind, since clearly his older brother must have told him not to mess with her and now he had.

"Cecil said he saw your mother making a map. That what she did, ain't it?"

Kate swallowed, her throat dry as sand.

"You got it on you, don't you? 'Course you do." He glanced at her backpack. She'd had the strap looped over one shoulder when he'd hit her. It had come off and landed a few feet from them.

She knew then that he was going to kill her. But first he had to be sure she had the map on her. If he killed her and he didn't find it, he would really be in serious trouble with his brother and he knew it.

He moved her hands until they were high over her head and grasped hold of both wrists with one hand, waiting to see if it held her.

She didn't fight, but bided her time as he reached for her backpack, pulling it over so he could unzip it.

The backpack contained a large bottle of water, gloves, a towel to clean herself up in the creek before she headed back into town, a small pocketknife, the county maps she'd collected, a small global positioning system and the infrared camera she'd purchased.

She tried not to think about what he would do to her when he realized that the map wasn't there.

She let him draw everything out of the backpack and sort through the other maps as she came up with a plan. She knew she would only get one chance so she couldn't blow it.

When his body weight had shifted to reach for the backpack, she'd felt the digging tool strapped on her belt. The handle dug into her side where it had shifted when he'd taken her down.

He started to clumsily unzip the side pocket on the backpack—the last place left to look. His weight shifted as he struggled with the zipper.

Kate knew it was now or never. She bucked with her hips, throwing him in the direction of the backpack as she wrestled her wrists free of his hold.

The move took him by surprise and with him already leaning in that direction, he fell sideways and had to catch himself.

The moment a hand was free, she went for the weapon at her waist. The hook-and-loop strap came open easily.

She pulled the small, sharp digging tool from its sheath as she rolled onto her side and scrambled to get her feet under her.

He took a swing at her, clipping her temple. She felt a gash open in the skin as blood began to run down in her eye. Before that moment, she hadn't realized that he'd grabbed the knife she carried from her backpack.

He came at her, brandishing the knife as he grabbed for her with his free hand. Instinctively, she lunged at him the moment the knife had passed by her, striking out at him with the wide, knifelike weapon.

The sound of the blade striking bone was followed by his horrible scream. The digger lodged in muscle on his arm and was jerked from her hand. He screamed again and wrenched the blade free, murder in his eyes.

Kate stumbled back, aghast at what she'd done and even more terrified of what she would have to do if she hoped to live. Wiping the blood from her eye, she saw a shovel propped against the side of the house. Not her shovel. As she snatched it up, she realized that Gallen had been digging before she'd come upon him.

He lunged at her. She hefted the shovel and swung

as hard as she could. The handle of the shovel rattled in her hands as the blade end connected with his skull. The sound would haunt her to her dying day, she thought as his entire body shuddered and dropped like a stone to the ground. A piteous sound escaped his lips and then he fell silent.

She stood over him, breathing hard, the shovel still in her hands. She'd watched too many movies where the heroine dropped her weapon and turned her back on the killer only to have him attack her again.

But Gallen didn't move, and from where she stood, she couldn't see his chest rising and falling—and she wasn't about to step closer to find out.

A MANHUNT WAS STILL ON for the missing and apparently wounded Cecil Ackermann. Sheriff Frank Curry had been in contact with his deputies, but there'd been no sign of Cecil. Or his brother Gallen.

As the hours went on, Frank was hoping both had left the county. Not that he expected that was the last he would see of them.

He was heating some soup on the stove after Tiffany left when his phone rang. It was the dispatcher. She hadn't been able to raise any of the deputies, but a rancher in the area had said he was driving the road by the Clark place when he saw what appeared to be a light up at Ackermann Hollow.

"I'd seen lights up the hollow a few times lately," Loralee had told him. "Thought I was just imagining it. But last night when I saw it again, I decided to investigate."

"I'll drive up and take a look," he told the dispatcher as he pulled his soup off the stove. He'd had his deputies watching the perimeter of the hollow, but had given them specific orders not to go inside the fence.

As he headed for the hollow, Frank wasn't too worried about any of the old booby traps or land mines Cullen Ackermann had laid for trespassers. He figured the military had found most if not all of them. He was more worried that if the man's sons had been staying up there, they might have built some of their own.

He didn't want to send a deputy into anything like that. Frank remembered too well the guilt his father had suffered after the raid on the place thirty years ago.

As he drove up the road, he saw tire tracks in the dirt on a jeep trail next to the fence. He turned up the trail, skirting the fence and the signs warning trespassers to stay off the property.

They hadn't kept everyone out, Frank saw as he slowed to a stop next to a place in the fence where the wire had been cut. He could see tracks where a vehicle had turned around. More than once. Kate? Or the Ackermanns?

He looked in the general direction of the house, but the pines were too thick here to see any lights. The last thing he wanted to do was go on the property. But if Cecil and Gallen Ackermann had been hiding out up here, they might still be on the property.

Frank grabbed his shotgun, climbed out and squeezed through the hole in the fence. Two sets of tracks were distinguishable in the dirt—a man-size boot and what could have been a woman's or a small man's.

He moved through the pines as quietly as possible. A light breeze moaned through the high boughs. Even in the twilight, heat still hung like a heavy black cloak over the hollow. Within a few yards of the house, Frank stopped, feeling the hair rise on the back of his neck.

Even as a boy, this hollow had given him the creeps.

Now he caught a familiar scent on the increasing breeze and felt his stomach roil. Nothing smelled quite like death. Violent death had always smelled stronger to him.

He took a few steps toward the house. The door stood open, a deep black hole inside. He heard a sound and froze again. A gust of wind caught the door, making it groan as it scraped across the weathered floor, and making him jump.

His nerves were like a live wire. His hands gripping the shotgun felt moist. Sweat ran down his face. He made a swipe at it.

He thought of his daughter and felt his heart rate kick up a couple of beats. He was just getting to know her. Suddenly he was afraid that he might get killed up here in this godforsaken hollow and that he might never spend another moment with her.

Bracing himself, he stepped around the corner of the house.

KATE STUMBLED INTO the back of the café. Only a small light near the large walk-in refrigerator glowed dimly. She didn't flip on another one, but went straight to the sink, where she turned on the water and let it run while she reached for a towel. Soaking it, she pressed the wet towel gently to her temple. The cold water felt good. But when she pulled back the white towel, she saw in the dim light that it was covered in her blood.

For a moment, she gripped the edge of the sink, waiting for the light-headedness to go away. Her head ached, but at least the double vision had passed. She knew she'd been a fool to drive all the way back here in the condition she was in. But all she could think about was getting back to the café.

Tears blurred her eyes. What had she done? Had she killed him?

He would have killed you if you hadn't stopped him. Even though she knew it was true, it made her sick to her stomach.

"I'm not doing this anymore, Claude," she said to the empty, dark café.

But she knew, whether she looked for the gold or not, that man in the woods would be coming for her. Unless she'd killed him.

And then his brother would be coming.

This wasn't over.

At the sound of the back door of the café opening, she turned, pressing her back against the edge of the sink and slipping into the darkness as the realization hit her. She'd failed to lock the door behind her—and she was unarmed.

Jack French stepped into the dim light at the edge of the room. It took a few moments for her heart to stop trying to pound out of her chest.

"Hey," he said, stopping just inside the door. He squinted in her direction, but she could tell he couldn't see more than her shape in the pool of darkness where she stood. "I wish you hadn't taken off so fast this morning."

"Oh?"

"I tried to catch up with you. I looked all over for you… Look, about me and Chantell—" He took a step toward her.

"It's none of my business," she said and moved deeper into the darkness of the café. She didn't want him to see her like this. Worse, she didn't want to need him, to want him now more desperately than ever. Even worse, she didn't want to fall into his arms and beg him to hold her until her shaking stopped.

"Damn it, Kate, I'm not involved with Chantell Hyett. Truthfully? I can't stand the sight of her. She only came to my cabin to talk to me about her father. It's a long story. As for that kiss, well…that was all Chantell's doing, not mine. That's when I came after you, but you'd torn out of there so fast…" He took another step toward her.

"What are you doing here, Jack?"

That's when he saw the bloody towel where she'd dropped it on the edge of the sink. "Kate?" He stepped to her, drawing her into the light by the back door. "My God, what happened to you?"

She willed herself not to break down, but the moment he took her in his arms, she began to sob uncontrollably. Jack swept her up and carried her upstairs to her apartment. Kicking open the bathroom door, he set her on her feet only long enough to turn a light and the shower on.

Kate caught a glimpse of herself in the bathroom mirror and almost passed out. She was covered in blood. Jack didn't even take off his lucky boots as he stepped into the shower with her.

The warm water ran down her face, soaking her to the skin, before draining dark red. He held her until they were both drenched and the water circling the drain was clear again, then he stripped off her clothes and wrapped her in her robe. He dug in her medicine cabinet and bandaged the gash over her left eye.

Carrying her into the bedroom, he carefully set her on the bed, promising to come right back. She thought she heard him on the phone, but a few moments later, he came into the bedroom wrapped in one of her towels.

She'd quit sobbing, though she didn't remember when exactly. The sight of him stirred a need greater than any she'd ever felt.

"Tell me what happened," he said as he lay down beside her on the bed.

She touched his handsome face, running her fingertips along his strong jawline to his lips. The memory of those lips on hers—

A banging at the door startled her. She jerked her fingers back. "It's him." Fear made her heart race and her voice break.

"It's just Carson. I called him to bring me a change of clothes and help me get you to the hospital."

"I don't need to go to the hospital."

He cupped her cheek, his gaze locking with hers. "You do, Kate. You need stitches and I think you have a concussion."

She stared after him as he went to answer the door. A moment later he was back, dressed and carrying her out to Carson's pickup for the ride into Big Timber to the hospital.

SHERIFF FRANK CURRY stared down into the dead man's face. The wind sighed loudly in the tops of the pines, making goose bumps ripple over his skin. The temperature was dropping quickly and soon it would be pitch-black in this hollow. He couldn't shake the feeling that they weren't alone, and yet after making the call for backup and a coroner, he'd checked the perimeter around the house and found no one.

The dead man was one of the Ackermanns, given his resemblance to Darrell. He had the same narrow ferretlike face, the close-set dark eyes. The face of a killer, Frank thought.

Only someone had killed this man first.

It appeared he'd been in some sort of altercation before the other party had ended the fight. A red-handled object that appeared to be a small spade was buried deep in the man's chest.

"What is this place?" Charlie Brooks asked behind him.

Frank hadn't heard the assistant coroner approach and couldn't help the way his body reacted.

"Sorry, didn't mean to scare you," Charlie said.

"It's this place," he told him. "I don't know if you've heard of Ackermann Hollow."

"I just got a brief history on my way up here via the EMT," Charlie said and shivered as he glanced toward the opening in the mountain behind the house. "That's where they found his first wife?"

Frank nodded. "She was in such poor shape she died shortly after she was rescued. My father always blamed himself for not raiding this place sooner."

"And the new wife died, too."

"One of her so-called husband's booby traps."

Charlie looked around as if expecting either a booby trap or a land mine to blow at any minute. Or worse maybe, one of the ghosts of this crazy-ass family to appear. Frank knew the feeling. "And this is one of the man's sons?"

"I'm not sure which. I'm hoping it is the one who ransacked Loralee Clark's house, the one she wounded. There's a knot on his head, but it could be a more recent wound from whatever altercation took place before he was killed."

"Well, it seems pretty obvious what killed him," Charlie said, crouching down next to the body. "What the hell is this thing?"

"I have no id—" Frank stopped as a memory surfaced. He'd seen Kate LaFond with something like this. It had a red handle and had been strapped to her belt the other day as she was leaving the café. *"Idea,"* he finished. "But I think I know where to find out."

CHAPTER TWENTY-THREE

KATE WOKE TO FIND JACK asleep next to her hospital bed. She touched the bandage on her temple. When she'd first opened her eyes, she'd been confused about where she was. The curtains were open on the first-floor window, a slight breeze blowing in the partially opened window next to Jack.

Sensing movement, he opened his eyes and smiled at her.

"Have you been here all night?"

He ignored the question and asked, "How are you feeling?"

"My head hurts."

"Doc says you have a mild concussion. With that and the gash in your temple and the loss of blood, I would imagine your head does hurt."

She stared into his handsome face. "You just keep saving me, don't you?"

"It appears to be my life's calling," he said, getting to his feet to come to the bed. He took her hand in one of his and brushed back her hair from her forehead with the other.

He was so gentle, so sweet. Tears welled in her eyes. She fought to curb the flow as he said, "Do you remember anything I told you last night before I brought you to the hospital?"

She did, but she shook her head slightly. Even that made her nauseous.

"I'm not seeing Chantell, haven't been since I got out of prison and have no desire to. She just showed up and tried to use her...charm...to keep me from going after her father."

"Her charm, huh?" Kate smiled, then frowned as she realized what he'd said. "You're going after the judge?"

"Already did. Not to worry. It's all legal. He was behind the trumped-up rustling charge. He wanted me out of his daughter's life, so he sent me to prison for two years."

"Apparently it didn't work."

He shook his head. "Chantell and I were never serious. The only reason she kissed me at the branding was to make you jealous. She couldn't stand the thought that I'd moved on. Chantell has this idea that all her old boyfriends are still pining away for her."

"But not you," Kate said quietly.

"Not me."

"Jack, what happened in your barn...it had nothing to do with—"

"Excuse me." They turned to see a nurse standing in the doorway. "I'm going to need you to step out for a few moments," she said to Jack. "I need to check the patient."

As Jack started to let go of her hand, Kate squeezed it. He met her gaze for a moment before he smiled, gave her a slight nod and left the room.

"WHERE'S MS. LAFOND?" the sheriff asked Bethany as she headed to a busy table with a large breakfast order the next morning.

"I don't know." Bethany glanced over her shoulder toward the kitchen. "I think Lou might know." She went on by with her multiple plates of food, and he walked back to the kitchen, where Lou was busy cooking.

"I'm looking for Ms. LaFond," he said.

Lou looked up from the grill, where he had hash browns, eggs, pancakes, sausage and bacon all going. "She's taking a day off." He flipped the pancakes with a large turner and then poured more grease on the grill to add another order of hash browns.

Frank glanced through the screen door and saw her pickup parked out back. As he started out the back, something caught his eye that brought him to a halt.

"Did someone cut themselves?" he asked Lou, pointing at a bloody white towel next to the washing machine.

"Not me," Lou said without looking at him. "Might ask Bethany."

Frank wanted to ask Kate. He stepped outside and saw that her pickup driver's door was ajar.

As he stepped to it, he pulled on a pair of latex gloves. He peered in, saw a stain on the seat and caught the strong smell of blood as he eased open the door.

Backtracking to the kitchen, he took a clean garbage bag and bagged the bloody towel. Lou was too busy to notice.

After dropping the evidence at his patrol pickup, he

climbed the stairs to Kate's apartment over the café. He knocked. No answer. He was ready to break down the door, his concern having grown with each step he'd taken since seeing the bloody towel and the blood all over the seat of her pickup.

His cell phone rang. Seeing it was the dispatcher, he answered the call.

"A man matching Cecil Ackermann's description was just seen on the corner of Hooper Street and Ninth Avenue in Big Timber. A deputy is headed that way, but you said you wanted to know if there were any sightings."

Before he could answer, Bethany appeared at the bottom of the stairs.

"She's not up there. Jack just called. She's in the hospital." With that, Bethany hurried back to work.

"Are you still there, Sheriff?"

"Yes." Frank doubted Cecil Ackermann was just strolling down a street in Big Timber. "Keep me informed."

"Also, Loralee Clark is here to identify the body?"

He swore under his breath, having forgotten that she'd offered. For all he knew, Cecil Ackermann was lying in a cooler with a toe tag.

"Tell her I am on my way," he said into the phone, and headed for his truck. Thinking about Kate and all the blood he'd seen in her pickup, he quickly called one of his deputies and asked him to go by the hospital and make sure Kate LaFond was all right and didn't go anywhere until he got to talk to her.

LORALEE WAS WAITING anxiously at the morgue when he got there. If he'd feared she might be squeamish, he had nothing to worry about. She took one look at the dead man and said, "That's not him."

"Don't you need a closer look?"

"No." She said it quickly and snapped her lips shut with a definite shake of her head. "There is nothing wrong with my eyesight. That's not the man. Believe me, I got a good look at him. I'd say it's his brother, Gallen." She gave him an impatient look. "The one I nailed was Cecil. You haven't found him yet?"

"Not yet." The dispatcher hadn't gotten back to him on that sighting in town, though.

Loralee pursed her lips. "Well, I suggest you get busy. None of us are safe as long as he's out there. Especially Kate LaFond."

He might have argued that none of the Ackermanns were safe with Kate LaFond on the loose, but suddenly he remembered the address where the dispatcher said there had been a Cecil Ackermann sighting.

It was just two blocks from the hospital.

JACK WALKED DOWN to the cafeteria, desperately needing coffee. He'd gotten little sleep last night. Kate could have died. She'd been delirious on the way to the hospital and yet he couldn't forget the things she'd told him about her life, about Claude, about how she felt about him.

He tried to tell himself not to believe any of it, especially the part about her having killed someone.

"It was one of the Ackermanns," she'd said. "I didn't see him at first and then..." She'd begun to cry, but he'd caught enough of the story through her tears to get the gist of it. "He was lying there. I didn't dare check to see. But I know he was dead."

While Jack had loved hearing how she really felt about him, if it was true, he didn't want to believe she'd killed anyone—even in self-defense. He had told himself the woman was talking out of her head.

The doctor had confirmed once they'd reached the hospital that Kate had a concussion and had lost way too much blood. The gash on her temple had taken fifteen stitches. By then, neither of them could make any sense of what she was saying.

It still made his heart drop when he recalled the way she'd looked standing in the café last night. What if he hadn't come looking for her?

He shook his head at the thought as he entered the cafeteria and went straight to the coffee machine.

"Jack?"

He turned to see Carson coming toward him. Jack had never been so glad to see his friend. They both got coffee, then took a small table in a corner, even though the place was nearly empty.

Carson looked around, then keeping his voice down, said, "I heard the sheriff and coroner were in Ackermann Hollow last night. Apparently they brought someone out in a body bag."

Jack felt sick. Was what Kate had told him true?

"Do you want me to call Arnie Thorndike?" Carson asked. Arnie didn't look like much of a lawyer, but apparently he was quite good. Or at least he had been when he was a trial attorney.

"Let me talk to Kate first."

WHEN THE HOSPITAL ROOM door opened, Kate looked up, expecting to see Jack. The smile that had instantly turned up her lips died on them the moment the man stepped into the room. He looked enough like the man who'd attacked her at the hollow that she thought for an instant it was him back from the dead.

Kate reached for the call button, but he beat her to it, tossing it out of her reach. He grabbed a chair and quickly stuck it under the doorknob, moving so fast she didn't have time to scream before he was at the bed, covering her mouth as he pressed her into the pillows.

Kate tried to fight him off, but she was too weak and he was much too strong. He was taller than the man who'd attacked her up in the hollow, she realized. Thin but strong with sinewy arms. He had the same narrow, pocked face, the same close-set eyes, the same hunger and hatred she'd seen in the other man's face. There was a goose-egg bump on his forehead and in his hand was her gun, the one he'd stolen from her apartment after he'd ransacked it looking for the map.

"Hey, little sis," he said, meeting her gaze. "You probably don't remember me. Cecil Ackermann? I used to pinch you to make you cry just to get a rise out of Teeny." He chuckled under his breath. "We don't have long, so we probably shouldn't take a trip down memory lane, huh. Where is the map?"

She tried to shake her head.

"I'm going to uncover your mouth, but if you scream I will snap your neck like a twig. You believe me?"

She did. He had to know that the map was pretty useless, since she hadn't found the gold. But in his arrogance, he would assume if he had the map he could do a better job of reading it than she had.

"Now," he said. "Just whisper it to me. Where is the map?" He uncovered her mouth.

She'd thought about screaming but only for an instant. Jack would be back soon. She needed to get rid of this man before then. If she could talk her way out of this... "I lost it up in the hollow."

Disbelief and anger twisted his features into an ugly grimace.

"I was up there looking for it when I ran into your brother." Remembering the nurse filling a large glass pitcher with water next to her bed, she snaked her hand under the covers toward it.

"You expect me to believe that?" Cecil demanded in a hushed tone as someone tried the door.

"It's the truth." She glanced toward the window and saw the sheriff had pulled up and was getting out of his truck. When she looked at Cecil Ackermann again she saw that there would be no talking her way out of this. He was going to kill her—probably had wanted to for years. All that had held him back was the thought that she'd find the gold for him.

Her hand was just inches from the pitcher handle when someone began to bang on the door. It was enough to distract Cecil for just an instant.

Kate grabbed the handle of the pitcher. It was heavy and she was still weak, but she managed to lift it and swing. She didn't even realize she'd screamed for help, but her voice filled the room as the pitcher caught the side of Cecil's head.

He let out a howl and grabbed for her throat. He would have strangled her or snapped her neck as he'd threatened to if the door hadn't burst open just then.

Out of the corner of her eye, Kate saw Jack and Carson come running into the room. Cecil spun away from her and dove through the window screen. She saw him hit the ground and run. The next thing she knew she was in Jack's arms and he was holding her, asking her if she was all right.

"I am now," she said into his broad chest. "I am now."

"WE CAUGHT CECIL," the sheriff said a few hours later, after pulling up a chair next to Kate's bed. "How are you?"

"I'm going to live."

"I need to ask you a few questions." Frank saw how pale she was, but then again she'd almost been killed twice in the past twenty-four hours, according to Jack French. He'd heard Jack's story already. Now he was waiting to hear Kate's.

"Tell me what happened. Why don't you start with what happened in this room today." He turned on the digital recorder and listened as she related Cecil coming into the room, blocking the door and threatening to snap her neck if she screamed.

When she'd finished, he said, "Now tell me what happened in the hollow last evening."

She told him about running into Gallen Ackermann and the fight that had ensued.

"You don't know if he was alive when you left?"

She shook her head. "I couldn't tell if he was breathing and I was afraid to check."

"You hit him with a shovel." She nodded. "Where was the digging tool with the red handle at this point?"

Kate frowned. "He pulled it out of his arm and tossed it aside. I didn't really see where it went."

"And you say you stabbed him in the upper arm— not in the chest?"

"Yes, the upper arm." She was still frowning. "Are you telling me he was killed with my tool?"

He looked at her for a moment, then shut off the recorder. "I might have more questions for you." He rose to his feet.

"It's not about the gold," she said.

He met her gaze. "Really? So does that mean you are going to stop looking for it?"

"My mother wanted me to have it."

Frank nodded. "So you will keep looking for it." He felt sad for her. "How will you know when to stop if you don't find it?"

She seemed to have no answer for that.

"And Jack?"

She didn't have an answer for that either, apparently.

"Well, I wish you luck. At least now you don't have to worry about the Ackermann boys. Cecil will be going back to prison, and the rest are dead."

"Did Cecil confess to killing his brothers?" she asked.

"He swears he didn't kill them." Frank again met her gaze. "He says you killed them."

"What now?" Jack asked later that evening after the doctor told him that Kate could go home. He wheeled her out to his pickup, helped her in, and then drove them toward Beartooth.

Kate didn't pretend not to know what he was talking about. She couldn't remember much of the ride to the hospital the night before, but she had a feeling that she'd bared her soul to him.

"Did I tell you last night that I'm in love with you?" she asked.

He glanced over at her in surprise. "You might have mentioned something like that."

She smiled and leaned back against the seat to close her eyes.

"Are you?"

Kate laughed softly, amazed how easy it was to distract a man with either the word *love* or *sex*. She opened her eyes and looked over at him. "I am."

He stared at her and almost ran off the road.

"You told me to be honest," she said, seeing his surprise. "I'm trying."

They drove for a while in silence. Kate knew she'd hurt him the other day after they'd made love. She should have told him the truth before that. Maybe long before that.

"While you're being truthful, how about answering my question," he said. "You haven't given up looking for the gold, have you?"

"No."

He sighed. "What if you don't find it?"

The sheriff had asked her the same thing. She hadn't had an answer for him. She didn't have one now.

"Don't worry, I'm not holding you to our partnership. I don't expect you to help me."

He glanced over at her again. "What is this really about? I just can't help feeling it isn't about the money. Am I wrong?"

"No." She stared out the windshield, watching the spring-green country blur past. Ahead, the Crazies loomed up, brilliant white-capped peaks piercing the big blue sky. It was a breathtaking sight that never ceased to capture her.

"I can't explain it," she said after a few moments. "At first it was just a case of not wanting my awful so-called stepbrothers to get their greedy hands on it."

"But they're out of the picture."

She nodded. "Now I just want to find it because my mother wanted me to have it." She knew what he wanted her to say. That if it meant losing him, she would give up looking for the gold.

But she'd made a promise a long time ago, long before she'd met Jack French. And she was hell bound to keep it. If she hadn't let the Ackermann boys stop her, then she couldn't let her feelings for Jack keep her from that promise.

She couldn't bear the thought of losing Jack from her life. But she feared she'd already lost him. He was planning to sell his ranch and move on, wasn't he?

And Claude had only made her promise to stay a year at the café.

Nothing was keeping either of them here.

They didn't talk about it the rest of the drive to Beartooth. Two whitetail deer came out of the tall grass and bounded across the road a few hundred yards in front of the pickup, their coats a beautiful buckskin reddish-brown. In a tall cottonwood, a bald eagle watched them, and several hawks circled in a pasture. Kate watched them rise on a thermal as Jack slowed on the outskirts of town.

"You're not planning to go to work yet, are you?" he asked as he parked beside the café in front of the old stone garage.

"Not today."

"The doctor said you should take it easy."

She nodded. "I will." She reached for her door handle.

"Kate?"

"Yes?" she asked, looking back over at him, hoping he would say the words she would have been thrilled to hear.

"I'm glad there are no more Ackermanns who can hurt you."

She smiled. "Me, too." With that, she got out and walked to the back door of the café to see how her crew was making out in her absence. Behind her, she heard Jack drive away.

FRANK DIDN'T GET HOME until late afternoon. He had two murdered Ackermanns and another behind bars. Cecil Ackermann had demanded a lawyer. Frank had been only mildly surprised when he'd asked for Arnie Thorndike's number.

Exhausted, he drove into his yard and was startled to see Tiffany's car parked in front of his house. Then he remembered that they were supposed to ride this afternoon, and he swore. He'd completely forgotten it was supposed to have been his day off.

As he got out of his patrol pickup, he saw Tiffany waiting for him on the porch. Even from a distance, he could see that she was furious with him.

"Tiffany, I'm so sorry."

She leaped to her feet. "You're always sorry," she said as she started past him.

He grabbed her arm to stop her from leaving. "At least let me—"

She jerked free. "I know. You were working. I called your office. Did you catch a speeder? Or was it a jaywalker?" she asked, her voice dripping with sarcasm.

"There was a murder. A woman was almost killed. I caught the bad guy and put him behind bars. You can make fun of what I do if you want to, but sometimes I have to do my job even on my day off. I'm the sheriff and I'm responsible for the people in this county."

She'd stopped a few feet from him and stood, arms crossed over her skinny chest. She looked so young, so fragile.

"I love you." His voice broke. "I'd rather cut off my right arm than hurt you."

Tears welled in her eyes. "You called my mother."

He nodded.

"She said you yelled at her, said you hated her, hated me—"

"That's not true." He said it softly, all the fight gone out of him. It shouldn't have surprised him that

Pam had lied or that she wasn't through hurting either
of them.

"She says she doesn't care if I come back or not."

"You can stay here as long as you want. I'll pay your
rent, or you can move in here at the ranch."

"What about my mother?"

He stared at her. "What about her?"

"She's all alone."

"Your mother is capable of taking care of herself,"
he said carefully, realizing how Pam had leaned on
this girl all her life, using her as a weapon as well as
pretending to be helpless so Tiffany could never emo-
tionally leave her.

"It's time for you to start your own life, Tiffany.
Maybe the best thing is putting distance between you
and your mother."

"She said you would try to turn me against her."

"That isn't what I'm trying to do." He took a step toward her and stopped dead in the dust. Lying on its side
next to her car was one of his crows. There was blood
on its dark wings and on the rock next to it. Someone
had smashed its head with the rock.

Frank looked up at his daughter. "Tiffany, what have
you done?"

An expression of satisfaction flickered across her
face. He felt his heart break. He stared down again at
the small black bird lying in the dirt, then up at his
daughter. "Why?"

Her face had taken on hard lines that belied her
youth. Her long blond hair floated around her face as

the breeze teased at it. She looked at the dead crow, then at him. "It's just a bird."

He realized then that he hadn't heard the crows. They were usually on the phone line waiting for him when he came home. Several of them would caw at him, one usually sounding as if welcoming him home, another one almost nagging at him for coming home so late.

He hadn't heard them because they weren't there. The line was empty.

"You hate me so much that you would kill something I loved." It wasn't a question. The answer was in the set of her jaw, the fury in her eyes. He'd seen it before, but he'd never dreamed how deep the poison in her ran.

"It's just a dumb bird," she said, raising her voice.

He took a step toward her. "I want to help you. Help us both. We'll go to counseling. I'll pay for it—"

"You think I'm crazy?" she demanded, taking another step back as she dug in her large shoulder bag as if searching for her car keys.

"No, I don't think either of us is crazy." He was too tired for this, too drained, too heartbroken. "I think we need to get a perspective on everything that has hap—" He stared in disbelief as his daughter pulled a Saturday night special from the bag, and gripping it in both hands, pointed it at him. "Tiffany, don't—"

Frank froze. It wasn't the first time he'd stared down the barrel of a gun. He told himself to forget this was his daughter. Forget everything except defusing this situation.

"You don't want to do this. I know you miss your mother."

A sound came out of her.

"But killing me will only bring you more pain."

She looked at him with contempt, as if he was wrong about that.

"Not because I'm your father, but because they will put you in prison. I don't want to see that happen to you. You have your whole life ahead of you."

"I won't go to prison. I'm only seventeen."

It shocked him to realize that this wasn't a spur-of-the-moment action. She'd planned it.

"They'll try you as an adult."

"Because you're a *cop?*"

"Because it would be premeditated murder."

She cocked her head quizzically, but the gun barrel never wavered. "How will they know that?"

"Your drawings."

Her eyes widened. She had her mother's big blue eyes. The girl had a fragile beauty, but she was broken. Broken by her mother's hatred and need for vengeance.

"Nettie," Tiffany said, her lips twisting in a grimace. "I should have known she would snoop."

Lynette had been worried about the girl's motives. Why hadn't he listened to her? She'd been afraid of what Tiffany would do.

Frank saw now that Tiffany hadn't come here to get to know him. She'd come to Beartooth to find him and kill him. She'd killed something she knew he loved. He didn't doubt she would kill him with even less concern than she'd had for the bird.

His heart dropped as a thought struck him. There was one other person Pam had hated as much as him. "Lynette, you didn't…" He couldn't bear to form the words.

She looked confused for a moment. "Lynette." Realization suddenly bloomed in her wide-eyed gaze. "Nettie is short for Lynette."

For a moment, the gun faltered and he thought about rushing her. But she quickly caught herself. Fury burned even hotter in her eyes.

"She's the woman you were in love with instead of your wife? Instead of my mother? Are still in love with her?" she demanded.

He expected her to pull the trigger right then. He would rush her. If he could. But he was too far away to reach her before she'd get off at least two shots.

He knew there was no appealing to her, father to daughter. They were strangers. The time they'd spent together had meant nothing to her, except to find even more ways to hurt him.

She hadn't known who Nettie was, so Lynette was safe. But he knew that Tiffany would go after her next. He couldn't let that happen.

"Tiffany, I love you. You're my daughter." He took a step toward her, needing to close the distance as much as he could.

"No!"

He saw her hand tighten around the gun, around the trigger, and braced himself for the impact of the shot as he prepared to launch himself at her.

But just as he started to make his move, Frank saw

something dark out of the corner of his eye. A crow flew at Tiffany, struck the side of her head, catching some of her long, silken-blond hair in its talons.

Her mouth opened in a scream, but it was drowned out by the boom of gunshot. Her face contorted into an expression of horror as the crow flew off, trailing several strands of her fine blond hair.

He felt fire tear through his shoulder as he tried to reach Tiffany before she could pull off another shot.

The crow swooped down again, making Tiffany's second shot go wild as she tried to cover her head.

And then Frank was on her, grabbing the gun, twisting it from her hands. She was still screaming. He felt hot, sticky blood run down his chest, soak into his shirt, as he pulled Tiffany into his arms to protect her from the crow.

The bird landed on the ground only a few feet from them. Frank stared into the dark beady eyes. He thought he recognized it. One of the uncles. He'd heard stories about crows attacking anyone who had hurt them or one of their own.

This one had saved his life. He felt the bird's pain. It had lost one of its own family today. So had Frank. They stayed like that for a long moment, Frank and the bird just looking at each other. Tiffany was crying and still screaming, both arms over her head. After a moment, the crow cawed twice at him, then flew away, disappearing behind the barn.

"It's going to be all right," he kept whispering as he held his daughter. A lie. He wasn't sure it would ever be all right. Tiffany needed help. He would see that she got it. He would be there for her.

When she quit crying, he looked into his daughter's face and saw only regret. Regret that she'd only wounded him. He dialed 911.

CHAPTER TWENTY-FOUR

KATE HADN'T SEEN JACK for almost a week now. He hadn't come into the café. Although she hadn't been working, she had been spending time there. The Beartooth Quilting Society had come in with the quilts Cilla had promised and put them up.

It had been good to see Loralee. "Thank you for trying to save my mother's life," Kate said to the older woman when she could get her alone.

"I failed."

"Only because my mother went back after she'd handed me through the fence. Apparently she'd made me a toy that I loved. I'd dropped it as we were fleeing...."

Loralee's eyes filled with tears. "But she got you out."

Kate nodded. "It wouldn't have happened if you hadn't gone to the sheriff."

"I always felt I should have done more. For eighteen months I—"

"We both have to let go of the past," Kate interrupted.

"Yes," the elderly woman agreed. "Those awful boys are either gone or in jail. I hope that oldest one never sees the light of day again."

"I'm sure he won't."

Loralee shook her head. "I heard he denies killing his brothers." She met Kate's gaze. "The awful man says you did it."

"It will be up to a jury to decide."

"Well, I'd love to be on that jury," Loralee said.

Kate had gone upstairs after the quilts were hung and the women had left. She felt sick to her stomach, not surprised that Cecil would lie the way he had but that the sheriff still had his doubts.

He'd come by, his shoulder bandaged, most mornings for breakfast. Kate had felt him watching her, wondering. His own problems were obviously weighing heavy on him as well. Everyone in the county had heard about his daughter. She'd been sent up to the state mental hospital for evaluation, but Judge Hyett was saying around town that she should be tried as an adult for trying to kill her father.

Kate hadn't been in her apartment long when there was a knock at the door. She thought it would be the sheriff. It felt as if it was only a matter of time before he would arrest her. He'd gotten a warrant and had searched her apartment and truck the day after she was released from the hospital.

Her heart had lodged in her throat. She'd forgotten to get rid of Darrell Ackermann's cowboy hat, but when Frank had searched the place, the hat hadn't turned up.

Jack, she'd thought. What a risk he'd taken getting rid of it. Her heart had swelled at the thought. She loved him. No denying that. A part of her was glad she'd told him, even if it had been too late. He felt she had chosen the gold over him and maybe he'd been right. The Ackermanns had scared her less than falling in love with Jack.

Now as she went to the door, she braced herself, wondering if that other shoe was about to drop.

"Jack?"

He looked her over before he said, "Nice to see you feeling better."

She smiled and stepped back. "Do you want to come in?"

He shook his head. "I thought you might like to go for a ride."

"A ride?"

"That is, if you aren't busy," he added quickly.

"No, I'd love to. I'll just grab—"

"You might want to change your clothes."

That stopped her. "You want me to dress up?" Jack was dressed in his old boots, the ones he swore were too lucky to throw out, worn jeans and a faded blue Western shirt.

"I want you to dress down. Wear digging clothes."

She stared at him, swallowing around the lump in her throat. "I beg your pardon?"

"You know, that map never made any sense to me and yet the Ackermann boys were willing to kill for it," Jack said. "It got me thinking that we were missing something. Then I happened to run into the sheriff the other day and he told me about a photograph that had been found of the Ackermanns. I asked to see it, and when I got the map out of the side zipper of your backpack, I compared the two."

"Jack—"

"Unless you'd rather not."

She looked into his blue eyes, eyes the color of faded jeans. "Are you sure about this?"

"I don't want to get your hopes up, but there's someplace I think we should check."

"No, I mean—"

"I know what you mean. I'm sure I want you to be happy. If I'm wrong about my hunch, then I give up. But if I'm not… Like you said, this gold is yours. Your mother wanted you to have it and now there is nothing standing in your way."

"HAVE YOU BEEN BUSY out at the W Bar G?" she asked after she'd changed clothes and Jack was driving them out of town.

He shook his head. "I'm working on my place."

Her heart dropped like a stone. "Right. To sell it."

"Actually, I'm going to ranch it. There's some good pasture there and with some new corrals…"

"So you're staying." She couldn't help her shock.

He glanced over at her. "Yeah."

She let that sink in for a moment. "I heard Judge Hyett was brought up before a commission on what he'd done to you. I can't believe he only got a three-month suspension. Are you going to file a lawsuit against him and the state for the two years you lost?"

"Nope." Once the news had come out, Arnie Thorndike had contacted Jack, offering to help him with a lawsuit. Jack had thought Arnie was busy enough with his client Cecil Ackermann. "I'm not interested," he'd told Thorndike, just as he told Kate now. "I can't get the years back. That's the past. I'm lookin' to the future."

Kate grew quiet after that and didn't speak again until he'd turned down the road along the edge of Ackermann Hollow and driven up into the trees to park.

"My mother died on this land," she said. "I knew that, but I don't think I let myself admit it until now."

"What are you saying, Kate?"

"Remember when you told me that all lost treasure is cursed?"

"Kate—"

"Look what this treasure has already cost."

He studied her openly. "Are you saying you want to quit?"

Kate looked out at the hollow. The last time she'd left here, she'd thought she'd killed a man. "I don't want it to beat me." She let out a small laugh. "I don't know if it is stubborn pride or just mule-headed determination. I've fought the fear and the feelings and…" She swallowed. "I've never cared about the monetary value. You were right about that. I just need to find it because she risked her life when she made that map."

"Then I hope I'm right," Jack said as he opened his door.

"TIFFANY NEEDS HELP," Frank told the county attorney. "Her mother programmed her to come after me. It isn't her fault. She's just a *child*."

"She's a few months short of eighteen, but even if she was much younger, she tried to kill you, Frank. She would have killed you if you hadn't stopped her."

He hadn't told anyone about the crow who'd saved him. No one who didn't know something about crows would have believed him.

Crows remembered faces. He'd read about a study where scientists wore masks when they captured and tagged crows. Whenever anyone wore the same mask for years after that, the person was harassed by crows.

Tiffany had killed a family member of one of his crows. The crows would know the person who'd hurt one of them. So it made perfect sense to him why the crow had attacked her.

The county attorney sighed. "Let's wait until we get the doctor's evaluation from the state mental hospital to see if she's deemed able to stand trial."

"I won't press charges."

"The state will. She shot an officer of the law. We know she planned to kill you."

"She's my *daughter*."

"Are you sure about that, Frank? You said your ex never told you about her, that she programmed this girl to kill you. I'll set up a paternity test."

Frank put his head in his hands.

"Where is her mother?" the county attorney asked.

"Probably long gone by now. I threw her address and phone number away, but Billy Westfall has it."

"I'm going to ask that a BOLO be put out on her. At the very least, she needs to be notified and questioned. It's possible charges will be brought up on her."

"I don't care about any of that. I just want to see Tiffany get help. Even if it turns out that Pam lied and she isn't my daughter. Either way, I'm going to do everything I can to help her."

THEY CLIMBED UP through the hollow. The afternoon sun fingered its way through the pine boughs to dapple the ground with splashes of gold. Nearby, Kate could hear the creek. It still ran high from snow runoff, but it was clearer now. She could see the colorful boulders beneath cold green water.

The day smelled of sunshine and pine trees. In the shade it was cool, a reminder that summer was still to come. Kate wished she and Jack were hiking up into the Crazies for a picnic lunch or a swim in Saddlestring Lake. For a moment, she could pretend they were. Lovers looking for a secret spot to lay down a blanket and make love.

The hair on the back of her neck suddenly prickled. She turned, stopping to look back. All she saw were the thick pines and part of the roof of the old barn. A squirrel chattered at them from a nearby tree. A shadow fell over her as a hawk glided in a circle above the tops of the pines.

"Anything wrong?" Jack asked. He'd gone a few yards on up the mountain and had apparently just now realized she'd stopped.

She looked again down the mountainside, then shook off the feeling that they were being watched. "Just being paranoid," she said under her breath.

"What?" Jack asked.

She shook her head. "Nothing."

"We're almost there." He was carrying all the equipment as well as the shovel. He'd insisted, saying she probably shouldn't even be hiking up here, that he'd waited a week on purpose so she could get her strength back.

Jack was true to his word. They hadn't gone far when the land flattened out a little and Kate saw that they'd reached an old logging road.

"We kept digging near the house because we were so sure Cullen wouldn't have dragged a bunch of gold bullion way up into the mountains," Jack said. He motioned to the old logging road. "But with a four-wheeler, all he needed was a way through the fence."

She followed Jack a few dozen yards and saw where someone had made a gate of sorts, then covered it with brush. Her pulse began to pound. "I think you might be right."

Jack smiled as he shoved back his hat to look at her. "We'll see," he said as he pulled out the map. "I think that one line isn't a creek, but this road."

Kate followed him and the road, going back and forth from watching Jack to watching the map. When he stopped, she held her breath. It definitely looked as if this was the spot.

"You should do this," he said, handing her the metal detector.

Her fingers were shaking as she took it. She shot him a look, then turned the metal detector on and began to move it slowly back and forth across the grassy ground.

THE METAL DETECTOR went off, strong and sure. Jack's stunned gaze came up to meet hers. Could he really have been right about this?

"Jack?" she said, her voice breaking as she went over the spot another time. No doubt about it. Something big was down there.

He grabbed the shovel and began to dig. Kate turned off the metal detector, put it down and dropped to her knees to begin moving the rock out of the way. Jack shoveled deeper, Kate moving anything she could out of the way.

Then she picked up the metal detector, and he stopped to watch as she turned it on and held it over the shallow hole he'd dug. The beep was stronger than ever.

He quickly went back to work. As he did, he tried to hold down his excitement, but it was hard. When he'd compared the map on the back of the photograph with the map Kate had given him, he could see where they made their mistake. Still, it had been conjecture until he'd hiked up here and seen the logging road and the hidden gate.

That's when he'd known he had to bring Kate up here, had to give her a chance to find the buried treasure her mother had wanted her to have so desperately that both had risked their lives.

Even as he'd thought about how excited he would be for her to find it, Jack knew what it would mean. She would leave Beartooth. The gold was the only reason she'd come here. The café had just been a blind to hide behind and keep her going until she found the treasure buried long-ago.

Digging was slow. The sun slipped behind the Crazies. A cool breeze stirred the leaves in the nearby aspens and made the pine boughs sigh softly. Jack finally dug the hole large enough to climb down into it.

He was a good five feet deep when his shovel struck something solid. His gaze flew up to Kate's. He saw the expression on her face. Fear and excitement tangled together with shock. Added to that, regret. The last thing he wanted was to see Kate leave Beartooth. Leave him.

"Before we do this," he said, his voice sounding strange to him, "there's something I need to say to you."

She looked at him as if he'd lost his mind.

"I love you. I think I've loved you since the first night I laid eyes on you and you told me what a fool I was for trying to save you. I know that sounds crazy, but it's true. I want to start a new family tradition. I want to build something, grow roots in the shadow of these mountains, dream about my future again."

Kate's gaze met his. "Now, Jack? You waited for this moment to tell me this?"

"Yeah, whatever is down here, I love you and I want you to be happy. If it takes a chest of gold, well, then I hope that's what we're about to find. But I need to know if you are in this with me."

"Jack, what are you saying?" Kate asked, laughing.

He looked toward the peaks for a moment before he looked again at her. "I'm asking you to be my partner."

"Partner?" she asked skeptically.

"Fifty-fifty." He stepped to the side of the hole and placed a hand on her knee. "See that land down there," he said, pointing in the distance toward the French place. "It's ours. We can tear down the house and build a new one, buy some cattle and raise a garden. We can plant trees and—"

"Jack, the café doesn't make enough money to—"

"I have money. My mother left me money I invested and have never spent." He met her dark gaze. "I never knew what I wanted to do with it, but I do now. I know my mother would approve."

"I don't know what to say."

"Say you'll marry me."

"Jack—"

"Fifty-fifty. Just think what you and I can do here in Montana, Kate. We can rewrite our family histories. Why not here?"

She looked down the hollow where she'd been born and her mother had died. "I don't know, Jack. I'm not sure I would make a good rancher's wife. I don't cook, clean or sew."

He laughed. "You don't have to do any of those things."

"I'd want to keep the café," she said. She thought of Claude. He'd said this place would grow on her. She smiled to herself. "It's what Claude would have wanted. What I want, too."

Jack smiled and pulled her down into a kiss. "This place has got to you, hasn't it?"

Or could it be this man? "Yeah, Jack, this place has gotten to me."

"Well, will you marry me?" he asked.

"You have to know *now?*" she asked, surprise in her tone.

He nodded solemnly. "I do, before we find out what is down here in this hole."

She glanced toward the trunk at his feet, then at Jack. "Yes."

As FRANK DROVE into his ranch yard, he automatically looked to the telephone wire, expecting to see a dark row of crows waiting for him.

The wire was empty. So were the clothesline and the barn ridge. The crows were gone. They'd been gone since that day one of them had died in the dirt just feet from his front door.

He'd once read about a town in Canada that had become a stopover for migrating crows and pretty soon a half million had invaded the town.

Unable to put up with so many crows, the town made a plan to kill three hundred thousand of the birds. Armed with guns, the mayor led the group.

They killed one crow.

That was all it had taken. The crows had warned each other. Word spread among the birds and their migration pattern changed to avoid the town. For generations, crows had been avoiding farms where one of them had been killed in the past.

Because of that, he knew his birds wouldn't be coming back. Nor would others come to take their place.

He knew it was silly, the horrible sense of loss that he felt for his daughter, for his family of birds.

He tried to minimize the latter, reminding himself they were just birds. But they were his birds, his family. Pam had stolen seventeen years with his daughter from him. Now his daughter had taken the only family he'd known.

His despair darkened as evening set in across the wide valley. He crossed the porch, stunned by the depth of silence in the crows' absence.

As he was pushing open the screen door, he heard the sound of a motor as a vehicle approached. An SUV he didn't recognize pulled into the yard, the driver cutting the lights and engine. As the door opened, he saw who it was.

"Lynette?"

She didn't speak as she closed the car door and started toward him. She didn't have to. He opened his arms and she stepped into them. He held her so tightly he feared she couldn't breathe.

She didn't try to tell him that everything would be all right. She didn't speak at all. She just let him hold her.

JACK'S WORDS FILLED her heart like helium. Kate felt light-headed from the sun, the climb up the mountain, the thought that this could be it. The inheritance Cullen Ackermann had stolen from her mother.

She had to sit down on the edge of the hole. Jack touched her leg, looked into her eyes and then shoveled away more dirt to expose an old wood-and-metal trunk.

Kate thought of Claude as she watched the clouds building over the Crazies. She felt what it must have been like for him that day here in the hollow. The woman he'd loved was dead. And now he had a toddler in his arms and all hell was breaking out with the sheriff and deputies storming the compound.

"You saved my life."

"If I could have gotten your mother out the moment she knew she was pregnant with you..." He shook his head. *"But Cullen was watching her like a hawk. Had the boys keeping an eye on her, too. I think he suspected something was going on with her."*

"You loved her."

He nodded.

"You risked your life for her."

He smiled and took her hand. "That is what you do when you love someone. You know that better than I do. Look what you did to save mine. I wish I could protect you."

She'd brought Claude more time but not near enough. He died less than a year later. His liver hadn't failed him, but his heart had.

"Are you all right?" Jack asked, looking up from the hole where he'd been shoveling.

She nodded. "I was just thinking about Claude. I wish he was here. He wanted this so badly for my mother."

This was it. She could feel it and could tell Jack did, too. Crazy as it was, she almost stopped him. She knew why he'd told her he loved her now. Because this could change everything. These stolen hours searching for the treasure with Jack had been the best in her life.

He began to dig around the clasp.

"Jack." She swallowed as he threw out another shov-

elful of dirt. "I don't want this to change things between us."

He laughed. "Too late for that, Kate." He kept digging. After a few minutes, the shovel blade clanged
against something. "It's padlocked."

Jack stopped digging and knelt down to brush aside
dirt and inspect the latch and padlock. "I think I can
break the lock with the shovel so we can see what is
inside."

She knew what he was saying. He didn't want to dig
out the trunk only to find it had nothing of value in
it. Best to see what they had before going any farther.

Raising the shovel, he brought the blade down on
the clasp and lock. The sound rang out and seemed to
drift across the hollow. Jack brought the shovel down
again. Then again. The sound was so loud neither of
them heard anyone approach.

CHAPTER TWENTY-FIVE

JACK'S HEART WAS POUNDING. Had he ever really believed the treasure existed, let alone that they would find it?

Now, though, he wanted to know what was in the box. Not for the sake of money. His curiosity was killing him. Kate, he'd noticed, had slumped onto the ground at the edge of the hole.

He looked up at her. "Do you want to—"

"You open it."

He nodded. A rusted padlock hung off one side. He picked up the shovel and again brought it down hard. The blade clanged against the lock, but didn't break it open. He tried again, putting more force into it.

Metal on metal sang, ending in a loud pop as the latch broke.

Jack swallowed, telling himself not to get his hopes up, but it was impossible. He glanced at Kate. She seemed awestruck, her brown eyes wide with disbelief and something else—awe.

He reached down and was forcing his fingers down along the edges of the trunk's lid to lift it when the shadow fell over him and he heard Kate let out a cry.

His already thundering heart kicked into overdrive

as he looked up. Kate was looking past him, shock and fear in her expression.

Slowly Jack turned to find a man silhouetted against the sky. He couldn't make out the man's face, but there was no missing the gun in the man's hand.

"Jack?" Kate asked, her voice breaking.

Jack froze, his mind racing. The sheriff had said that only three of the four Ackermann boys had survived the raid thirty years ago. Two were now dead and one was in jail. Unless this was a friend...

"Nice work, Jack."

He felt a chill careen down his spine as he recognized the voice.

"You, too, Kate," Arnie Thorndike said. "I was starting to lose faith that the two of you would ever find it. Which would have been disappointing, since I put all my money, so to speak, on you."

"Being a lawyer wasn't profitable enough for you?" Jack asked. The shovel was in reach, but he was at a distinct disadvantage, since he was in a hole and Thorndike had a gun.

"I thought you were Claude's friend," Kate said.

"I was," the man said, sounding indignant. "His *best* friend. This really has nothing to do with Claude."

"How can you say that?" Jack demanded. "Kate is his daughter."

Thorndike nodded. "But the money in that chest is *mine*. Cullen owed me."

Jack scoffed. "I know lawyer's charge a lot but—"

"Cullen and I had a business arrangement. He left

me holding the bag. I'm here to collect what is right-fully mine."

"Pot," Kate said. "Of course. He and his sons raised marijuana. But they had to have someone outside the compound distribute it since Cullen seldom left the property, according to Claude. Who better than an ex-hippie lawyer?"

Thorndike smiled and tipped his hat to her.

"Claude couldn't have known about your arrange-ment with his brother," Jack said.

"Seems Claude and I both had our secrets," the law-yer said, looking at Kate. His attention quickly shifted back to Jack, though. "Come on, I'm dying of suspense up here. Open the trunk, Jack."

KATE COULDN'T BELIEVE this was happening. She and Jack had come so far only to have it end like this.

"Open it yourself," Jack said.

Thorndike wagged his head as if disappointed. "Don't be like that. You owe me."

"How's that?" Jack asked.

"Who do you think has been saving your girl-friend?" the attorney said. "When Darrell and Cecil got to town, their plan was to kill her, get the map so they could compare it to the one their father had left behind, get the gold and disappear for good."

"They came to you?" Kate asked in surprise.

"I was their father's attorney and business partner," Thorndike said, "plus they'd hoped their old man had left them something in his will." He shook his head. "I gave them advice instead."

"Did you tell them to kill each other?" Jack asked.

"No, that was their doing. Apparently Darrell didn't like my advice. He and Cecil fought." He shrugged.

"And Gallen?" Kate asked.

"He had to be dealt with after he attacked you. He could have killed you and ruined everything."

"Isn't that what you're planning to do—kill us?" Jack asked.

"The trunk, Jack," Thorndike said, motioning with the gun. "I'm tired of this chitchat."

Jack glanced at Kate. She held her breath as he bent over, grabbed the lip of the trunk lid and pulled. The rusty hinges groaned, complaining loudly.

"Wait," Kate cried.

Jack stopped, the trunk lid open only a fraction of an inch.

"You can have whatever is in the trunk," she said.

Thorndike laughed. "I know."

"No, I'm saying, let us go now. Jack and I will walk away. No one will ever know what happened to Ackermann's buried treasure."

The lawyer seemed to study her for a moment. "Do you think I'm a fool? You'll go running straight to the sheriff."

"And tell him what?" she said. "That we found the gold but you took it away from us? Who would believe that? Even if we did, by the time the sheriff got up here, you and the gold would be gone. There's a gate behind that bush down there, and a road where you could drive a four-wheeler."

"You expect me to believe you would give up whatever is in that trunk just like that?" he asked with a snap of the fingers on his free hand.

Kate nodded. "Just like that."

Thorndike laughed. "Aren't you even curious what you would be giving up?"

"No." Kate looked to Jack. "I've actually found what I've been looking for and didn't realize it."

Jack looked at her in surprise. He gave her a smile.

The lawyer studied them for a long moment. "You'll tell the sheriff I killed Gallen."

"Even if we did, the sheriff would never be able to prove it," Jack said. "With all the Ackermanns now dead, Frank isn't going to keep looking for their killers. You won this one. Quit while you're ahead. If you kill us, it will be a whole different story and you know it."

"You should have been lawyers," Thorndike said as he lowered the gun. "You two make a very convincing argument."

"Just help me out of this hole and it's all yours," Jack said and extended his hand.

EPILOGUE

SUMMER CAME TO BEARTOOTH on a sweet, warm wind that blew down out of the Crazy Mountains. Three things happened that would be remembered and talked about for years.

The first and biggest event of the season was the wedding of Destry Grant and Rylan West. High school lovers finally reunited, their story was told time and again during the three-day celebration in Beartooth.

Shortly after that glorious reception, the second thing happened. Ruth McCray died from a tragic fall down the stairs at her ranch. At her funeral service Sunday at church, Hitch wept openly. Now who would save Hitch from himself? everyone wondered.

Jack was surprised when he got a call from a Bozeman lawyer telling him he'd been mentioned in Ruth's will. He'd driven to Bozeman, more out of curiosity than anything else. As he was going into the lawyer's office, he passed an extremely upset Hitch coming out.

"You all right?" Jack asked, but Hitch only ducked his head and pushed past him, hurrying away.

The lawyer gave Jack the shocking news in a letter, handwritten and signed by Ruth.

"I bequeath Jack French my ranch, although I know it won't make up for what I've done. I will never forgive myself for what happened the night his father died. I am responsible for running Delbert French off the road. Once I realized that he was dead, I panicked. I got rid of the old pickup I was driving and let my son Hitch discover it gone and report the truck as stolen. All these years, I've lived with the guilt and fear that I'd be found out. I know the land can't make up for what I've done, but at least I can rest in peace knowing that I bared my soul and gave what I could."

Jack was too shocked to speak. He'd been so sure it was Hitch who'd run his father off the road, and all the time it had been Ruth. Not even Hitch had known the truth. Until today, apparently.

"I don't want her land." He stood to leave.

"It's yours. You can sell it, give it away, but it is yours," the lawyer said.

Jack thought of all the years Hitch had put up with his mother's tyranny so he could inherit the ranch. "What about her son? What did she leave him?"

"She saw to his security," the lawyer assured him.

It wasn't until later, back in Beartooth, that Jack heard Hitch had been going all over town saying that he was finally free not just of his mother but the ranch. The last Jack saw of Hitch, he was headed for the Yellowstone Airport, threatening to see the world.

This was followed by the third and most shocking

event. Arnie Thorndike's body was discovered in a deep hole up in Ackermann Hollow.

"He appears to have been killed by a makeshift booby trap after opening an old trunk that had been buried up in the hollow," the sheriff was quoted as saying in the newspaper. "This is one of the reasons that residents have been warned to stay out of that hollow. The booby trap is believed to have been constructed by the late Cullen Ackermann.

"The trunk," according to the sheriff, "was found empty, except for the booby trap paraphernalia found inside. The device appears to have been triggered when Mr. Thorndike opened the lid."

People in Beartooth were shocked by the news.

"I never took Arnie Thorndike as a treasure hunter," one rancher said at the café after the news came out. "Can't imagine that old hippie getting off the couch, let alone climbing all over the hollow looking for gold. And then to find something only to get yourself killed." The rancher shook his head. "Guess there never was any gold up there."

Jack and Kate never told anyone any different. But Kate threw away all the lost-treasure magazines after that and sold her metal detector and infrared camera on eBay.

Their engagement was hardly mentioned, just like their small wedding, at the café with only a few close friends. The two moved into the apartment over the café until Jack completed the home he was building for them on the French ranch. Carson had talked Jack into taking the land Ruth McCray had given him.

"Do something good with it for your father," his friend had argued.

Meanwhile Kate was running the café and looking for a waitress to take Bethany's place. Bethany was pregnant with her and Clete's first child.

Life in Beartooth was so uneventful after that that there was hardly any gossip to pass along. Nettie had been so upset over Frank being shot by his daughter that she didn't even get up and look out the window the night Jack and Kate buried a heavy, large box next to that old garage by the café.

To Kate's and Jack's surprise—and of course Arnie Thorndike's—there had been more than a booby trap inside the trunk hidden in Ackermann Hollow. The gold Kate's mother had wanted her so desperately to have was finally hers for that rainy day when she and Jack might need it.

"JACK?"

"Yes, Kate?"

The two of them were lying naked up in the hayloft. A light breeze blew out of the Crazies, smelling of summer and pine.

"What would you think about having a baby?"

He turned his head to look over at her. His blue eyes shone like sunshine on Saddlestring Lake. She thought of the picnics they'd had up there, of the long horseback rides, of the garden the two of them were nurturing behind the house.

She had settled well into being a rancher's wife, the

café was thriving and she'd even taken a quilting class from the Beartooth Quilting Society.

"Kate?" Jack rolled onto his side to look at her. "Are you telling me you're…"

She smiled as she turned on her side to look at him. Only minutes before, he'd made passionate love to her. Now he ran his fingers along the length of her. Desire sparked again as she nodded.

He touched her face with such tenderness, then looped his hand around the nape of her neck and drew her to him. His kiss was sweeter than the strawberries that were turning red in their garden.

Kate curled into his arms as his hand brushed over her scar to settle on her stomach, and she closed her eyes. Jack said she gave him back his ability to dream about the future. He'd given her so much more. She often wondered what would have happened if she'd never come to Beartooth. She couldn't stand the thought that she might never have met Jack.

But fate had thrown them together, so maybe it had always been written in the stars, all the way back to the day Claude Durham had walked into that café in Nevada looking for her. She'd had more than a different name back then. She'd been a different person.

Claude had offered her a new life, in a new place. He'd also given her a piece of her past that had been missing. She'd loved him at the end, something she'd been afraid to do since losing both her adoptive parents.

Her only wish now was that Claude could know how it all turned out, she thought as she looked into her husband's eyes. Maybe he did.

"Aren't you worried about my genes?" Jack asked.

She laughed and shook her head. "Trouble isn't in your genes."

He gave her a look that said he wasn't so sure about that.

"I'm not worried. You and I... Well, we can handle most anything as long as we are together."

"Love saved us," Jack said, meeting her gaze, their secret passing silently between them.

Kate nodded. She often thought about that day in Ackermann Hollow. She didn't let herself think about what would have happened if she hadn't been willing to give up everything for the love of Jack French.

But sometimes, if your love is strong and the stars are aligned perfectly, you don't have to give up anything, she thought as Jack kissed her and they lost themselves in each other in the shadow of the Crazy Mountains. Sometimes you get it all.

* * * * *

Read on for an excerpt from HARD RAIN,
the newest book in the exciting
MONTANA HAMILTONS *series by* **New York Times** *bestselling author B.J. Daniels!*

CHAPTER ONE

Thunder cracked overhead in a piercing boom that rattled the windows. As she huddled in the darkness, rain pelted down in angry drenching waves. Lightning again lit the sky in a blinding flash that burned in her mind the image before her.

In that instant, she saw him crossing the ridge carrying the shovel, his head down, rain pouring off his black Stetson. It was done.

Dark clouds blanketed the hillside. Through the driving rain, she watched him come toward her, telling herself she could live with what she'd done. But she feared he could not. And that could be a problem.

BRODY MCTAVISH HEARD the screams only seconds before he heard the roar of hooves headed in his direction. Shoving back his cowboy hat, he looked up from the fence he'd been mending to see a woman on a horse riding at breakneck speed toward him.

Harper Hamilton. He'd heard that she'd recently returned after being away at college. Which meant it could have been years since she'd been on a horse. He was already grabbing for his horse's reins and swinging up in the saddle.

Runaway horse.

He'd been on a runaway horse when he was a kid. He remembered how terrifying it had been. With that many pounds of horseflesh running at such a deadly speed, he prayed hard she could hang on.

He had to hand it to Harper. She hadn't been unseated. At least not yet.

Harper, yards away on a large bay, screamed. He spurred his horse to catch her, and as he raced up beside her, her blue eyes were wide with alarm.

Acting quickly, he looped an arm around her, dragged her off the horse and reined in. His horse came to a stop in a cloud of dust. Her horse kept going, disappearing into the foothill pines ahead.

Brody let Harper slip to the ground next to his horse. The minute her feet touched earth, she started screaming again as if all the wind had been knocked out of her when he'd grabbed her but was back now.

"You're all right," he said, swinging out of the saddle and stepping to her to try to calm her.

She spun on him, leading with her fist, and caught him in the jaw. He staggered back more from surprise than the actual blow, but the woman had a pretty darned good right hook.

He stared at her in confusion. "What the devil was that about?"

Picking up a baseball-sized rock, she brandished it as she took a few steps back from him, all the time glancing around, seeming either to expect more men to come out of the foothills or looking for a larger weapon.

Had the woman hit her head? He spoke calmly as he

would to a skittish horse—or a crazy woman. "Calm down. I know you're scared. But you're all right now." It had only been a few months since the two of them were attendants at her sister Bo's wedding, not that they hadn't known each other for years.

She peered under the brim of his hat as if only then taking a good look at him. "Brody McTavish?" She stared at him as if in shock. "Have you lost your mind?"

Brody frowned, since this hadn't been the reaction he'd expected. "Ah, correct me if I'm wrong," he said, rubbing his jaw. "But I don't think this is the way most women react after a man saves her life."

"You think you just saved my life?" Her voice rose in amazement.

"You were *screaming* like either a woman in trouble or one who has lost her senses. I assumed, as any sane person would, that your horse had run away with you. No need to thank me," he said sarcastically.

"Thank you? For scaring me half to death?" She dropped the rock and dusted the dirt off her hand onto her jeans. "And for the record, I wasn't *screaming*. I was...expressing myself."

"Expressing yourself at the top of your lungs?"

Harper jammed her hands on her hips and thrust out her adorable chin. He recalled her sister's wedding back at Christmastime. While both attendants, they hadn't shared more than a few words. Nor had he gotten a chance to dance with her. His own fault. He hadn't wanted to get in line with all her young suitors.

"It was a beautiful morning," she said haughtily. "I hadn't been on a horse in a long time and it felt so good that I couldn't resist expressing it." She looked embarrassed but clearly wasn't about to admit it. "Do you have a problem with that?"

"Nope. But when I see a woman riding like a wild person, screaming her head off, I'm going to assume she's in trouble and needs some help. My mistake." Didn't she know how dangerous it was riding like that out here? If her horse had stepped into a gopher hole… A lecture came to his lips, but he clamped his mouth shut. "You have a nice day, Miss Hamilton." He tipped his hat, grabbed up his reins and started toward his property.

"You're just going to walk away?" she demanded to his back.

"Since you aren't in need of *my* help…" he said over his shoulder.

"I thought you would at least help me retrieve my horse."

He stopped and mumbled under this breath, "If your horse has any sense he'll keep going."

"I beg your pardon?"

Brody took a breath and turned to face her again.

Her blond hair shone in the morning sunlight, her blue eyes wide and filled with devilment. He recalled the girl she'd been. *Feisty* was an understatement. While nothing had changed as far as that went, she was definitely no longer a girl. He would have had to be blind not to notice the way she filled out her jeans and Western shirt.

She shifted her boots in the dust. "I'd appreciate it if you would help me find my horse."

"By all means let me help you find your horse then. As you said, it's the least I can do. Would you care to ride... *Miss Hamilton*?" He motioned to his horse, glad he hadn't called her Princess, even though it had been on the tip of his tongue.

Looking chastised, she shook her head. "And, please, my name is—"

"Harper. I know."

"Thank you for not mistaking me for my twin." She sounded more than a little surprised. "Not even my own father can tell us apart at times."

He could feel her looking at him, studying him like a bug under a microscope. He wondered what she'd majored in at college. Nothing useful, he would bet.

"Thank you also for helping me find my horse," she said into the silence that fell between them. "I really don't want to be left out here on foot if my horse has returned to the barn."

He thought the walk might do her some good but was smart enough not to voice it. "The last I saw of your mare she was headed up into the foothills. I would imagine that's where we'll find her, next to the creek."

She glanced up at him. "I should probably apologize for hitting you." When he said nothing, she continued. "With everything that's been going on in my family, I thought you were... Anyway, I'm sorry that I hit you and that I misunderstood your concern." He could hear in her voice how hard that apology was for her.

And, he had to admit, her family had recently definitely been through a lot. The family had seemed to be under attack since her father, Senator Buckmaster

Hamilton, had announced he would be running for president. Three of her sisters had been threatened. Not to mention the mother she'd believed dead had returned out of the blue after twenty-two years—and her stepmother had been killed in a car accident. It was as if tragedy was tracking that family.

"Apology accepted," he said as he picked up her cowboy hat from the dust and handed it to her.

As they walked toward sun-bleached cliffs and shimmering green pines, he mentally kicked himself. He'd had a crush on Harper—from a distance, of course—for years, waiting for her to grow up, and now that she finally had and he'd managed to get her attention, he couldn't imagine a worse encounter.

Not that he wasn't knocked to his knees by her crooked smile or the way she had of cocking her head when she was considering something. Or the endless blue of her wide-eyed innocence—all things he'd noticed from the first time he'd laid eyes on her. He smiled to himself, remembering the first time he'd seen her. She'd just been a freckle-faced kid.

Somehow, he'd thought… She'd be grown-up and one day… He told himself someday he and Harper would have a good laugh over today's little incident, before he mentally kicked himself.

He'd actually thought he'd rescued the woman of his dreams—until she'd hit him.

BRODY MCTAVISH. HARPER grimaced in embarrassment. She'd been half in love with him as far back as she could remember. Not that he had looked twice at her.

He'd been the handsome rowdy teen she used to spy on from a distance. She'd been just a girl, much too young for him. But Brody had come to parties her older sisters had put on at the ranch. She and Cassidy were too young to attend and were always sent up to bed, but Harper often sneaked down when everyone else, including her twin, thought she was asleep.

Several times Brody had caught her watching, and she'd thought for sure he would snitch on her, but he hadn't. Instead, he'd given her a grin and covered for her. Her nine-year-old heart had beat like a jackhammer in her chest at just the thought of that grin.

She'd seen Brody a few times after that, but only in passing. He'd graduated from high school and gone off to college before coming back to the family ranch. She'd been busy herself, getting an education, traveling, experiencing life away from Montana. When she'd heard that her sister Bo was dating Jace Calder, she'd wondered if he and Brody were still best friends.

It wasn't until the wedding that she got to see him again. She hadn't been surprised to find that he was still handsome, still had that same self-deprecating grin, still made her now grown-up heart beat a little faster. She'd waited at the wedding reception for him to ask her to dance since they were both attendants, but he hadn't. She'd told herself that he probably still saw her as a child, given the difference in their ages.

Glancing over at him now, she didn't even want to consider what he must think of her after this. Not that she cared, she told herself, lifting her head and pretending it didn't matter. He probably didn't even remember the secret they had shared when she was a girl.

As they walked, though, she couldn't help studying him out of the corner of her eye. Earlier, she hadn't appreciated how strong he was. Now that she knew he wasn't some predator who had been trying to abduct her—something she'd been warned about as a girl since she was the daughter of a wealthy rancher, not to mention US senator—she took in his muscled body along with the chiseled features of his handsome face in the shade of his straw cowboy hat.

No matter what he said, he hadn't accepted her apology. He was still angry with her. She'd given him her best smile when he'd returned her hat from the ground and all she'd gotten was a grunt. Her smile was all it usually took with most men. But Brody wasn't most men. Wasn't that why she'd never been able to forget him?

"I feel as if we've gotten off on the wrong foot," she said, trying to make amends.

Another grunt without even looking at her.

"My fault entirely," she said, although she didn't really believe that was true and hoped he would agree.

But he said nothing, nor would he even look at her. He was starting to irritate her. She was doing her best to make up for the misunderstanding, but the stubborn man wasn't giving her an inch.

"You can't just keep ignoring me," she snapped, digging in her boot heels as she stopped shy of the pine-covered hillside. "Have you even heard a word I've said? If you don't look at me right this minute, Brody McTavish, I'm going to—"

He swung on her. Had she not been standing flat-footed she would have stumbled back. Instead, she was rooted to the ground as suddenly he was in her face. "I've *been* listening to you and I've *been* looking at you for years," he said, his voice deep and thick with emotion. "I've *been* waiting for you to grow up." His voice faltered as he dropped his horse's reins. "Because I've been wanting to do this since you were sixteen."

Grabbing her, he pulled her against his rock-hard body. His mouth dropped to hers. Her lips parted of their own accord, just as her arms wrapped around his neck. Her heart hammered against her ribs as he deepened the kiss and she heard herself moan.

The sudden high-pitched whinny of a horse only yards away brought them both out of the kiss in one startled movement. Turning, she could see her horse in the trees. Her first thought was that the mare had gotten into a hunter's snare, because the whinny was one of pain—or alarm.

Brody grabbed her arm as she started past him to see what was wrong with her horse. "I think you should wait here," he said, letting go of her arm as he took off toward the pines.

"My horse—"

"Stay here," he said more sternly over his shoulder.

Still stunned by the kiss and anxious about her horse, she set off after him. The ground was soft under her feet. She saw where fresh soil had washed down through the pines, forming a dark, muddy gully.

Her horse was partway up the hillside near where the rain a few nights ago had loosened the soil and washed it down the hillside. As Brody approached, the mare snorted and crow-hopped away a few feet.

"She's afraid of you," she called to his retreating backside. She could hear him speaking softly to the horse as he approached. She followed, although she was no match for his long legs.

An eerie quiet fell over the hillside as she stepped into the shadowed pines. She slowed, frowning as she finally got a good look at her horse. The mare didn't seem to be hurt and yet Harper had never seen her act like this before.

"I thought I told you to stay back," Brody said as she came up behind him. "You've never been good at following orders, have you?"

So he did remember her sneaking downstairs at her sisters' parties. She felt a bump of excitement at that news, but it was quickly doused. Past him, she saw that her horse's eyes were wild. The mare snorted again, stomped the ground and shied away, to move a few yards back from them and the gully.

"What is wrong with her?" Harper demanded, afraid it was something she had done.

"She's reacting to what the hard rain dislodged and sent down the hillside in an avalanche of mud," Brody snapped. What was he talking about? As she started to step past him to get a look, he put a hand out to stop her. "Harper, you don't want to see this."

She *did* want to see whatever it was and resented him telling her she didn't. Protective was one thing, but the man was being ridiculous. She'd been raised on a ranch. She'd seen her share of dead animals, if that was what it was. She stepped around him, determined to see what the storm had exposed.

At first all she saw were old grimy, weathered boards that looked like part of a large wooden box. Then she saw what must have been inside the container before it had washed down the slope and broken open.

Her pulse jumped at the sight, her mind telling her she wasn't seeing what her eyes told her she was. *"What is that?"* she whispered into the already unnerving quiet as she took a step back.

"From the clothing and long hair, I'd say it was the mummified body of a woman who, until recently, had been buried up on that hillside."

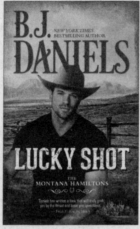

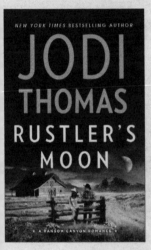

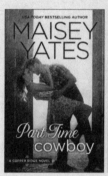
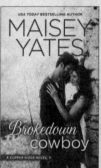

Turn your love of reading into rewards you'll love with
Harlequin My Rewards

B.J. DANIELS

78855   LUCKY SHOT   ___ $7.99 U.S.   ___ $9.99 CAN.
77846   ATONEMENT   ___ $7.99 U.S.   ___ $8.99 CAN.

(limited quantities available)

TOTAL AMOUNT	$ _____
POSTAGE & HANDLING	$ _____
($1.00 FOR 1 BOOK, 50¢ for each additional)	
APPLICABLE TAXES*	$ _____
TOTAL PAYABLE	$ _____

(check or money order—please do not send cash)

To order, complete this form and send it, along with a check or money order for the total above, payable to HQN Books, to: **In the U.S.:** 3010 Walden Avenue, P.O. Box 9077, Buffalo, NY 14269-9077; **In Canada:** P.O. Box 636, Fort Erie, Ontario, L2A 5X3.

Name: _____
Address: _____ City: _____
State/Prov.: _____ Zip/Postal Code: _____
Account Number (if applicable): _____
075 CSAS

*New York residents remit applicable sales taxes.
*Canadian residents remit applicable GST and provincial taxes.

HQN™
www.HQNBooks.com

PHBJD021 6BL